A fantasy novel by
S. Johnson

Cover art by
Gavin T. Gardner

Cover design and page layout by
S. Johnson

The Never Story
by S. Johnson

Acknowledgments

The Never Story was born on a bitterly cold day as an experiment to see if a girl with wings, that just wouldn't work, could find her way to the sky.

Her story remained a secret for weeks, with the exception of a few close friends and family who watched me descend into what must have seemed like madness. They could never have guessed it would get worse when the writing was done, but it did, and they loved me anyway.

The long coffees and phone calls, encouragement, idea-bouncing, editing and critiques are gifts I will always cherish.

Never is presented, finally and with much agony, only because of the support and love of my children, the reason for it all and who remind me daily that life is always worse for teens; my parents, who have been remarkably open-minded and loving; my brother, an amazing artist and friend; and my dearest friends and colleagues who give me far more than I could ever give them. Also, I would be remiss if I forgot my horses, dogs, cats and wild things, all of whom remind me daily of what a truly beautiful world it is.

Without those who surround me, neither Never or I would be trying to fly at all.

And most of all, thank you for taking the time to get to know Never.

I hope that you enjoy The Never Story as much as I have and I look forward to us sharing Never's future as we continue to journey through the challenges she faces together.

S. Johnson

"Verily all things move within your being in constant half embrace, the desired and the dreaded, the repugnant and the cherished, the pursued and that which you would escape.

These things move within you as lights and shadows in pairs that cling.

And when the shadow fades and is no more, the light that lingers becomes a shadow to another light.

And thus your freedom when it loses its fetters becomes itself the fetter of a greater freedom."

Kahlil Gibran, On Freedom

●● Prologue ●●

"Call it," he said toward the deepest shadow.

He received no response.

Dwindling light made its way through the small windows up above; occasionally a stronger ray glimmering off the oily surface of his scalp.

His anger was contained, but it gave a rigid edge to his pose where he leaned against the cold stone wall peering into the darkness with his lips pursed. Held that way, his lips made him appear birdlike, his dark eyes seeming frozen where they stabbed into the shadows before him.

Sneering, he pulled away from the wall and turned his shoulder against the dark, but only for a second, his head snapping back to stare again while his index finger traced the mating line of the smooth blocks he had just abandoned.

He snatched his hand back with a scowl and leaned again, this time folding his arms across his chest – not because he wished to withdraw into himself, but rather as a measure of control.

His anger was beneath the surface, yet vibrating through the tissue it found there. The air nearly snapped around him.

"You will call it and bring it here," he said, his voice measured and so sickly sweet it threatened to violate masculinity.

Still there was no answer from the darkness.

"You are a traitor, and yet I protect you and give you this chance to redeem yourself and you refuse?"

Swinging his fist down to his side, it met the wall with a powerful sound that cut, then reverberated through the room. The aftershock was a match to his rising voice.

Even in his anger, he still kept his distance, not that his bellowing fury didn't crawl across the stone tiles of the floor and into the darkness of its own accord.

It was the explosion he had needed to blow out the fire and his demeanor once again found cold composure.

Pivoting, this time he turned his back on the dark and kept it there, making his way to the door with soundless steps of purpose.

Pausing, he pressed his hand to the door, then pushed it open.

"Call it and it has a chance – refuse and, you have my word, we will hunt it, we will find it and *we will kill it!* ... And then, there will be no need for you."

Long after he was gone, his words remained trapped in the room, only fading when the darkness split, one shadow moving away to hang its head in the silence.

1

•• Chapter One ••

The still air was only broken momentarily as he glided by, the gentle motion of his wings sending a quick breeze to tickle her cheek.

Nev stretched her feet in front of her in the silky grass, smiling and leaning back on her hands as she watched the hawk dip, then climb like a perfectly orchestrated crescendo, feeling the familiar tug of excitement.

Warm morning sun soaked through her skin, tingling as it moved through her body and closing her eyes, she let her head fall back, still tracking his movements.

Her stomach fluttered, sharing in the sensation of the air's pressure against his chest.

Ah... There it was!

The current rushed through her body, bringing every nerve to life as she arched her back, and her own wings began to unfold behind her.

Eyes still closed, she slowly sat forward and wrapped her arms around her folded knees, hugging them to her as the wings began to stretch, muscles contracting then pushing against their own resistance.

Tightly coiled, her bare back shivered involuntarily as the translucent sections lightly grazed her skin and shifted her hair in their effort to extend.

The hawk felt it too, his excitement rushing through her as she planted her palms on the grass in front of her and pushed to her feet.

There was no need to open her eyes.

Avec pulled at her, showing her the way, and Nev felt his eagerness and encouragement.

She flexed them once, twice, then began to sweep them in unison – curling them as they drew in, extending and opening them as they moved out.

The wind they created was growing as he coaxed her with his mind.

It worked – the weight of her feet gave way to the top of the grass blades, tickling her soles.

Faster and faster she moved her wings, bringing her body level with the ground as it fell away.

Nev knew better than to open her eyes, reaching her arms out to the sides with her fingers spread wide for balance.

She didn't need to see to know he flew close, for it was enough that she felt him stir the air beneath her, sending a brief flash of coolness along her belly as she rose even higher.

Slowly, she opened her eyes, unable to resist a peek. Oh she was high this time, probably the highest yet.

But as she focused in on the ground below, it began rapidly rising up to meet her and her flapping turned futile against the speedy descent.

Overpowered by the opposing pressure, her wings folded backward and Avec faded to a glimmer in the back of her mind, snuffing out like a candle flame as she slammed to the earth.

Her knees did little to break her fall as her face met with the grass and the smell of dirt was quickly followed by the hard reality of it.

Tears gathered in her eyes in response to the stinging sensations spreading out from the bridge of her nose, punctuating the failure. Her will to move lost, she lay there, eyes closed against the once silky grass that now felt like a million needles on her skin. A sob coincided with the retraction of her wings, melding into the skin of her back as if they had never been there at all.

Feathered legs reaching out, Avec landed on her right shoulder, talons gently gripping her skin and he burrowed his head through her tangled, black hair in search of her cheek.

"Next time. It will happen next time," he told her silently, Stroking her bruised flesh with his cool beak.

Avec stood sentinel as she lay there for what seemed like hours before she finally gathered herself to her knees. Avec took to the air, moving a short distance away.

His watchful eyes upon her, she pushed to her feet, pausing for a moment to look down at them with disdain.

Curling her toes in the grass, she shot a sideways glance at him.

"It won't happen and you know it," she muttered.

Now perched on a nearby rock, he tilted his russet streaked, gray head and looked at her with piercing, loving gray eyes.

"Yes, yes it will.

You did better this time."

Turning her back to him, she ran her fingers through her hair, angrily tugging past a snarl.

When it was smooth again, she carelessly braided it, then leaned down where she had discarded her tunic to grab the beaded leather hair tie her mother had made her all those years ago.

Pausing to admire the simple design as if she were seeing it for the first time, she sighed and reached up to wrap it around the braid, tying it securely with care.

It was the only piece of her mother she had left. That and a few fleeting and intangible snippets of memory.

He felt her sadness but said nothing while she slipped the tunic over her head, maintaining his silence when she reached down to knock dirt clumps from her breeches.

His pity reached her, though, causing her to reel around and glare at him for a moment before she turned her back and started angrily walking the other direction, toward the grassy rise that blocked her view of home.

Avec's chuckle had the effect of a finger poking against her.

"What could possibly be funny?" she spat over her shoulder, refusing to look at him as she trudged forward.

Gliding to a position near her shoulder, Avec kept pace and curled his head to make eye contact with her when she stubbornly turned her head away.

Chuckling again, he darted around her head to catch her eyes.

*"That hot head of yours won't let you quit. **That** is why I know you'll get it next time."*

Before she could get the growl from her throat, he was above her head and carving a path through the air in front of her, his straight line interrupted by a brief, playful roll as he wiggled his white tail feathers at her, then cut left into a patch of trees.

His taunting, flippant disregard fueled her march as she made her way down the hill, weaving around the occasional rock in her path.

Try as she might to hold on to her anger, the long walk started chipping away at it.

Loosing a reluctant sigh, she allowed her mind to find him, briefly sharing an empty twinge in her gut followed by an excited flutter as a small rabbit raised its head then turned tail and darted through the underbrush.

She enjoyed the sensation as he gathered speed and dipped down, but she pulled away as the rabbit's back came within reach.

That was something she couldn't share with him, or rather, didn't want to.

She had been with him on his first hunt and had refused to watch since, enjoying the thrill of the chase with him but always severing their connection before the defining moment.

There was a violence to the death of his prey that her compassion just couldn't quite overcome no matter how hard she tried.

Of course, she herself had hunted and killed, but there was a cleanness to those deaths – mercy and regret blended with success that showed the greatest difference between them.

Well, that and the fact that he could fly.

That was an injustice she couldn't quite come to terms with.

She had been present for his first flight, the culmination of weeks of nurturing and mothering after his own parents failed to return to the nest where she found him, a days-old hatchling with no hope.

To see him now – the smooth white underside of his black-tipped, broad wings so capable and strong, stretching more than four feet in either direction as he soared through the air – it hardly seemed possible he had ever been so ruffled and awkward. .

She could still remember the day she climbed up to the highest branches of her favorite tree and pushed him off her arm, watching him panic, flutter and tumble before he steadied himself and realized what he could do.

He had outgrown the vulnerability of those early days, somehow turning the tables on her – his independence and self sufficiency redefining their connection as now she turned to him in her quest to understand the purpose of it all.

Nev's frustration came in part from her flawed perception that he didn't need her anymore, but mostly from the utter helplessness she felt as her reliance on him grew, seemingly more and more each day.

And he didn't – couldn't understand – even though he thought he did.

Regardless of some of the similarities, his experience was very different than hers, particularly in the fact it had followed a natural progression – and each stage had been accomplished exactly as it should be.

But not her.

First she had to crawl, then walk, talk and overcome awkwardness, only to have what little confidence she found in those accomplishments cut short with the discovery of those damn wings – their existence sending her right back to the cradle again.

As if at nineteen summers, life wasn't awkward enough in that she remained unmarried and lived alone with her father with no apparent movement toward a life of her own.

Though it might have seemed the wings would give her an advantage of some kind, in all reality they made her more vulnerable than ever, especially because she couldn't use them and absolutely couldn't explain them.

She'd only discovered them a few months before, though it felt like an eternity.

She had taken a break from swimming to sit on the edge of a cliff and watch Avec fly, touching his mind with hers as he soared and dove, clipping the surface of the water below.

As she closed her eyes and dipped with him, she felt two pinpoints suddenly radiate like fingers in her shoulders.

She gasped for air, her eyes snapping open as webs of energy connected the finger-like lines, and she felt the flesh on her back began to lift and stretch.

Rising up from a swoop, Avec froze and let out a shriek, sinking in the air before he righted himself and flew toward her.

She heard and saw nothing as she tried to crawl to her knees and fell, her attempted cry for help only a low broken moan as she clawed at the dirt beneath her.

It wasn't pain she felt, but a maddening surge of energy, pushing from every inch of her body to the area between her shoulders like the billions of pinpoints that burst and tingle when a sleeping limb wakes.

A shadow covered her as the wings stretched above her and she discovered the more they stretched, the more the tingling subsided.

Willing them to stretch farther, she found the sensations faded, giving way to the coolness from a light breeze as it touched damp new skin.

Shivering, she regained her breath but lay still, afraid to move.

Not knowing how to communicate what lay before him, Avec opened his mind and showed her.

She saw herself naked and shivering, her stomach flat against the ground and her eyes open in empty shock. Stretching about four feet on either side of her body were pale, bluish wings that glistened in the sun – an image forever emblazoned in her brain.

The question of what the wings meant was one she was beginning to believe she would never answer.

Morning was giving way to afternoon, the sun growing hot overhead as she made her way through the valley toward home.

Squinting against it, she could vaguely make out the hills of Roden that housed the burrows of her people, and she caught herself sighing as she tried to envision what the rest of her day would hold.

Anxiety piled on top of the already heavy feelings from her failed flight, knowing with little doubt she had a reprimand or worse coming from Delsin, for she had been gone too long already.

Since her youthful days, she had spent much of her time away from the village, preferring Avec's company to the cold and judgmental eyes of the others, who seemed almost relieved to have her gone and never truly challenged her leaving.

Only Delsin's disposition had never been one she could lay bets on. One day he couldn't care less. The next day he might view her absence as tantamount to murder.

She and Avec chose the other side of the rise as a good location for her to test her wings because it was secluded, and no one from the village had reason to venture that far. It meant quite a hike back home, but the walk gave her time to reflect on things, an activity she treasured.

She and her raptor went there almost every day but they knew little more about her wings than they had the first day.

Well, that wasn't entirely true. She now knew how to recognize the signs her wings would emerge and understood that it was somehow triggered when she linked to Avec and shared in his flight.

And when the link was broken, she lost control, and her wings became useless, retracting.

Unfortunately, that almost always seemed to happen when she was hovering off the ground, sending her crashing.

It seemed the more times that happened, the harder it became to maintain her link to the hawk and the quicker and more often she crashed, a vicious cycle she couldn't seem to break free of.

Concluding that the problem was one rooted in her mind and will, they quickly decided against a first flight such as Avec's, knowing that a plunge off a cliff or a jump out of a tall tree would be too dangerous and probably fatal.

So, close to the ground they stayed while she worked to strengthen the connection to Avec and improve her concentration.

Any other time she had no trouble staying linked to him. They had been sharing thoughts and experiences for years, something that had become second nature to them since she scooped him from the abandoned nest.

But when her senses overloaded, as they did when she realized she was defying gravity, her focus would split from his, and down she went.

Luckily, the same dynamic made it easy to keep her wings from being exposed around the villagers.

Usually Avec was close by, but on the rare occasion he went out on his own, she was careful not to stay linked to him long enough to share in his exhilaration, connecting to him only for brief moments to make sure he was all right.

Nev's connection with Avec was yet another of those things about herself she couldn't explain and knew better than to try.

Though she'd learned at an early age she could exchange thoughts and feelings with the creatures around her, the connection she had with him was far deeper than any other and uniquely special to her.

She still couldn't forgive herself for Slipsy, who's brutal death it had taken to teach her to hide the truth of herself from everyone around her – her first and hardest lesson in the fact she wasn't like them and they didn't understand.

The memory made her shiver, fresh as if it had just happened, though in truth it had been more than fourteen years.

She could still feel the cool silk of his length twisting through her fingers as she sat playing in the warm summer grass at the edge of the village.

They had just met that afternoon; his sleek green body slithering by when she plopped into the grass to watch after the other children had made it clear there wasn't room for her in their game of hide and seek.

"*Oooh, you're pretty,*" she'd thought silently to herself as she laid down on her belly to watch him cut through the sea of grass. "*Thank you.*"

The small thin voice had rang through her mind so clearly, she'd looked around to see who spoke before realizing the snake had stopped and turned to look at her.

"*Did you talk to me?*" she tested the thought, leaning in to see if his mouth moved.

Slithering closer, the snake rose up, coming within inches of her face.

"*Yes, I said thank you,*" he said, turning his head to one side so he could get a better look at her, seeming as confused as she was by their exchange.

A flood gate opened as they explored their ability to communicate, asking questions of one another in rapid succession.

Even though he had only hatched a month before, he was alone, she learned, spending his time moving across the ground in search of crickets and spiders and other things to eat.

"*I live in the village with my father. He doesn't like me so I spend a lot of time with my friend Nina,*" she said, leaving out the part about her mother leaving. She'd learned not to talk about it because it made people look at her funny.

"*How do you move like that? Can I touch your skin?*" reaching out her hand, she'd waited for him to say it was all right, then scooped him up before he changed his mind.

"*You're warm. I like to be warm,*" he said, rolling over on his back then curling back to his stomach in her hands. The cold feeling of his scales moving fast against her skin made her giggle.

Having spent his life alone, he didn't have a name and had seemed proud when she'd asked if she could call him Slipsy.

"*Do you have bones Slipsy?*" she'd asked.

Rabbits had bones, so did deer. She knew because she had seen them while she watched the women clean and trim the meat after the hunts. And Nina said people had bones too, but she couldn't twist and turn the way Slipsy could.

Slipsy coiled his body in the palm of her hand so he could look up at her.

"*What are bones?*"

"*Bones are hard things inside of you that are all connected and help you move, but I don't think you have any or you couldn't wiggle like that,*" she said, making her voice sound as wise as possible. "*I know I have bones because sometimes they make popping sounds, like this...*" pushing her thumb hard into the palm of her hand, she smiled proudly at the loud crack it made.

"*Oh I can do that! Listen...*" Slipsy straightened his body tight until he looked like a green stick, then started at his neck in a sharp turn.

Leaning her ear down, Nev giggled as a series of tiny little crackling sounds reached up to tickle her ears like water drops hitting hot grease in a frying pan.

"What do you have there girl?"

Bellan's harsh voice sounded behind her.

Too old to do much work anymore, Bellan had been sent out with the children so the other village women could harvest bramble berries in the small patch of woods without having to worry about them getting in the way.

"Nothing," Nev answered quickly, closing her hand over Slipsy's tightly coiled body.

"What are you hiding? Show me what's in your hand now girl!"

Rolling to a seated position, Nev tucked her hand under her leg and looked up at the old woman. Bellan was mean and always had been, or at least she was mean to Nev. While the other children got smiles and treats, the twisted wood cane that helped the bent old woman walk had thumped Nev more than once.

"I don't have anything Bellan."

Nev tried to look as innocent as possible, but couldn't help a small jolt of surprise when she felt Slipsy sliding through the opening between her thumb and forefinger.

"I don't like her, let me go back to the grass," he said, pushing his body out to climb up her wrist.

"No, don't go, she will go away and then we can play more," in her haste to keep him from leaving, she glanced down at him.

Bellan's scream of terror made her realize her mistake, but it was too late.

Before she could stop the old woman, she was knocked to her back – Bellan slamming her cane into the grass as Slipsy tried to get away.

"Nooo!" Nev cried, crawling forward and trying to grab the cane at the same time. "Don't hurt him, he's my friend!"

Bellan didn't hear her, or couldn't, her shrieks of panic so loud they attracted the attention of the other children, who moved in closer to watch.

Slipsy slithered from side to side trying to avoid the thumping cane, but Bellan was surprisingly fast.

Bellan lifted again and Nev reached forward, trying to cover Slipsy with her hands, but she wasn't fast enough and fell onto her stomach, her face just inches from the snake as the cane came down.

Frozen, she couldn't close her eyes, watching as the wood slammed down on his head, pounding him into the dirt and all she could hear was the sound of his bones shattering.

"*Slipsy!*" she screamed, pushing the cane away.

But it was too late.

One look at his eyes and misshapen head and she knew he wasn't there anymore.

"I'm sorry ... I'm so sorry," she wailed, ignoring the laughter of the other children who had drawn in closer to see.

When a satisfied Bellan leaned down with her knife to cut Slipsy's head from his body, Nev covered her face with hands.

After Slipsy, her mind replaced the image of him on the ground with one of herself because for the first time, she knew that just like Bellan, the people around her feared what they didn't understand.

And they didn't understand her.

A new world opened up to her when she realized Slipsy wasn't the only creature she could communicate with, but from that point forward she was careful to hide it from everyone, even Nina.

Nearing the edge of the village, Nev was briefly distracted by a group of children playing in the tall grass. The sound of their happy laughter breached her isolated thoughts.

For a moment her eyes lingered on them, nostalgia and a touch of envy creeping into her chest.

It snapped away like a cord pulled too tight when one of the children, a particularly light haired little girl, noticed her watching and turned away to say something quietly that sent the whole group into a fit of laughter.

They continued to stare at her as she passed, her gait suddenly feeling jerky and uneven as if she had forgotten how to put one foot in front of the other.

Everything about her seemed to fuel ridicule from the other villagers. Even her name, which she had shortened from Never to "Nev" provided an endless source for their cruelty.

"Never gonna marry – Never gonna be pretty – Never -Never-

Never," the children chanted in whispers as she moved farther away.

She should have grown used to it by now, but try as she might, she wasn't able to block out the sting.

What was it this time, she thought, trying to turn it into a game to distract herself from the hurt.

"Maybe it was my knobby knees," she muttered to herself, "or my boney legs."

"No, it must have been my filthy hair, blackened by the fire dirt," she repeated the insult she had heard more times than she could remember.

Only in the last few months her black hair, which usually hung like an unhemmed shroud about her shoulders, had developed silver streaks. She had no explanation for it, but it had added fodder for the insults.

She tossed around possibilities all the way through the village, her low-volume debate intensifying a little every time she felt eyes on her.

She had no human friends, but Nina, an eccentric and reclusive traveler who, as tales were told, had appeared out of nowhere some 16 summers before and taken up residence in the village.

Nev had come to embrace her isolation, keeping to herself and avoiding interaction with the other villagers as best she could.

They, on the other hand, seemed to delight in seeking her out as a target for their jokes made easy by the fact she was quiet and withdrawn and made no effort to fit in.

Another part of the problem, though she couldn't see it, was her easy mastery of challenges. From cooking to tests of agility, things her peers struggled to learn and accomplish she did with the slightest effort.

Ironically, her peers might have seen her differently had she shown even a hint of arrogance or bragged. But her quiet ways gave too much room for interpretation and to them, her lack of pride seemed like callous disregard for that which took enormous investment for them.

And rather than acknowledge her aptitudes, they looked for faults and when they thought they had spotted one, they dug at it like a splinter – whether it was the fact she was motherless, dressed like a boy or that she spent all her time with a bird and crazy old Nina.

Roden was a small village, built into the facing sides of two elongated hills and had it not been for the modest wooden doorways and windows, one might not realize they had life within them at all. A quiet people, the hundred-some occupants kept mostly to themselves, growing and making what they needed. What they lacked or couldn't make, they supplemented through trade with travelers and by making the two-day journey to the closest town.

Rounding the curve of the hill to her right, Nev came to the last door and paused before she pushed it open and walked inside the only home she'd ever known.

The musty smell of damp earth greeted her, a stark contrast to the lighter smell of flora and sunshine outdoors.

Patches of color shone through dyed pieces of animal skin embedded in the walls and roof, which except for a small window near the door, served as the only light perforating the darkness.

Sparsely furnished, the small space was laid out with function in mind, the rough support beams that held the hard packed dirt cluttered with randomly hung tools and miscellaneous items.

A small wooden table sat just inside and to the right of the door situated between two matching benches and against the wall nearest the table a shelf housed jugs, pots and utensils.

Other than the table, there was a single chair that sat off to the side of the fire pit in the center of the room.

Straight ahead, on the other side of the fire hung two rope ladders leading up to curtain covered holes that served as sleeping areas, from one of which issued a series of low groans and slurred curse words.

The sounds reminded her of listening from beneath her blankets as his cup banged against the table, time and time again the night before, repeatedly filled and then drained of wild flower wine until well past the high moon.

"N-e-v-e-r. Where the hell have you been?" was followed by a dull "thunk" then another string of disjointed cursing.

"I just went to pray, Papa," she said quickly, easing the door closed behind her back, knowing any loud noises would only aggravate him more.

Her father was the one and probably only person she truly feared.

His ill-tempered ways had certainly taught her to avoid confrontation with other people, keeping her own stubborn and hot-headed nature carefully contained.

She often thought that the injustices she endured living with him had made her stronger than most, for there was little doubt it took a lot of mettle to withstand his fury.

The curtain over the hole on the left shifted and his feet emerged, feeling clumsily for the ladder.

Finding a foothold, he began descending the rungs, shaking and swaying a couple of times before he made it to the floor, surprisingly on his feet.

Had it been anyone else, it might have been funny, but Nev knew better than to laugh.

Delsin was not a man who could laugh at himself and she had long ago learned the quickest way to discover his ire was to insult his pride.

When he turned to face her, his short, peppered brown hair was sticking up in awkward tufts and his cheeks were flushed.

"Your place is here," he said, the heat in his eyes showing as the muscles in his jaw clenched.

He kicked at the near empty jug of wine he had left sitting on the floor next to the leg of the table.

Nev winced, then sighed in relief that it didn't break when it tipped and rolled, with a hollow sound.

"Let me guess, that fool bird is more important to you than living in a clean home," he said, closing the space between them so he could tower over her.

"Or did you run off with one of these idiot boys that are always around here?" he gestured toward the door with his hand, then brought it back to poke his finger at her chest. "You better stop lying to me, because I know you weren't praying, you stupid girl."

She tried to steady her nerves, knowing if she showed her fear he would mistake it for a sign of dishonesty, and things would get worse quickly.

Speaking at little more than a whisper, she looked down at the floor.

"No, Papa. I walked north to the valley. There's a rock there that I like to sit on to watch the morning fog lift. It helps with my prayers because it's quiet," she said, a tinge of pleading coloring her words. "I was alone. There are no boys that hang around here."

That part at least was true. None of the village boys had even the remotest interest in her.

And, really, the rest was true to a degree.

While she hadn't exactly been praying, something she'd never seen much purpose in, she had been worshiping in her own way.

Maybe it was the pathetic tone in her voice or the way she looked down at the ground, but when he could see her hurt or fear of him, his guilt would fuel further anger.

Turning around, he kicked the shelf by the table as hard as he could, sending pottery flying to the floor.

"Well I'm sure as hell not going to stay here in this mess," he growled, not making eye contact.

"If you can find time to care about something other than yourself, maybe you'll clean up this pigsty and start thinking about what we'll eat for supper. I'm starting to wonder what good it does keeping you around."

In a final show, he knocked a pot of ground meal from the table, then stormed out the door, no doubt smoothing his hair and forcing a smile on the other side for the benefit of anyone who might be watching.

Feeling as if her arms and legs were being moved by a puppeteer, Nev set about picking up the meal-coated shards of broken pottery, not pausing for even a second out of fear he might return.

Avec broke through the fog.

"He's at Edric's place."

His words tugged on the thread that was holding her together and she sank to her knees in the center of the floor and silently cried.

●● Chapter two ●●

Darkness was descending by the time Nev finished.

Cornmeal dough balls sat on the table waiting to be fried and the smell of celery and potatoes tinged with a warming hint of hot peppers and spices spilled out from a boiling pot over the fire, filling the room.

The floor was clear of reminders, the shards and mess swept away and carted off to the village's trash pit behind the hill. Had it not been for the ominous energy permanently embedded in the dirt walls, it might have felt almost homey.

Using a concoction of boiled deer sinew and starch, she had been able to mend a plate and pot, but the rest of the dishes had been destroyed beyond repair. She would have to work out a trade for more.

She still had a bit of hide left from her last hunt. Perhaps she would be able to interest Doba in a new satchel or belt.

The aging potter could still turn her wheel with skill, but the aching in her arms and fingers made it too difficult for her to do small, detailed work like sewing.

She decided in the morning she would slip over while Delsin slept and see if she could replace the broken dishes.

Weary, Nev sat down at the table and sighed.

Avec was napping above on the crest of the hill and the quiet was becoming almost eerie.

Nev hated night time more than anything.

It wasn't that she was afraid of the dark, but night was usually when she was stuck inside with no reasonable excuse to leave and consequently most vulnerable to Delsin's fits of rage.

He was a strange blend of utterly predictable and completely unpredictable at the same time.

After so many years of being on the receiving end, she could usually gauge his attacks and figure out how to calm or redirect him. But what she never knew was when or what would bring on his anger – a question she often thought even he lacked the answer to.

It made life about as stable as walking on a fault line, waiting for the inevitable earthquake but not knowing when it was coming or how bad it would be.

Sure, there were the predictable triggers – any type of embarrassment, insult to his pride, a threat to what he considered to be his or not having what he needed or thought he needed at the exact moment that he wanted it – but otherwise, it was anyone's guess what frame of mind he'd be in at any given time.

However as long as one remembered to focus on what interested him, he could be a remarkably friendly man and easy to talk with.

Which was what he had probably been doing at Edric's place all afternoon.

There was usually a group of three or four men gathered at the old man's table every day.

They drank their wine and took turns bragging, telling war stories and showing off their weapon collections and scars while talking about the glory days.

Delsin fit right in.

She hadn't had to go to Edric's much since she was a young child that needed watching, but she could picture them all as clearly as if she was there, their glasses full and smoke from their pipes hanging in the air as they laughed and ribbed at one another in a futile show of trying to prove themselves.

Thankfully, those hours spent at Edric's gave Delsin something to do away from home, buying her peace from time to time, and, this day, it gave her the opportunity to clean and prepare food without him towering over her.

Nev went to the window and pulled the small wooden shutter closed. Dusk had quieted the village except for occasional sounds of laughter or a child crying.

She fastened the latch, deciding to begin working on a satchel for Doba, knowing a bargain was always better struck with goods in hand rather than a promise.

Fetching the last remnant of deer hide from her bed chamber, she laid it out on the table and marked out a pattern with a small piece of white rock.

She had almost finished cutting when she heard a giggle outside the door.

"Is your daughter here?" she recognized Meena's voice, the words squeezed between a series of breathy giggles.

She heard their bodies impacting the wooden door and the rustle of shifting of clothing before Delsin's affirmative response brought forth another series of giggles punctuated by noises that sounded remarkably like pig snorts.

"Come with me," she heard the fat woman say right before they headed toward her burrow, their noisiness slowly fading with them as they walked away. He would be gone hours, if he returned at all before morning, and, when he did come back, he would more than likely be in a pleasant mood, the monster inside him pacified – if only for a little while.

"Disgusting," she muttered, unable to fathom what, beyond her too-eager availability, Delsin found appealing in such a repulsive woman – or for that matter any of the women that seemed to so easily find their way into his bed.

Her mother had been nothing like that, she thought, sighing as she cut the last of the pattern with a sharp knife.

No, Lannera had grace and a quiet way about her that commanded admiration from those who saw her and never since had Nev met anyone who exuded such a feeling of bearing and gentle strength.

In the same way she wondered about her father's choices in women through the last few years, she often wondered what her mother had seen in him.

But in as much as he was now defined by past accomplishments, likewise, at some point something inside the beautiful Lannera had been terribly broken and wounded.

Her pattern cut, Nev glanced up as she felt Avec stirring above on the hillside.

Staring back down at the soft leather cutouts on the table, she suddenly felt the walls closing in on her and knew she needed a diversion.

Rising to her feet, she walked over to the fire and wrapped a thick cloth around her hand, pulling the pot of soup from the center of the coals by its handle. It would keep, she thought, setting it on the table and placing the last, mended plate over top to protect the contents.

As an afterthought, she grabbed the pieces of leather, her knife, a needle and a spool of thread and shoved them in a small bag she slung over her shoulder before she slipped out the door.

Avec joined her as she made her way to the other end of the village, lighting on her shoulder, his talons clenching the strap of her bag to steady himself.

"Have a good nap?" She asked.

She could tell he was still in a bit of a haze, though he was waking quickly.

"Yes. Once I knew you were all right I was finally able to relax," he said. *"You know someday it will change. You don't have to live this way forever."*

"Oh really? And where will I go?" she retorted angrily, her voice dripping with sarcasm. "You know, you're right. Shall I find myself some nice young man in the village who will let me cook for him and raise his fat babies? That would be a fine turn, wouldn't it?"

She felt guilty for the words as they were forming because she knew striking out at him was unfair, but she couldn't seem to stop herself. Though Avec was not always but often right, he had this uncanny way of making her responsible for everything when she wanted to believe otherwise.

He took it in stride, responding in the steady way that was uniquely his.

"You're better than that, and you know it," he said, flying ahead and disappearing into the darkness.

The walk to Nina's wasn't far, though her frustration made it seem longer.

While the others in the village either downright resented her or kept a cool distance, Nina was an exception and had been for as long as she could remember.

A widow and happily a loner, she did things in her own odd way which often accentuated the distance between her and the other villagers and probably explained why she and Nev got along so well.

As Nina's door came into sight, she saw Avec waiting for her on a small clump of dirt over the top of the window.

He tilted his head and cocked one eye at her, issuing an innocent pattern of tweets as if he were a song bird.

He knew how to make her blood boil like no one else and she knew without a doubt she would have thrown something at him if there had been any such thing at her disposal, but somewhere deep inside, she knew it was probably that fury he continually stoked at that kept her going.

Lifting her fist to rap on the door, she stopped briefly to look over at him and smiled sweetly.

"Go suck worms, little robin," she said, hooking her left index finger under his chin and rubbing before her right hand descended on the wood of Nina's door.

When Nina saw Nev standing in her doorway, she pulled the door wide, her face breaking into a broad smile like a child handed a sweet.

Looking down at the small woman, Nev felt instant warmth fill her.

Nina had a near magical air about her that became obvious with one look into her lively blue eyes.

Her spirit cut through the wrinkles of her face, making them seem as ill a fit as the thin yellow-gray locks that were swept into a permanent twist at the back of her head.

She had this way of making Nev feel she was in the presence of some other-worldly being trapped in a human casing.

"Come in, girl," she said, stepping back to clear the doorway. "It's a perfect night for a visit!"

Nina's words were fast, always tumbling from her mouth as if they were competing to get somewhere before the ones that followed.

Stepping inside, Nev pulled her bag from her shoulder and clenched it in her hand as she stood waiting for direction, overtaken by a sense of reverence as she always was in Nina's home.

The smell of mint and an unidentifiable musky scent curled up her nostrils, and she glanced around – for even after years of visiting, she saw something different every time.

Candles lit the small space, giving it a warm glow that softened the edges of things, though it already had a softness beyond the light.

No slave to practicality, the sprightly woman had hung brightly colored, mismatched curtains from the ceiling to cover the dirt walls, the long lengths of fabric meeting scattered pillows and cushions on the floor, exotic textures and unusually patterned animal skins mixed throughout.

"Would you like a cup of tea?" Nina asked, her dulcet voice breaking in like chimes rustled by a surprise breeze.

"Yes, thank you," Nev responded as the woman ushered her to an overstuffed pillow by the low table in the corner.

Settling in, Nev dug into her bag and pulled out its contents, setting about threading the needle. Her ears perked to a lively tune Nina whistled as she clanked and clanged, cups brought to join saucers and spoons on a small wooden tray.

Needle threaded, Nev cut the thread loose from the spool and tied a knot in the tail.

As she pushed the needle through the double thickness of leather, Nina set a cup in front of her and turned to pull a pot of water from the fire.

Effortlessly, she transferred the steaming liquid into the cups, and Nev sniffed, pinpointing the origin of the smell in the air.

"Mint and mushroom. The mint settles the nerves and the mushroom anchors the mind," Nina said lightly before setting the pot back on the fire.

She always knew what life was like with Delsin, or at least Nev believed she did, eliminating the urge to discuss that which had no solution.

Besides, Nina wasn't one you had complicated conversations with, not because she wasn't intelligent, but because she just worked differently, her thoughts organized more like whimsical rabbit trails than well-traveled paths.

"Another bag?" Nina settled onto her own cushion, watching Nev stitch.

"I'm taking it to Doba tomorrow to hopefully trade for some dishes," she nodded, looking up through a shadowy tendril of hair crossing her forehead and eyes as she reached for her cup.

She quickly replaced it after the tea singed the tip of her tongue, jolting her in her seat.

"Ah," Nina said, looking off at the wall for a second before she sparked back to life.

"Did I ever tell you the story of the time my horse's feet got stuck in mud," she said, less of a question than it was a segue.

Of course she had, but Nev smiled and listened as Nina spun the tale, theatrically consuming every inch of her seat and more as she attempted to show herself kicking at the mired horse while a huge, monstrous and angry creature bore down on them.

Knowing Nev had never seen such an animal, Nina hooked her hands to her ears and flapped her elbows slowly back and forth to illustrate the creature's ears during the hostile stampede.

"POP! That horse pulled his leg out just in time, and off we went!" She exclaimed, clapping, then launched into high pitched giggles as she used her hand in the air to show their careening escape across the flatland.

Despite her exhaustion and frustration, Nev found herself laughing along, her tea finally cool enough to sip cautiously. Perhaps it was merely because of the suggestion, but the strange blend of savory mushroom and pervasive mint did seem to calm her and help her head to clear.

While an ever-so-small part of her always questioned the woman's fantastical stories – for the creatures and places she described were certainly imaginative – Nev was quick to tamp the thoughts.

All it took was one look at the sparkle in the petite giant's eyes to know they were real to Nina, and that was all that really mattered.

One story after another, Nina entertained Nev while she stitched but when she felt a small lull between tales, Nev abruptly asked a question that always burned at the back of her mind.

"Why did you end up on your journeys?"

Nina seemed to sense the earnestness in the question and sat back against a pillow, reaching down to tug loose a bit of curtain pulled tight by her changed posture.

Her head rested against the wall and her eyes appeared to look through the ceiling and beyond, causing Nev to again focus on her hands as they automatically plunged, then pulled the needle.

"I think the better question is why wouldn't I? It was the way my life was meant to be," her voice grew wistful with a tinge of pride. "One day I just did it – I left my home and I just did it!"

Nev felt a shift in the air and knew the woman's eyes were on her, looking up from her sewing to meet the bottomless gaze.

"That world out there is a wonderful thing, and life is to be lived," she said, her words spilling like water over rocks in a down-hill stream.

And for the first time, Nina told Nev the story of how the world became her playground, making her suddenly and acutely aware of how little she truly knew about the woman she thought she had known all her life.

In a far away western city, born the third child of humble parents, Nina said she tried but never really mastered her school lessons, finding only awkwardness between the pages of books and scribbling of pencils.

"I just didn't have use for books and I had too much energy to be sitting in a seat all the time," she said with a mischievous grin. "All I ever got out of school was in trouble."

Smiling, Nev could almost picture a younger Nina wriggling in her seat at the most inappropriate times not entirely unlike she just had during her stories.

Nina said she made it through her schooling somehow and was always a hard worker with the best of intentions, but her wild and unpredictable nature made marriage seem a distant if not impossible future for her.

"I told my parents more than once they could forget marrying me off, not that they didn't already know it because there weren't any young men calling on me. They all said they'd rather try to tame a wild horse than spend a minute with me," she said, breaking off into giggles.

When her older brother announced to their family he was striking out into the world to seek his fortune, Nina said she began to fantasize about going with him.

"And that's what I did!" She said grinning, and smacking her hands together to emphasize the pivotal moment that changed her life.

"I packed a bag full of clothes and an empty journal and that was it," she said. "When Pritt was done saying his good-byes, I followed him to the ship, sneaked on behind him and found me a nice spot down below in between the cargo crates."

By the time she was discovered on the ship, it was too late for him to send her back and Pritt was forced to pacify the angry captain by paying her way, making her promise she would board another ship and return home the moment they arrived.

"But Pritt got sick twelve days in. At first we thought it was just sea sickness, but I tended to him for a week and he just got worse and worse. I knew he was bad, but it never crossed my mind he wouldn't make it." she said, her voice losing its cheerful tone.

"He was so out of it, he hadn't said a word in days, then one night I was trying to give him some water and he grabbed my hand and he looked me in the eyes and told me, '*Make it your life Nin.*' Then he was gone."

Misty-eyed, Nina got caught up in the memory, pausing for a moment before she resumed her tale.

"The captain and his men adopted me after that. I think they felt sorry for me being out there all on my own so they tried to keep me busy," she said, her voice regaining strength as she continued. Memories of the crew brought a smile to her face.

"They liked to play jokes on me. Their favorite was to call me out on deck and tip the mop bucket over the railing above my head or chase me with the dirty mops."

They succeeded in cheering her up, Nina said, but the remaining month aboard the ship was still a bittersweet one and the crew became a strange extended family to her.

Nev hung on every word, awkwardly reaching for her cup when a tear gathered in Nina's eye as she described the long awaited day when the ship arrived at its destination.

The busy crew never noticed her slip away, hours later finding a note of heart-felt thanks for their care along with a letter for her parents informing them of her brother's death and apologizing for her own departure.

"I never looked back," Nina said, for by then she said she was fully committed to having the adventure of not only her life, but the one her brother had been cheated of. "And girl, I lived enough for both of us and more!"

It was the first time mention of her brother's death seemed to affect Nina. Her voice choked a little as she feigned interest in the bottom of her cup, using its emptiness as an excuse to rise and fetch the pot from the fire again.

It was the first time Nev had ever seen Nina vary from her childlike enthusiasm to venture into sadness.

As if she caught herself, Nina looked at Nev and resumed her sing-song tone, her features light again.

"Yes, I had adventure, learned to speak in other tongues, saw creatures and places I never saw in books and I had love," she said with a secret giggle that led to a smile spreading across her face and a far away look in her blue eyes as she poured Nev another cup of tea.

"Have you thought of love?" she asked, startling the pensive girl with her question, for usually Nina showed little curiosity in the thoughts of others.

It was a stunning question for Nev.

"No, I guess I haven't," she said, looking down into her cup to take a diversionary sip.

Between pacifying Delsin, the efforts she devoted to trying to learn to use her blasted wings, daily life and her satisfying if not all-inclusive bond with Avec, love was simply not a concern.

For Delsin, who also was not concerned with her finding love, his most recent onslaughts had been split between preventing her from going anywhere so she could see to his needs and a desire to be rid of her by passing her off to some other man.

But without having to probe the concept too deeply she knew there were no candidates in the vicinity who even remotely caught her eye, much less her heart.

A high pitched giggle from Nina made heat rise in her cheeks as she sought to crawl further into her cup.

"That's good, child, because true love isn't something you plan or think into existence, that's for sure. My fella just appeared out of thin air one day, and we didn't have to think, we knew," she said, sounding a little dreamy. "Bring love to life and it will bring love to you."

Changing course in that strange way that was uniquely hers, Nina pulled the satchel from its spot on the table in front of Nev. The bag was lacking only a handful of stitches in the strap, and, while it wasn't her best, it was nothing to be ashamed of – had it been made by anyone else, that is.

Looking down at the table while Nina silently inspected the seams, she became acutely aware of how little attention she had paid to her handwork, having been so engrossed in the old woman's stories.

"You sew like your mother. I used to have to hunt for her stitches because she did them so tight and neat," Nina said. Ignoring the look of surprise on Nev's face, she pushed her index finger through the bag to the bottom in an effort to expose the thread.

Though she really didn't know why, her mother was a topic the two never broached, and keeping with tradition, Nina skipped past the reference, leading Nev to tell herself she had imagined it.

"Doba will be proud to have that bag," she said, setting it back in front of Nev and patting it. "I'm sure she'll make you a fine trade for it, just don't let her try to short you. That is good leather and even better sewing you've done there – worth at least two plates and three or four cups. Maybe more considering how sloppy she's gotten."

Nodding obediently, Nev couldn't help but smile a little at the woman's compliments for Nina was one of the few people whose opinions she valued, and to be compared to her mother by such a person had even more significance.

"I should go Nina. I need to be home before my father gets back," she said, placing her cup back on the table.

A single furrow in her brow was the only sign of Nina's disdain at the mention of Delsin, but she moved past it quickly.

In all her years of story telling and tea with Nev, she had never asked or intervened, and this night was no exception. It was almost as if she knew the tea and stories did more good than anything else she might offer.

"Well, go on then, child. Come back tomorrow and maybe I'll see if I can get you to blush again. You look pretty with a flush in your cheeks," she said with a wink and a giggle as she rose to her feet, a slight delay in her final stretch to full height serving as a clue that her body, as always, lagged behind her mind.

"Nina?" Nev said, pausing and looking up through her hair as she restocked her bag with it's contents and folded the satchel for stowing.

Seeing the woman's eyes fix to hers, she knew she had Nina's attention and her words plunged forward.

"When I come back tomorrow, will you tell me about my mother?"

She almost felt ashamed to ask, her timidness playing out in the question as she braced for a blow that never came. Instead, Nina took the same somber tone she had used to talk of her brother and met Nev's eyes squarely.

"I would be honored to tell those stories," she said, reaching to pull the door open as Nev stepped toward it with a smile on her face.

Embracing the small woman and walking into the night, she spent the distance to her home trying to quell the fluttering in her stomach at the thought of tomorrow's promise.

"Do you think she will do as she says?" she asked Avec, stepping around an exposed tree root in the path.

"Nina's a little kooky, perhaps, but good to her word," he said in a matter of fact way as he coasted through the night air up above.

So warmed by the idea was she, Nev didn't even feel the night chill in the air. Arriving home, she tried to push away the discomfort of the place with her new found optimism, climbed up to her bed and drifted off to sleep.

Unfortunately in her sleep, the thought of learning more about her mother only stoked pain that was buried in the dark recesses of her mind. And, though she didn't know it at the time, the dreams of blood and sorrow that resulted were a prelude to the day when Nina would trade one promise for another.

•• Chapter Three ••

Specks of dust glimmered in the ray of summer sun that grew wider as she pushed the door open.

Paying more attention to the pretty rock in her hand than where she was walking, Nev felt something wet under her bare feet and looking, came to a sudden stop in the center of the room.

It was blood, and a lot of it.

Panic rising in her throat, she tried to cry out but her voice wouldn't work. Breath quickening, she dropped the rock in her pudgy hand and lifted her head. There, on the far side of the fire pit in a dark recess of the wall she saw her mother's empty, crumpled cloak.

Filled with terror and confusion, Nev dropped to her knees and crawled to it, sitting beside it and wrapping it around herself. She paid no mind to the blood that coated her hands, face and everywhere else the rough wool made contact, instead finding safety and comfort inside the thick blood drenched folds that also held the smell and feel of her mother.

The sliver of light that remained from her passage through the doorway spread, filling the room, but the sounds that followed had difficulty reaching her inside the cloak.

Starting as whispers, the voices grew to mumbles then shouts, but tucked safe inside, Nev was an island to the waves of noise that crashed around her.

It was only when a hand reached inside the safety of the folds that she became part of the activity around her, letting loose a piercing scream.

Only now as she screamed, instead of lifting her from the floor to pull her close, the hand grabbed hold of her hair and pulled.

The sensation of pain ripping through her scalp jolted Nev from her sleep and she instinctively reached behind her to grab at the source while her eyes opened wide, searching for an answer in the darkness.

The hand let loose its hold, and Delsin's voice ripped through the sanctity of her sleeping cubby..

"Get down here idiot!"

Mumbling in response, Nev's heart felt like it would explode in her chest as she struggled free from her covers and backed toward the opening, trying not to hit her head on the low ceiling while her bare feet pushed aside the curtain and sought hold on the ladder.

Reaching the bottom, she became aware of a faint light filling the room. It was an indication dawn was coming outside, but it felt a world away as fear swirled around her.

The shaking in her hands was uncontrollable as she tried to smooth her hair, hoping he wouldn't notice her sheer terror.

Delsin had settled in a corner chair while he waited for her. Leaning it back so its weight was balanced by his feet, he bit at his thumbnail and glared, his cheeks red and the muscles in his jaw clenching as if of their own accord.

Still numb from sleep and at a complete disadvantage, Nev stood waiting without a word. The excruciating silence in the room was broken only by the rhythmic sound of his teeth biting through a segment of nail followed by the sticky sound as he adjusted the saliva in his mouth before the next clench and pop.

Finally he spoke, leaning further back in his chair as if to exemplify his control of both gravity and the moment.

"Things are going to change around here," he said, the sentence lying in the room like a rug on the floor.

She said nothing, knowing more was coming.

"I've had it with your wildness. You act as if you're the only person in the world and just do whatever you want, lying and carrying on all the time.

You will get rid of those ridiculous breeches and wear a skirt like a real woman. And I expect you to be here. Maybe you wouldn't be so bad at keeping this place up if you practiced at it a little more."

Nev couldn't stop the tears that gathered in her eyes and though she managed to keep her face from showing her pain, it was too late – he had seen.

"Are you crying?" he bellowed. "Did you honestly think you could run around like a spoiled child forever, playing with your bird and drinking tea with that crazy old hag? I've had enough and I don't have to put up with this. You should be grateful for all I've done for you. If it weren't for me, you'd have nothing!"

Delsin's words were the manifestation of all the little attacks and hints he'd been making for years, yet here he'd strung them all together. But what Nev couldn't figure out was what was his goal other than to strip her down to nothing, something he'd accomplished long ago.

"You are not to see Nina again, and it's time to let that bird go. I don't want to see it around here anymore. If I see it I will kill it."

Unmoving from his chair, Delsin demanded food, glaring at her while he picked apart every move she made while she struggled to prepare it.

While she worked, he grumbled about how crazy Nina had put all these ideas in her head, twisting the truth and making her forget what was important. And how that bird of hers was nothing more than a selfish waste of time, taking her attention from the things she needed to be doing.

When her eyes grew blurry with tears she could no longer contain, she dropped the frying pan, and he laughed cruelly.

"Clumsy idiot! Watch what you're doing!"

Nev's only reprieve came from the fact that as long as she was working, she didn't have to look at him.

It took what seemed like an eternity before she set the soup and fried bread in front of him, having re-cooked the previous night's meal in the desperation of the moment.

He scowled, but lifted the bread to his mouth anyway, loading a spoon with soup to chase it down.

She poked at the fire with her back turned to him while he ate, and hoped for a diversion of any kind to break the tightness in the air... A knock at the door, anything, but none came. Even Avec remained silent, though she could feel him anxiously observing from the hilltop.

For hours Delsin demanded from his seat, tirelessly driving her from one chore to the next with cruel insults, throwing things at her when she didn't move fast enough. Throughout, he sat and picked at what was left of his nails with his hunting knife.

When golden light around the closed window shutter signaled the dropping sun, Delsin told her to stop as soon as she finished changing the bedding, but she quickly realized that it in no way meant he was done.

"Go dress yourself," he growled. "And try not to look like a girl who thinks she's a boy.

We're going to find a man who will have you. And maybe if you can try not to look so homely we'll be lucky enough to stumble on one foolish enough."

He crossed his arms over his chest, staring and waiting.

Frozen in place, Nev waged an inner battle, torn between knowing she should listen and hoping something would change in his mind and he would rescind the order.

"No, Papa, please," she begged. "I will find a husband, but please, not like this."

Delsin laughed genuinely and deeply, but his eyes remained mocking and cruel as he leaned forward.

"Who said anything about a husband?" he squeezed the words between closed teeth.

"MOVE!" he shouted as he stabbed the blade of his knife into the table.

Nev had no idea what that meant but she knew it wasn't good.

A whole new level of fear crept up in her throat as she made her way to her bed. Even once she was safely behind the curtain and away from his penetrating stare, her defenses were so engaged that she found herself far past tears, feeling more empty than anything. Empty and terrified by the uncertainty but painfully aware she had no choice.

Once inside the small hollowed cubby that served as the only place where she could retreat within the burrow, she sat for a moment and tried to steady her breathing, knowing she needed to rejuvenate what little control she had left.

Reaching out to Avec for the first time all day, she sent him an overwhelming surge of confused emotion that was wrapped in questions she knew he couldn't answer.

"I'm here," he said simply in response.

She felt her grief gripping her face at the feel of him, but she resisted the urge to break down, just glad to have the comfort of a loving friend.

"What is he talking about?" she asked the hawk. "What is he going to do to me?"

There was a short pause before Avec responded softly and with sad regret.

"I don't know, dear one."

At the sound of Delsin impatiently tapping on the table below, Nev snapped back to reality and began rooting through her small bundle of clothing in the corner as she felt Avec fly off into the dusk.

She had one dress she had made from a length of silky fabric Nina gave her as a gift to commemorate the day of her birth a few months back.

At the time she had sewn it, she knew it was only appropriate for a gown, even though she had no use for one herself. Rich and delicate, the purple cloth was covered in tiny golden flowers, lovingly hand-stitched by some unknown craftsman from some faraway land.

Though she had used herself as a guide in making it, she had never truly intended to wear the garment making it more out of respect for the craftsmanship than anything else.

The fabric had a cool glassy feel in her hands as she pulled it from underneath her modest pile of well-worn breaches and tunics.

She wriggled out of her filthy clothes, still damp in some places from the scrubbing she had done around the burrow, and tossed them near the opening. Feeling Delsin's scrutiny through the curtain, she quickly slipped the dress over her head.

It was a long gown with a straight skirt that became tangled around her legs as she shifted.

Tugging the skirt so it pooled around her where she knelt, she felt for the small ribbons she had added to it, made from the leftover pieces of fabric she hadn't had the heart to waste.

In the low light of the cubby, she cinched them gently but tightly under her breasts, still able to admire the luxurious way the fabric draped even in her distress.

She had only one set of shoes, worn leather slippers so well traveled they maintained the shape of her feet even when they weren't filled. Reluctantly, she slipped them on, knowing they were no match for the dress.

Finished, she paused, unable to force herself back through the curtain and into Delsin's eyesight again.

Reaching for Avec, she felt a lonely pain shoot through her as she realized he was out flying along the edge of the forest, feeling deserted, even though she knew realistically there was nothing he could do for her here but share in her suffering.

If only she could fly with him, she thought, wishing more than ever she had mastered use of her wings so this reality could drift off below her as she soared away.

Breaking off from Avec, she took one last, deep breath, then pushed the curtain aside and backed down the ladder, the intensity of Delsin's critical eye heating up her backside as she went.

Reaching the bottom, she turned his way but looked at the floor in front of him rather than meet his eyes.

Humiliated, the dress that should have made her feel royal instead made her feel like a sour apple – plucked, polished and held for inspection.

"Where did you get that?" he growled, his eyes lingering on her briefly as he eyed her up and down much like he was evaluating a horse to determine if it could travel, but certainly not like a father looking at his daughter.

The closest she had ever come to seeing that look on his face was in the moments before he slipped off with one of those disgusting cows of his, a thought that sent a jolt of fear through her and at the same time turned her stomach.

"I made it. Nina gave me the cloth," she responded in monotone.

Walking over, Delsin looked down at her shoes and scoffed, kicking at her foot. "Take those off. They are disgusting and you won't be needing them anyway."

Circling, he made noises to indicate he was mulling a thought;

returning back to stand in front of her, he raised his knife in his hand.

He brought the knife toward her chest and let the tip of the blade nick her flesh. When she flinched, he scowled and simultaneously slapped his open palm against her face, ordering her to be still.

The stinging heat on her cheek pulsed as she fought to stand like a statue, watching as he brought the knife to the edge of the fabric between her breasts.

Sawing at the delicate threads, he worked intently until the fabric parted, exposing her flesh, stopping right before it fell open completely.

Satisfied, he bent and examined her skirt.

Choosing a spot on the side, he grabbed the hem and cut into it, pulling the fabric apart so it tore in a straight line to the top of her hip. He repeated the action on the other side, then again on the front and back, tearing those only about half the length of the first two.

"Turn around," he ordered, stepping back..

Doing as she was told, Nev pivoted clumsily, wishing she could crawl away and hide as the fabric opened up, exposing her legs.

"Well you still look ridiculous, but it might be enough," he said, his eyes sending a different message as he stood back and examined her, consuming the sight. He swallowed hard, but then coldness snapped back into his eyes as if he realized he was showing his inner thoughts.

"Wash yourself, and be done by the time I return," he said, eyes flashing.

Then he turned and left, slamming the door behind him.

All at once Nev's mind raced. Something very bad was about to happen and she knew she needed to run but couldn't make her feet move toward the door. Her mind convinced her she would never get away before he caught her – and whatever horrible thing she faced by staying would pale in comparison to his wrath if she defied him and failed.

It was a horrible feeling that surged through her as she washed her body, working carefully to keep the dress dry; for even though it was now ruined, she still treasured what remained as a last fragment of something beautiful.

Washed, she stood, waiting in the center of the room like a sheep for the blade, wishing she could just die and escape the feeling of dread that enveloped her and numbed her senses

It was Avec's urgency that jerked her back to awareness as his voice penetrated her paralysis.

"Nev, you must leave, NOW!" he practically screeched through her head.

She suddenly lost control of her mind to him as her thoughts tumbled, coming to rest on the darkening dirt road that cut alongside the village.

There she saw Delsin, standing beside a horse-drawn wagon with his hand extended to grasp a bag of coins being offered by a towering figure of a man, but it was not Delsin, or the cold pock-marked, face of the stranger that drew her in. It was the eyes that stared out from the carriage.

Empty and pushed far beyond pain, the eyes were those of young girls, their fingers wrapped around metal bars in narrow slats at the top of the otherwise enclosed box being pulled by a pair of broken and tired bay mares.

Avec swooped down, using his sharp eyesight to show her what lay inside the carriage, and her soul fragmented at what she saw, the last few hours suddenly making sense.

Squinting through the dark shadows, a girl so small she couldn't have reached her sixth summer lay in the corner like a broken doll, her eyes hauntingly empty, legs flopped apart with dark blood staining the folds of her dress that stretched between them. Shallow breaths in her small chest indicated she was alive, but only in the literal sense of the word.

Another girl, probably twice the age of the first and likely a sister based on the shared blond hair and slender build, huddled naked beside the broken child, her arms embracing her folded legs; a look of stale anguish on her tear stained face.

Nev gasped as she saw the puncture wounds and long gashes that ran the length of the girl's back.

The horror was repeated throughout the box which was filled from corner to corner with mostly young girls and a couple of women, all battered and wounded in the most unimaginable ways.

'He has sold you to him!" Avec's voice shattered the picture, afraid she wasn't understanding as she lingered too long, overtaken by the sheer horror of what she saw.

A sudden rush of air burned in Nev's lungs as she returned to life and Avec showed her another image, this time of Delsin making his way back through the village, the coins fattening his pocket.

The image of the ravaged child in the cart was enough to close the gap in Nev's mind as risking Delsin's rage shifted to a lessor concern than that of knowing the alternative.

He was too close to the door for her to get through it, she thought, backing toward the dark recess of the wall where she had sat wrapped in her mother's cloak only hours before in her dream.

Propped against the wall a few feet away, she reached for the long knife she sometimes used to make paths through the underbrush of the forest and pulled it from its sheath.

Delsin's hand reached for the door and with Avec's full fury mingling with her own, she braced herself, knowing with absolute certainty that, regardless of what took place in the moments to come, she was not getting in that cart.

●● Chapter Four ●●

Entering the room with purpose, Delsin looked around confused when he realized Nev wasn't where he had left her.

She watched from the shadows on the other side of the burrow as he turned his back to her and pulled the coin bag from his pocket to set it alongside his knife on the table.

Turning back, he looked up toward her sleeping hole and bellowed.

"Get down here, girl!" he said, his posture oozing cockiness as she waited in the darkness.

Taking one last deep breath, she straightened to her feet and stepped forward, stopping just inside the pocket of orange glow cast by the low fire.

"How could you?" she asked, posing the question while his face still moved through shock at seeing her before him, the long knife by her side.

She stared at him a long moment, meeting his gaze fully for the first time she could remember.

"You sold me," she stated matter of fact, her eyes flickering over to the bag of coins on the table, then back to his.

Her blunt words stunned him, and, not knowing how, but realizing he'd been found out, he bristled.

"So what? Your value to me is in that bag," he said. "I have no use for you otherwise."

"Now what are you going to do? Kill me?" he said, with an unsteady laugh as he looked down at the knife in her hands. "You'd better strike and you better not miss, girl, because I will hunt you to the end of time for this."

But Nev wasn't ready yet. She could feel the shift in power and knew she had more questions for the pathetic man she saw before her.

"Is that what you did to my mother? Did you sell her too?" she demanded, years of contained anger giving push to her words.

Delsin's bravado melted away for a fraction of a second and his eyes took on an earnest look, but he quickly pushed it away and scowled at her.

"Your mother? Now she was a thing I would have kept, if she hadn't been so lost in the head," he said.

"No, girl, I didn't sell your mother, and I didn't kill her, she killed herself."

Enjoying the look of shock on Nev's face, Delsin mocked her.

"Oh, you didn't know? She cut open her veins with a knife and bled to death right where you're standing." He pointed to the dirt beneath her bare feet.

"When I found her, you were out playing, so we carried her out and dumped her in the woods for the crows to eat," he scoffed, his expression showing his utter contempt for the woman whose memory she treasured above all else. "By the time we got back and you had curled up in the corner screaming with her blood all over you. She didn't care about you any more than she cared about me or anything but herself. She was a useless woman who thought too much of herself... just like you."

Delsin's revulsion and disgust was obvious as he spat the words at her, but it was the underlying ring of truth that fueled her as she rushed forward, shrieking and throwing her full weight at him.

In his surprise, Delsin lost his balance and they tumbled as he fell backward into the table, Nev's elbow catching his mouth.

He shoved her away and struggled to get to his feet, but Nev had regained her footing, quickly backing up a step so she could tighten her grip on the knife.

"You're a monster!" she screamed, her voice filled with venom born of a lifetime of pain.

"If you're telling the truth and she did kill herself, I have no doubt it was because of you – you're a heartless, selfish pig."

Nev leaned in, her clenched knuckles whitened on the handle of her knife.

"I wish she'd taken the knife to you while you slept, but I'm sure you ruined her so badly she couldn't see a future – not even one without you. There is nothing of you in me, and I promise you, you will have your turn with the crows."

Laughing, Delsin wiped a little blood from the corner of his mouth.

"Well you're right about two things," he growled. "There is nothing of me in you and we'd all be better off if she'd taken a knife to me, but she didn't."

Nev was so stunned by his words, she didn't realize Delsin had grabbed his knife from the table until he was already lunging toward her.

Pivoting backward off her right leg, she side-stepped the blow and brought her own knife down in a sweeping motion. The blade cut through Delsin's wrist without slowing on its way back to her side.

He roared in pain and grabbed at the bleeding stump, cursing her as he fell to his knees.

"GET OUT NOW!" Avec's cry snapped her back to reality as she realized what she'd just done.

Nev scrambled up the ladder to her bed, finding the largest bag she had and blindly shoving everything she could fit inside it, topping it off with her blanket.

Half falling, half jumping, she missed the ladder on the way down and stumbled to her shoes, which she stuffed in the bag she had taken to Nina's the night before. Last, she slid the blood stained knife back into it's sheath.

Almost to the door, she stopped, turning to take one last look at Delsin where he lay on the floor. His eyes moved in and out of consciousness, his body wracked with pain.

"I'm... sorry," he said, the sound of true regret mixed with low moans.

She froze as his words sent guilt washing over her and for a brief second she felt compelled to comfort him, but it was short lived as Delsin continued speaking, staring at her, his good hand gripping what remained of his arm.

His pain caused spittle to gather on his lips as he struggled to form the broken words.

"Your mother was a bitch! ... She thought she was too good for me ... and I'm sorry ... I let her bring you into this world," he practically hissed.

It was the final push she needed. Nev darted across the room and grabbed the bag of coins from the table, pausing for one last look at Delsin before she opened the door and ran into the night.

The path was a blur and the distance seemed shorter than ever before.

Nina's door swung open before her fist made contact with the wood, and the woman practically yanked her inside, shutting it quickly behind them.

Nina grabbed Nev's hand tight and closed her eyes and Nev gasped as she felt the woman enter her mind, only it wasn't Nev she was there for, it was Avec.

"Watch," was all she said.

The equally startled hawk said nothing but obeyed without hesitation, launching himself into the air from the clump of dirt above Nina's window where he'd perched on Nev's arrival.

Nina let go of Nev's hand and stepped back, taking note. The girl's torn dress, tousled hair, bare feet and the long knife in her hand told the story well enough, even if not the details.

Nina reached down to grab the hem of the dress, and, bringing it up to the light, examined the dark stains of blood that had soaked into the purple fabric.

"Do you have a change of clothes in there?" she asked, eying the bag on Nev's shoulder.

Nev could only muster a slow nod, the shock setting in.

"Snap out of it, girl," Nina said, grabbing the bag and rooting around until she found breeches and a tunic.

Tugging the dress over Nev's head, Nina tossed it to the floor and dressed her as if she were a child.

"I need you with me now, child, we only have a few minutes and they will come. Someone's bound to hear him crying like a baby if they haven't already. You should have killed him while you had the chance."

The words somehow reached Nev and she turned to look at the little woman who had transformed from the child-like story teller into something all-together different – something formidable and competent.

Nina looked up from where she had crouched to slide the slippers on Nev's feet and chuckled, then she stood and moved over to her pantry, grabbing things and shoving them into bags.

Turning, she abruptly threw a bag at Nev and ordered her to get the books on the table and anything else she thought important enough to carry.

"Come on girl, time's a-wasting!"

Unsure of what Nina meant for her to pack, Nev did as she was told and scooped up the small stack of books then added a writing stick, some animal skins, a couple candles, trinkets, Nina's slippers and a couple of the smaller pillows.

Rushing passed Nev, Nina pulled a curtain aside, revealing an hollowed recess that contained a brown leather book, a knife and a small drawstring pouch.

Placing the items in a bag she had slung across her body, Nina stopped and looked at Nev, her face beaming with the broadest smile she had ever worn.

"Let's go!"

Then she turned and pulled aside another curtain, revealing a low tunnel in the dirt.

Before Nev could say a word, Nina's backside disappeared into the hole, leaving her alone in the room.

"People have heard Delsin," Avec said, urgently sending her the image of a man stepping outside his door and walking toward the sounds of Delsin's wailing.

Nev grabbed her two bags and one Nina had left her and dove toward the tunnel, dropping to her knees to crawl as the old woman had.

Moving as fast as she could while half dragging, half carrying the bags along, Nev reminded herself that at the first opportunity, she needed to have a real talk with the strange woman that moved ahead of her in the tunnel.

Time seemed to stop while she crawled, temporarily immune to the fact that outside the tunnel were a series of happenings she had set in motion with her act of defiance.

The two old bays were pulling their box of shattered souls,

pushed faster than they should have been capable of along the small road that curved south, then west of the village.

Sitting high above their backs in the splintered cart seat, the pock-faced harbinger leaned forward – his whip snapping in time with the seasoned senses that were telling him something was wrong.

And back in the hillside, the burrow came to life like a tapped beehive right about the time the tunnel gave way to moonlit pastures.

"Hurry," Avec said, showing her the activity as he flew to join them on the far side of the hill.

Nina wasted no time, dropping her bags just outside the opening and scrambling toward the pen where the horses were kept.

"Find us three and ask them to come to me," she shouted over her shoulder as she ran.

"Did you tell her?" Avec asked as he landed on one of the bags at Nev's feet.

"No, but she knows," Nev responded.

Reaching out, she felt among the herd, searching first for Mica, a spirited but loyal gray that she had won in a hunting contest three summers before. Once he answered, she looked further, searching for the minds that were most receptive.

She found them quickly, a smallish black mare named Soot and a large bay named Barge mostly named for his build, though partly for his habit of always pushing to the front. Asking them to meet Nina at the gate, she turned her attention to Avec, checking to be sure Nina wasn't nearby.

Even though she had enormous affection for the woman and had no reason not to trust her, she also realized everything she had always known to be true was changing with every moment that ticked by.

"I don't know what she knows, and until we know who or what she is, we need to be careful," she told the hawk, who had arrived at the same conclusion on his own.

"Are you all right?" he asked.

His question made her shudder as she pictured Delsin lying on the floor, whimpering in pain.

"You can't feel guilt for that," he said. *"Long before tonight he turned his back on you. He was prepared to send you off to a life of horrible things."*

"I know, and I know he was cruel, but why did it have to be like that?" she asked, knowing he couldn't answer.

"There must be some good in him or my mother wouldn't have been with him and she wouldn't have left me there."

"Not necessarily," he said. *"She's not here to tell us, and you can't believe him."*

"I know you're right – shhh..." she said, hoisting bags to her shoulders as Nina approached, horses trailing behind.

Saddles would have certainly made the coming ride more comfortable, but they would have to make do without.

Barge was selected to carry the bags, which Nev tied across his back, balancing the weight equally on either side. By the time she was finished, Nina had already mounted Soot and was waiting impatiently.

"Come on, child, we have to go!" she said, Soot turning tail and heading west at a fast clip.

As she climbed onto Mica's back, Nev didn't need Avec's help to see the flickering lights or hear the angry voices rising out from between the hills.

No doubt by now Delsin had told them some quickly contrived story about how his crazy daughter had attacked him and run off – and no doubt they'd have no trouble believing him.

Turning her back on the village of her birth, Nev told Mica to follow Nina and leaned down against his neck.

Alone with her thoughts, she buried her face in Mica's mane and as home grew smaller behind them, she finally allowed herself to shed tears, realizing as they soaked into his coarse hair that they were not just for her, but for Delsin, too.

●● Chapter Five ●●

With the village long since out of sight, they slowed to let the horses rest, but continued pushing on at a steady pace, knowing if anyone came after them, whatever ground they'd gained might be easily closed by a fast horse.

They had covered a lot of distance, but were still out in the open, with nothing to hide them from the glow of the moon. Nev sent Avec back to check the path behind them.

Shortly after they'd left, a group of men had ridden from the village, combing the surrounding hillsides but so far they hadn't ventured out beyond the immediate area. No doubt their desire to find them would increase when they realized they had taken the horses.

Waiting for a new report from Avec, she caught up alongside Nina and slowed to keep pace.

"How far should we go until we stop?" she asked.

She didn't want Nina to think she couldn't keep up, but in truth, the events of the last several hours had begun to weigh heavily on her muscles, and as the urgency melted away, all that was left was sheer exhaustion.

"We have to make it across the open. Once we get to the forest, then we should be able to stop and rest," Nina replied, her eyes staying focused on the nothingness ahead.

The woman must have heard her sigh, because she turned toward Nev and looked at her for the first time since they'd fled the village.

Sympathy crept into her eyes.

"Hold tight to your horse girl and try to close your eyes for a little while. I'll wake you if there's trouble," she said, reaching down to pat Nev on the thigh before nudging Soot ahead.

It wasn't easy finding a comfortable position. Mica's sweat had soaked through her breeches, and the hard ridge of his spine was almost unbearable if she didn't situate just perfectly.

After multiple attempts to find a better angle, Nev finally gave up and lowered her head to the crest of his neck, wrapping long sections of his mane around her clenched fists.

Closing her eyes, she remained aware of her balance for only a moment until the darkness reached through her and she no longer cared if she fell.

The deepest sleep possible that only comes when the body has no choice, Nev's mind swirled, a jumbled mass of broken thoughts speeding through her brain until they fell away like leaves from a tree and she felt herself rising.

She instantly recognized the strange sensation of being in contact with nothing that only came with flight – no tethers, no support, no weight. It was exhilarating like nothing else.

Finally!

She sailed, moving effortlessly through the air, enjoying the success with which she defied the rules – rising up then down, rolling and turning at will.

"Never..." a female voice drifted toward her.

She tried to ignore it, preferring to revel in her mastery of the sky, but try as she might couldn't move far from it.

Instead, she found herself unable to break away, growing confused when familiarity began tugging at the edges of her memory.

"My sweet Aleta, you must listen,"it probed urgently, pleading with her.

Reluctantly, Nev paused in mid-air and turned toward the voice, almost insolently facing the nothingness from which it came.

"Tell Nina to take you to Aileron. She will understand," the voice rushed at her like a gentle, but persistent breeze.

"Why? Who are you?" Nev demanded only to have her questions ignored.

"Use the bird to watch along your way. You are not safe," it continued. "Trust only the bird and the old woman – no one else."

"I don't understand," she said, frustrated. Even though in the haze of her dream she couldn't remember the details, somehow she knew the only threat to her safety was not near the concern it had been.

"You will sooner than you think." The words tickled her ears before growing faint. "Take care Aleta."

Suddenly Nev inexplicably knew she was alone again.

Relieved, she stretched her arms and smiled, trying to return to the bliss that had been interrupted by the voice.

Only now the air felt abruptly cold and thin and the heavens turned uninviting, shaking and rumbling as if to knock her loose.

"No!" she cried out in defiance, angry at the thought of losing the wonderful feeling she had enjoyed only a moment before.

But it was not a battle she was going to win, she realized as the rumbling grew stronger and more violent – so violent it shook her, jarring her brain against the base of her skull and knocking her teeth together.

Then came the one feeling she knew all too well... falling.

"No, no, NO!" she said as if the word could somehow intervene on her behalf.

She was still chanting it when her shoulder made contact with the ground, striking with enough force to make her cry out. Gathering her breath, Nev lay still, wiggling the fingers of her right hand to be sure they still worked.

Groaning, she was taking stock of Mica's hooves and legs when Nina came to stand above her, reaching down a hand to help her to her feet.

"You all right child?" the old woman asked, blocking her lips with her other hand as if her fingers could somehow stop the giggle that she quickly suppressed by a snort.

Glaring, Nev grabbed her hand and struggled to her feet, grimacing from the pain it sent through her shoulder and back.

"Yes, I'm fine," she replied, averting her eyes and wondering silently as she dusted herself off if there would ever be a day where she stayed out of the dirt.

"You slid off before I could get to you," Nina told, throwing the words casually over her shoulder while she walked away – as if Nev wanted or needed an explanation.

Nev took a moment to look around at the unfamiliar territory so far from Roden.

They had stopped on the edge of a thick forest. To their backs was the seemingly endless plain they had crossed through the night, and, though it was still dark, the absence of the moon in the sky and the glimmer on the horizon told her morning was coming.

"We will find a place in the forest to rest for a couple of hours and have a meal, but we can't dally long," Nina said as she moved inside the tree line, the horses following behind.

Nev found the walk comforting, though initially her muscles resisted the stretching, locked in place from hours spent on a horse.

As they moved, the density of the darkness faded and was replaced with a growing, hazy light.

They had to choose their footing since there was no path, but Nina wove in and around the trees as if she knew the way, selecting passages the horses could easily maneuver.

Still foggy from sleep and stinging from the fall from her horse, Nev slowly regained her bearings as they walked, bits and pieces of her dream returning to her.

She had been flying in a wide open sky, she recalled, momentarily filled with a warmth that quickly dissipated as she remembered it had only taken place in her mind.

As she pushed aside her disappointment, Nev's mind dredged up the memory of the voice.

"Nina?" she called out ahead as the woman bobbed in and out of view between the trees.

"Yes, child?" the woman replied, not pausing to look back.

"Where is Aileron?"

Nina came to a sudden stop, causing a chain reaction as the horses snapped from their mindless plodding to come to an abrupt halt.

Following suit, Nev watched the small figure turn around and look her in the eye, unable to hide her surprise.

"Why do you ask?" she said, solemnly, turning the question back before Nev could enjoy having the advantage.

Nev could only manage to stammer the word "dream" in response.

Shooting her a final, piercing look, Nina turned her back and continued walking forward without a word.

The rest of the walk was silent, the only noise created by the sounds of their feet swooshing and crunching through the leaves on the forest floor.

Nev felt a bit wounded by what had obviously been a mistake on her part in mentioning her dream. Reaching out to Avec, she found he had momentarily stopped circling the forest edge to perch on a high limb and eye a plump mouse.

She felt the bird's heart speed as the rodent abruptly ceased foraging and rose to its hind legs to look around, somehow aware it was being watched.

So much for hope of a conversation, she thought, silently growling in frustration as she left the hawk and reluctantly rejoined the uncomfortable silence beneath the trees.

By the time they heard the trickling of water, the morning sun was beginning to weave through the trees.

The silence continued as they found a flat dip along the bank of the stream where the horses could easily approach the water and untied the bags so Barge could join the others in a drink.

Nina found a rock to sit on and dug around in one of her bags, smiling as her hand came forth with something wrapped in cloth.

It was strange, but in the hazy morning light, Nev noticed the lines in Nina's face had softened as if she had grown younger through the night.

Convinced she was seeing things, Nev focused instead on the bundle in Nina's lap, watching as she opened it to exposed a round loaf of bread, quickly joined by a similarly wrapped chunk of cheese and a small jar of jam.

The sight of the food suddenly made Nev suddenly and painfully aware of how long it had been since she'd eaten. It had almost been a full day ago that, while Delsin ordered her about, she had managed to choke down some of his leftover soup and a half-eaten piece of fried bread while she worked.

Nina fed her first, spreading the jam on a torn piece of bread paired with a sliver of cheese.

The savory sweet taste in her mouth went a long way toward

softening the silence as Nev took bite after bite, pausing only to half chew before taking the next.

It was Nina's voice that finally broke through the sounds of chewing that filled her head. Licking the last jam from her fingers, Nev looked up.

"Tell me about this dream," Nina said, leaning forward intently, her meal finished and the leftover food packed and returned to its bag.

Swallowing, Nev brushed a couple of small crumbs from her shirt and told Nina what she could remember, focusing on the message given by the voice rather than the flying and the feeling of familiarity, which for some reason, seemed far more personal.

"So I'm supposed to take you to Aileron," she said, contemplating the message and seeming for a moment as if she forgotten Nev was there.

"Well then, I guess that's what we'll do." Mind made up, she slapped her leg to seal the deal and opened a bag in search of something. "Take some rest, girl, it's a long way."

"Um, Nina?" Nev asked, still bewildered.

"What is it, child?" the woman said, pulling out one, then another of the pillows Nev had packed and staring at them with a quizzical look on her face.

Nev's question left her, and the woman's perplexed face when she next pulled her slippers from the bag was more than Nev could take, giggling when Nina, looking truly confused, peered down into the bag as if she next expected to pull out a broom.

The realization she had actually packed decorative pillows and slippers for a harrowing escape was enough to send Nev into uncontrollable laughter.

By the time Avec returned, landing in a nearby tree, he was taken aback at the sight of the pair doubled over with tears rolling down their cheeks. He cocked his head to one side then the other, studying them with growing panic until he realized they were laughing.

"What is so funny?" he asked Nev.

Even in her thoughts, she was unable to answer him, the explanation coming out in broken pieces that made no sense, making her laugh even harder as she tried to tell him.

By the time she and Nina stopped laughing, they were both lying on the ground clutching their stomachs as they tried to catch their breath.

Rolling over to look at Nina, Nev reached out to block one of the pillows the woman tossed her way with a last, burst of laughter that she closed with a sigh.

It was only after Nina tucked a pillow under her head and closed her eyes, with her arms folded on her chest, that Nev followed the example.

Content and remarkably comfortable against the pillow, she suddenly remembered the question she had started to ask before.

"Nina?"

She turned again to watch the woman, who remained unmoving, looking as if she were in a deep sleep.

"Where and what is Aileron?"

Nina responded without opening her eyes.

"It's your mother's homeland and it's very, very far away. With any luck, we'll be there by the end of summer," she said in a matter-of-fact tone. "Now sleep child. There will be plenty of time for questions later.

"You know, this pillow isn't half bad."

With that, Nina rolled onto her side and began snoring.

Avec was as stunned as Nev, who stared up at the trees, her mind spinning.

"My mother's homeland? I always thought she was born in Roden like me," she said, glad she could speak to Avec silently, for even though Nina seemed to be sleeping deeply, she had a feeling it wouldn't take much to wake her.

"*As did I,*" he answered, his tone letting on that his mind was whirling as much as hers.

The bird's only knowledge of Lannera drawn from what Nev had shared with him, which in turn were the memories of a three year old child.

Those few memories were enough, however, to leave Nev shocked that she had never made the connection before.

Conjuring one of those images now, she realized looking at

Lannera was almost like looking in the surface of still water.

Though she had been teased about it all her life, it had never struck her as odd until now that she had her mother's black hair, a contrast to the villagers, for whom brown hair was the darkest among them.

And she had worked hard to overlook her tall, slender build when it became increasingly apparent in the last few years as she matured, putting her at the height of most men in the village.

Holding her hands in front of her face, she stared at her long, thin fingers and realized for the first time that they were nothing like the short, thick fingers most of the people in Roden had.

"Could there really be others like me?" she asked Avec, her mind running wild with comparison after comparison as the loss of her home gave way to the hope there was another home out there for her.

The thought that there were people who would understand her was one Nev had never dreamed possible and she found herself imagining a world free of the scrutiny she had battled all her life.

Of course, Avec chose that moment to interject a thought that she wasn't ready to hear.

"Nev, if your mother's home was so wonderful, why did she leave it, and why didn't she take you there?"

The thought hit her like a punch in the stomach.

Hurt and angry that he had seen her childish enthusiasm and so quickly turned it against her, she flopped onto her side and curled into a ball, squeezing her eyes closed and pushing him out of her mind.

The hawk loyally watched over the two women lying on the forest floor, and Nev drifted into a fitful sleep, trying with all her might to hold onto the warm feeling of belonging, but unable to deny, even to herself, that Avec's point made too much sense to be ignored.

●● Chapter Six ●●

It was the sound of Nina's humming that brought her back, her eyes opening to the light of the sun being overtaken by the shadows of dusk as it withdrew into the trees.

The woman must have noticed her stirring, because by the time Nev had pulled herself into a seated position, a warm cup had been thrust under her nose.

As she sipped at the dark pungent drink, Nev saw a small fire nearby, smelling the meat before she saw it roasting above the flames.

"Good, you're awake just in time."

Nina pulled the meat down, using a knife to cut off a few pieces, which she put on a cloth and held out to her.

Setting her cup on the ground beside her, Nev stretched to reach, then sat back and took a bite, savoring the tenderness even though her senses hadn't quite woken yet.

"We'll get going as soon as we eat," Nina told her, settling in on a tree stump nearby to eat her own serving.

"Thank you, bird. It's an excellent rabbit," the woman said with her mouth half full, looking up at Avec where he sat perched in a nearby tree.

Nodding in response, Avec looked sideways at Nev and winked before launching into the air.

"She cares for you very much," he told her, disappearing into the thick leaves of the treetops above.

Turning back to face Nina, Nev continued eating in silence.

The numbness was falling away, replaced with questions she could tell the woman was not ready to answer from the way she stared off into space as she chewed.

When she finished eating, Nev again sipped from her cup, noticing that the liquid almost tingled as it rolled down her throat.

"What is this?" she asked, looking down into the cup, noticing it was almost black.

"It's a tea made from a root," Nina said casually. "It gives energy."

Nev could have already answered that herself, noticing her skin and the roots of her hair coming to life.

With the silence ended, Nev decided to go ahead and try a little conversation. She wasn't sure how to handle the awkwardness she now seemed to feel more and more with the woman who obviously knew a lot more about her than the other way around.

"What are we running from exactly? Delsin was in no condition to do anything, and it doesn't seem like anyone from the village followed us," she asked.

Nina's face broke into the wide smile of hers that Nev was beginning to understand hid a secret, but then, as if she caught herself, the woman grew serious again.

"You're right about that, child. You've certainly stopped Delsin for now, but he will heal in time and do not forget for the rest of your days that to injure someone creates an enemy for life who will hate you like none other."

"Some enemies are best dealt with through death," she said, punctuating the warning with that penetrating gaze of hers.

"But also know Delsin was nothing but a fool who was keeping you safe from the true dangers you now face," Nina threw her hand out as if to indicate the world at large, then shook her head as if in disbelief and looked off into the trees. "We just never expected he would pull a stunt like that. To think he actually thought to profit from you! He's a bigger fool than we ever thought possible." Her eyes came back to rest on Nev, and she reached out a hand to pat her knee.

"I'm truly sorry you had to endure so many years with him child. It's hard to understand now, but I promise you will see the reason in it."

Frustration overwhelmed Nev, quickly boiling to anger at the evasive way the woman spoke to her. Nina was always giving her partial bits and pieces of things but never really telling her anything.

Coupled with the realization she had never told Nina what Delsin had planned for her it was more obvious than ever before that Nina was not what she seemed at all – as if there were any question at this point.

Her love and respect kept her from striking out at the woman but it was growing increasingly difficult to keep control as Nina danced and wove around the obvious secrets she kept.

Rising to her feet, she turned her back.

"Nina," she said, struggling to control her tone.

"Yes, child?"

Nev didn't hesitate in response. "Please tell me... Who... What am I?"

There was silence behind her, amplifying the trickle of the stream and the movement of the horses' feet in the carpet of leaves as they picked around for shoots of grass among them.

Just as she was about to snap, she heard Nina sigh.

"I cannot completely answer that, because I don't know yet. What I do know is you are the only one of your kind," Nina sounded sincerely, but spoke slowly, as if unsure of how to choose her words.

"The story of how you came to be is full of pain and sorrow, but there is hope too, and no one knows how those things will work together – or what you will do with them," she said.

Darkness was falling, and the shadows between the trees were pulling together to consume the few remaining pockets of light.

"The story of who you are extends beyond you or your mother or your father. For you to understand, I must start at the beginning," Nina said, rising up and placing a hand on Nev's shoulder.

"We need to travel at night for now so we can stay under cover. Let's clean up here and get moving. While we journey I will tell you what I can. We have a long road ahead and plenty of time to talk about it."

Nina met her eyes, waiting for affirmation.

Letting loose a deep breath, Nev nodded and turned back toward the camp, grabbing her cup and downing the last gulp then moving to repack the few things that had been taken from the bags.

She silently called to Mica and let him know it was time to move again as she tied the last of them.

While Nev strapped the bags across Barge's broad back, she noticed Nina covering the small fire and taking steps to eliminate evidence they had been there. She hoped the woman's story would include an explanation for all the caution.

When they were ready, Nev sent a quick thought to Avec to let him know and climbed onto Mica's back.

Looking back to where Nina sat on Soot fumbling around with something, Nev pondered the darkness around them. It was already getting difficult to see, and the dense trees were going to make the way worse in the dark, especially for the horses.

"Nina..." She stopped as the woman withdrew her hand from what Nev realized was the small drawstring bag she had retrieved from the hidden cubby back in her burrow.

Giggling like a child with a treasure to share, Nina opened her hand.

Small white eggs the size of corn kernels vibrated and bounced off one another in the cup of her hand and she looked up at Nev, shrugging her shoulders together, her eyebrows raising to a pucker in the gleeful center of her face.

Nev gasped and watched in amazement as the tiny eggs cracked and little white birds began to rise out of them from Nina's hand, dispersing into the air like bees.

One of the tiny birds zoomed, then came to a stop by Nev's head, floating at eye level and she noticed the others had positioned themselves similarly near Nina and each of the horses. Even though they were suspended in mid-air, they continued vibrating, their whiteness so bright they almost seemed to glow.

Turning her head to the side, Nev peered into the forest and drew a sharp breath through her teeth when she realized the impossible had occurred and day had returned.

"What is this?" she managed, pushing her words past the shock as she looked around near frantically.

Nina broke into musical laughter and clapped her hands together, urging Soot closer to where Nev and Mica stood.

"I call them fireflies because they have always reminded me of the little glow bugs of summer," Nina said, still smiling.

"They sleep in the day and fly only at night. Now that they have each chosen one of us, they are bonded and will stay with us for the rest of their lives, short as they may be."

Curious, Nev reached out to her firefly and gently probed at its mind, pulling back in shock when an intense vibration filled her head.

Nina laughed when Nev shut the connection and made a small sound of surprise.

"Try it again right before it settles in to sleep," Nina said with a knowing smile. "They function at a very high energy level that you'll be hard pressed to make sense of. In fact, their energy is so high that they constantly need more and actually feed off the energy of whoever they've bonded to.

"All living creatures generate energy that we interpret through things like warmth or sound or movement. They can absorb that energy when they are close by. It's a good thing they are so small, because they need a constant feed that would drain you if they were larger."

Nev watched her little firefly hover in front of her right eye, amazed at the miniature perfection of it.

Pure white with the exception of a yellow patch on its breast, it was so darling she felt overwhelming affection for it.

She stared closely, appreciating the details and realized it was emitting a high pitched hum and the yellow patch on its chest grew brighter in time with the sky above her.

Nev's perplexed expression brought more laughter from Nina.

"Their energy returns to you through your bond, making your vision bright," she said. "The more you give them, and especially the more positive it is, the brighter your vision becomes, but they can manage on the unintentional energy you always carry."

Not wanting to look away, Nev continued to study the marvelous creature as she asked Nina the only question she hadn't yet heard an answer to. "What happens if the person they're bonded to dies?"

"Well, child, they die too." She said. "If their bonded one gets sick or dies or shuts them out of the bond, they cannot survive."

Avec lit on a nearby branch, surprised to see Nev staring blindly at nothing with the most intense scrutiny he had ever seen.

"Have you gone mad?" he asked, genuinely concerned.

Nev couldn't help but giggle at his question, hearing hints of Nina's characteristic laugh in her own.

She sent Avec a brief, distracted explanation, including the concept of the bond and energy exchange that Nina had just shared with her.

Her attention snapped away from the firefly when she could have sworn she heard him snort in distaste.

"That's no bird. It looks like more like a bug to me," he said, his tone taking on a snide, aristocratic air.

Turning her full focus to Avec, Nev blinked in surprise.

"Are you jealous?"

She felt the hawk bristle at her question, and immediately knew she had guessed correctly but also knew enough not to say another word.

The firefly became muted, and the air around her grew gloomy as concern with a touch of guilt overtook the enthusiasm she had felt just seconds before.

"Jealous?" he repeated her question with a harrumph. *"I'd say I'm more disappointed that you can't tell the difference between a bird and a bug. Just keep that thing away from me or I might snap it up as a snack... by accident of course."*

A little startled by his vehement snobbery, Nev didn't try to stop his speedy exit through the treetops, though she did cringe a little when his screech reached her ears, having the effect of a slammed door.

She knew Avec was reacting to a multitude of things including hurt because he wasn't used to sharing her and even though he often seemed more unflappable than she, truth be told, he was no more accustomed to change than she was.

Marking a note in her head, she vowed to give him more positive attention when he came back from the sting to his pride, recognizing that because her life always seemed so much more urgent and complicated than his, she often took their bond for granted and forgot to show him how much she appreciated him.

"He'll come around, girl," Nina chimed in reassurance as if reading her mind. It was a trait that was starting to make her wonder in fact if the woman actually was reading her mind.

She decided to say as much.

Nina brushed the idea aside with a laugh.

"No, child, I'm not reading your mind, I just know you," she said. "That and more summers than I care to tell you have made me a pretty good judge of what is going on inside a person."

Clucking gently to Soot, Nina started off through the trees, and Nev tapped Mica with her foot in an effort to keep up. While she rode, the little firefly hovered beside her face.

She noticed the same was true for the horses who had accepted their fireflies and the change from night to day almost instantaneously, which wasn't entirely a surprise. While horses were easily one of her favorite animals, Nev knew from the conversations she'd had with them that, for lack of a better explanation, they weren't overly complicated.

When she leaned in to take a closer look, the little bird zoomed in so close he had to angle his beak up to avoid poking her in the eye with it. Basking in her gaze the little guy seemed completely smitten, and though she couldn't share his thoughts, she knew without a doubt if a bird could smile, he was.

Straightening, she decided to test her firefly. She moved her head to the left, the right, bobbed up and down and even swung her upper torso in a circle, causing Mica to tilt his head back to see what all the ruckus was. Everywhere she moved, the firefly followed, staying within inches of her head.

"Is the firefly magic?" she called out to Nina where she rode a few feet ahead of her.

Confusion lay the foundation for Nev's question. For over the course of her life she had heard of magic from people in the village who claimed to have seen mystical things, and while she had never seen magic herself, at the same time, the existence of her wings and her connection with Avec had primed her for the possibility long ago. That, and the strange happenings with Nina in recent hours seemed to be confirming it.

"Yes and no," Nina answered. "Most of what people call magic can actually be explained, as in the case of the way energy is exchanged with the fireflies, but there is a point where explanations fall short. I can tell you how it works but not how it happens or why, which is where magic comes in.

"And yes, child, there is magic and there are people who can harness it, but I prefer to think of magic as questions lacking answers. Most of what people think of as magic is really just an ignorance of how the world works."

Nev mulled it over in her mind and for the most part, it made sense except that she had seen more strangeness in the past day than in all her time in Roden.

Life in the village was simple, predictable and everything worked in an understood way leaving no questions of how. If you needed light, you lit a candle or used the firelight, not a bird the size of a fingernail that somehow made your brain turn dark to light. The inconsistency was one she couldn't reconcile.

Nina seemed, yet again, to understand.

"The world is full of creatures you've never seen or even imagined that can defy the rules you know to be true," the woman said. "You have been isolated in the village, and only seen a small fragment of what exists, child. That doesn't make it magic. Take yourself for example. Can you fly?"

The words sucked the air out of Nev's lungs and left her as dazed.

"No, of course not," she stammered, her shock delaying her response.

Nina laughed, as if she recognized the lie before it was even told and looked her dead in the eyes.

"Does it feel like magic when you try?" she asked with a half smirk, albeit friendly.

Nev couldn't meet her eyes, looking down at a tuft of long hair that had grown between Mica's withers, apart from the rest of his mane. Exhaling deeply, she sighed and felt her shoulders sag.

"No, there's nothing magical about it. It's a lot of work that usually ends with my face in the dirt," she finally admitted, feeling a strange sense of relief at making the confession to another human being for the first time.

And Nina, skipped right past it, ignoring what should have been a shocking revelation, not even pausing for a second to let Nev to process what had just happened.

"You have known since childhood that you are different from the people in the village, both through your communication with the bird and other creatures and the growth of your wings, which I'm guessing happened recently," she said with a wink. "So you must certainly understand that you too are a creature that at one time even you yourself would never have imagined. But being you still takes practice and muscles in the right places and sweat and tears. When you look at it like that, it's all really quite simple, right? Just like lighting the fire or digging a hole – not like magic."

Nev lifted her eyes to look at Nina, listening intently as she spoke.

"So again I say magic is only an excuse for ignorance," she said with a smile. "Well, most of the time anyway...And while you can expect to feel very ignorant for a while and even at times after you've learned more, understand that just because it wasn't in your sheltered village doesn't make it magic."

The words might have seemed condescending if Nev hadn't known Nina meant them in a loving and nurturing way intended to open her mind, not close it.

And it did go a long way toward helping her bridge the chasm between the normal of yesterday and the fantastical of today, granted it was a shaky bridge.

"How long have you known about my wings?" Nev asked softly, still feeling timid about the topic, though of course she expected the giggle that introduced Nina's answer.

"I didn't actually know until you confirmed it, but I had assumed they would have come in by now," she said.

"It sounds like you're a little late developing them, but that's to be expected, since you weren't exposed to the proper teaching and environment. Most have developed by 15 or 16 summers."

Nev drew a sharp breath.

"Most? ... 15 or 16?" she blurted incredulously. "So you're saying there are more like me?... And I'm... slow?" she said, her mouth hanging open as if it would help catch the answer when it came.

Nina tossed her head back and laughed from deep within her belly.

"No child, you're not slow," she said, rubbing her face with her hands as she chuckled again. "You are anything but slow. And yes, there are many more who share that characteristic with you, but I wouldn't say there are more like you."

"How do you know so much about me? Do you have wings like me?" Nev's head was spinning.

"All right, child, slow down and let me start from the beginning. Or at least where it began for me," she said.

Unbeknownst to Nev, the story that unfolded was not only the keeping of Nina's promise to her but a step toward keeping a more important one she had made long ago.

●● Chapter Seven ●●

"First let me say that no, I'm not like you. I'm just plain-old human with a lot up here – " Nina tapped her temple with her finger to emphasize the point "– and with a few tricks up my sleeve."

Moving south through the forest, the women had pulled their horses side by side and were trailing behind Barge, who pushed through underbrush between the trees like a downhill moving rock crushing grass beneath it.

Nev listened intently as Nina spoke, the woman's words drowning out the night sounds of the forest.

"The people of Aileron, your mother's people, are a militant winged race," she said, explaining the Aile ability to fly and mental communication were really the only things that set them apart from humans, though they would never admit it, for they believed they were superior to all others. It was a belief that had some truth to it since their pure bloodlines and careful breeding had honed intelligence, motor skills and beauty in their offspring.

"Proud, rigid, cold and they keep their world closed to the rest of us, making sure that while many know of them, few truly know them."

It was clear that Nina had a grudging respect for the Aile, but didn't have a high opinion of them making it a surprise when her tone turned wistful and she looked away, voice breaking a little.

"There are a few exceptions who have learned kindness and joy," she said. "My husband was one of them."

Nev gasped at the revelation, for though of course she knew Nina had been married, beyond that she knew only that she loved him deeply and he had died long before Nina came to Roden.

Nina continued her story, the emotion of it apparent as she seemed to get lost in the telling.

Their paths crossed in a cold mountain village in the north. The village was used as a rally point where travelers stopped to wait out the harsh winter months until the mountains were safe for passage. While passing the days they would socialize, tell tales, share news of the world and trade their wares in a large indoor market at the village center.

Nina had fallen in with a group of traders and was peddling animal skins when Alcedo, working as a guide, came in with a group of wealthy southerners he was taking on a climbing adventure.

The dark, quiet Alcedo had shown particular interest in a large, thick fur she had been trying to sell for months at a price most couldn't pay. It wasn't until later, after several appearances by him in a feigned attempt to bargain with her, that she said she realized it wasn't the pelt Alcedo was interested in.

Though it did eventually serve as their blanket, she told with a girlish giggle, bringing a blush to Nev's cheeks.

"Girl, I wasn't always this wrinkled thing before you now. Once upon a time, I had golden hair flowing down my back and a figure that got more than a second look," she said with a wide grin and a twinkle in her eye.

Her attention drawn to them, Nev noticed as she had back at camp that Nina's wrinkles, while still there, were growing even more subdued and her skin appeared tighter and almost healthier than it had back in Roden.

Either Nina thrived on stress and urgency or she was indeed in a strange pattern of reverse aging, Nev thought, making a mental note to ask later.

The bond between Nina and Alcedo came on quickly and with an intensity she had never experienced before, the woman was saying.

They spent the cold nights secreted away from their companions, sharing the warmth of both body and spirit.

When the spring months melted the ice and snow, signaling time to move, Alcedo broke the news to her that he had a secret, knowing he had a choice to make.

"I had heard of the Aile, but never as more than a legend or a child's tale," she recalled. "When Alcedo told me the truth of who he was, it was the most heartbreaking moment of my life and I knew for certain that I would never see him again after that night."

But she quickly learned the pain Alcedo was demonstrating was not coming from dread of parting with her at all.

"He chose me," she said, the pride of the realization still within her.

The feeling that Alcedo had the night he told her the truth of who he was, could only be described as anguish, for staying with her meant turning his back on all he had ever known, Nina recalled, the pain she shared with her mate still clear.

Masquerading as innocent travelers, Alcedo and his group were a detachment of hunters from Aileron who had been sent to assassinate the son of their arch enemy, the leader of the Fauho.

"Who are the Fauho?" Nev interjected.

Nina turned and looked at her with a strange touch of sadness hiding behind her eyes.

"Patience, child. Trust me, we will get to that part," she said.

"Now, remember I told you the Aile are a harsh people with little use for any but their own kind, which is important if you are to understand how much that weighed on Alcedo in his decision," she said. "He knew that it was the end of one life in exchange for another."

Alcedo had fallen in love with a human woman, an offense that back in Aileron would have earned him death but out in the world and far from home, the question of how to handle his offense was far less clear and it was his hope that his love would have a chance.

His group of five had been sent to gain knowledge of their enemy, something of a test by the Aile, who had created an entire society around annihilation of the Fauho.

Usually hunters flew out from Aileron alone or in pairs, returning back often, but Alcedo' group had forsaken flight – instead living as humans for ten years. Their communication with Aileron limited to rare reports or instructions from the council, filtered through their commander.

Isolated and detached from home, it was a life that changed their way of thinking and though the group remained loyal above all else to the Aile, they became a family that shared a bond through their experience and trials that the Aile hadn't anticipated and wouldn't have approved of.

Alcedo took Nina with him to tell them of his decision to leave the group and abandon the mission.

Gathered in a small timber cabin they had rented from one of the villagers, they looked different to her as she viewed them for the first time since discovering who they really were.

Jovial and polite out in the village, their mannerisms and interactions they convincingly cast themselves as four wealthy fools with more money than sense. Alcedo too had played well the part of the opportunistic mountain guide helping them part with their coins.

But inside the cabin away from view, the polarity was frightening.

The moment they stepped through the door into the small room, four sets of eyes cut through Nina, the sudden tension in the air making it hard for her to breathe.

No sooner had she crossed the threshold than Teesa, the prankster of the bunch, grabbed her and pulled her into a corner where he stood behind her with an arm locked tight around her neck.

She was too afraid to cry out and smart enough not to resist, she recalled, instead standing silent while the others glared at Alcedo.

The woman who led the group was the first to speak, springing from the top of the table where she sat sharpening her knife beside the fire.

"What have you brought here?" she hissed, coming to stand inches from him where he stood frozen in the doorway.

Nina recalled Alcedo's face, covered in pain as he met the woman's anger with all the strength he could muster.

"I'm leaving Lannera, I've chosen this woman," Nina repeated his words. She spoke without pause, but looked over to take measure of Nev's shock at the reference to her mother.

"What?!" Lannera responded, her voice a blend of shock, fear and violent anger.

Nina paused to describe the group, making Nev wait for what she was really aching to hear.

They ranged in ages, Lannera clearly the youngest – probably no more than twenty-four summers old – with the tawny-headed Teesa and Buteo not far ahead of her. The thin Calvus, whose sharp features and stringy, dull red locks had always made her a little uneasy, was probably about thirty summers, making Alcedo the oldest.

Each member of the group brought with them a unique skill, and though Lannera was young, she was also the most skilled fighter and the best strategist – without a doubt, the smartest among them – and to top it off, she was a natural leader.

Tall and slender, Lannera moved like folds of silk sliding against a smooth surface, but there was a spring to her step that showed every muscle in her body was ruled by a calculating mind. The only thing about her that lacked control was the long black hair that hung in ringlets to the middle of her back and over her shoulders, framing a deceptively sweet face that contained brown eyes so light they at times appeared instead to be a deep yellow.

"She was so beautiful, your mother, but she was a thing to be reckoned with," Nina said laughing. "If you had asked me that night, I would have told you she would sooner slit my throat and laugh while I bled than have a cup of tea with me. But time teaches first impressions aren't always a window to the future."

Her humor waned as she moved back to the story, describing the scene inside the cabin that followed Alcedo' statement to his companions.

Buteo, muscular and reminiscent of a tree trunk, jumped to his feet and shoved Alcedo against the wall right about the time Teesa let loose his hold and threw Nina to the floor, moving across the room, obviously with the same intentions.

"You can't just leave, Alcedo!" Buteo bellowed down on him as he stood pinned against the wall by his neck, his hand tightening on Alcedo's throat.

While Teesa and Buteo shouted, Lannera quietly kept her back to the fray, her face hidden from view. In the far corner, Calvus chewed on a piece of bark, watching with a strange look of amusement on his face.

"Let him go, Buteo," Lannera ordered sharply, turning around with a stony look on her face.

Her words sent a ripple through the room, and the others calmed reluctantly.

Looking at Alcedo, Lannera visibly softened though she still maintained control.

"Brother, have you thought of what this means?" she asked him.

Alcedo straightened and smoothed his shirt as if embarrassed to stand before her in disarray.

"Yes, sister, I have. I love this woman. It is a connection like none I have ever known," he said, his words strong and sincere.

Watching from the floor where Teesa had tossed her, Nina was filled with pride at her love's admission.

Lannera, too, seemed to respect it.

Bowing her head, she lowered her voice so the others had to strain to hear her.

"Alcedo, I have no choice but to kill you. You know we cannot accept you leaving," she said, the regret in her voice muffled by a blanket of conviction.

"I respected you enough that I took that chance in coming to you, but I had hoped you could see another way," Alcedo answered.

"Lannera, this is not Aile, and we are far beyond the closed-mindedness of that place! Have these years together meant nothing? Can you not be happy for me and move past the venom they bred into our blood? This woman is beautiful, and she loves me, and I see joy for the first time in my life," he pleaded. "Please open your mind and your heart, I know that you hear me, I know you understand."

Nina could have sworn she saw a tear in the corner of Lannera's eye as she reached her arm out to lay a hand on Alcedo shoulder.

"Brother, I wish you had chosen differently. I will miss our bond," she said, lowering her forehead to rest against his.

"I saw the knife before anyone else, not that they seemed to care," Nina said bitterly. "Your mother drove the blade into his chest as hard as she could."

When she was sure she'd met her mark, Lannera pushed Alcedo to the floor and began barking orders to the rest of the group, telling them it was time to leave.

Only Buteo and Teesa even glanced at the limp body of their fallen brother as they hustled about.

It took only a few minutes for the men to pack their bags, even though it felt like hours to the seemingly forgotten Nina, where she lay sobbing on the floor, afraid to move to her love who lay dying just feet away.

"I will take care of the woman," Lannera snapped to the others, ordering them outside to load the mule.

Nina shivered on the floor, for even though it was spring, the night air still had a cutting chill as it drifted through the open door into the cabin. Watching Alcedo struggle to breathe, consciousness long past, she felt anger instead of fear when Lannera turned and walked toward her.

Reaching into her boot, Nina quietly pulled her knife free, keeping it between her side and the wall.

When Lannera was close enough, Nina reached out to grab her ankle, pulling her to the ground, springing to her knees with a rage she'd never felt before.

Straddling the downed woman, angry tears blurred her eyes as she pushed the knife point under Lannera's chin, but she waited too long to strike.

Lannera grabbed a handful of Nina's golden hair and yanked her head to the floor, in one swift motion, half rolling, half springing to reverse their positions.

Gripping Nina's wrist, Lannera squeezed tight until she dropped the knife on the floor, then leaned down, placing her lips next to her ear.

"Be still, you fool," she whispered, and Nina obeyed.

"My brother loves you, and if you want to have a life with him, you will shut up and listen. There is a small pouch tucked on top of the supports under the table," she said. "I am going to cut you, but if you do as I say, you will not die. After we are gone, pack the contents of the pouch into your wound and his, and you will heal."

Nina nodded, not saying a word.

With that, Lannera pulled away, looking into her eyes as she sliced her blade across Nina's throat.

There was no pain, but Nina could feel the wound was deep, her life draining from it with each pulse in her veins.

"Lannera, let's go," Calvus' voice pierced the silence.

Nina could see him leaning in the doorway, a satisfied smirk on his face at the sight of her bleeding on the floor beneath Lannera.

"I'm almost done here," Lannera answered, her tone sending him ducking back into the night.

"You bleed for him now, but I promise you nothing will save you if I ever find out you betrayed him or me from this night forward," she said quietly, through clenched teeth.

"Never! He is my love, and I will die for him," Nina responded weakly, her tears trickling from her eyes to mingle with the blood spilling onto the floor around her. "Thank you Lannera. I will never forget."

Leaning down, Lannera placed her lips against Nina's ear and whispered softly, "Never."

Nina didn't see her leave but heard the door slam shut.

Rolling to her side, she crawled toward the table through her own blood to feel for the pouch that would bring Alcedo back to her.

Her fingers explored the splintered wood until they encountered the soft leather and in their fumbling, knocked it to the floor. Struggling through her darkening vision, she found it again, this time gripping it tightly in her fist as she crawled toward Alcedo where he lay lifeless on the floor.

Her hands shook uncontrollably as she drew a fistful of pungent powder out of the bag and clumsily pressed it first into the blood soaked hole in her lover's chest. Then, their blood mingling, she pressed more into the crimson line along her own neck.

She felt a tingling along the wound as, energy spent, she collapsed beside Alcedo and lost consciousness in his limp arms.

"He woke me hours later, and we spent three days in that cabin together while we regained our strength. The compound your mother gave me healed the wounds but couldn't replace the lost blood," Nina recalled, a punctuating sniffle the only indication of how painful the memory was.

"Once we were healed, we left the mountains and set out into the world. We had nearly ten summers together, exploring and soaking up every ounce of life we could, thankful of the gift we had in each other. We always made sure the Aile didn't learn we had survived, for that would have meant death for Lannera."

Nev listened in awe at hearing a side of her mother she had never known and overtaken with reverence for the bittersweet memory that had defined Nina's life.

"We never had children. We were happy enough with just each other and had already defied the Aile enough. We had no desire to be the first to bring mixed blood into the world," she said.

"I was living by the sea asking death to come for me six days after my Alcedo died in my arms when Lannera called me to Roden," Nina said, the tears unmistakeable as she paused a moment to clear her throat. "I said a final goodbye to my love where he lay at the bottom of the ocean floor and left immediately. I arrived two days before your mother called death to take her, but those two days were enough time for her to remind me of my promise."

Nina stopped Soot, and Mica followed the example. Reaching out to place a cupped hand under Nev's chin, Nina stared deep into her eyes. A single tear gathered then trickled down her face.

"You are that promise, Never," she said, not looking away as more tears followed the first.

●● Chapter Eight ●●

They had been riding for an hour in silence and Nev found herself in a strange state, her thoughts so muddled and thick, they lay heavy on her mind, making her sleepy.

It didn't help that Avec, still keeping an emotional distance from her, had settled in for a nap on top of the bags lashed to Barge's back.

Even though Nev had asked for answers, it was almost too much to process with each answer creating a new question and though she had reciprocated Nina's heartfelt emotion, inside she felt empty.

Her last memories of Lannera were from about three summers old, the year she disappeared, and in those memories she was nothing like the woman Nina described, but her recollections were also those of a child with simple wants and perceptions.

Even still, the Lannera that Nev remembered had been sad and withdrawn, the only joy she'd ever shown reserved for her child and fleeting at that.

Granted those small pockets of joy had somehow been enough for Nev, and even the absence of the empty and sad Lannera had created a deep pit within her.

Most days, Lannera had sat in the single chair of the burrow, staring at nothing, and only Nev could rouse her from her stupor. She'd even appeared immune to Delsin's tantrums, though Nev remembered being terrified of the man as he stormed through the burrow demanding dinner or some other thing Lannera wasn't going to respond to.

There was only one time Nev could recall Lannera even speaking to Delsin – the one and only time he raised a hand to Nev before the night she left the burrow.

She'd attracted Delsin's anger when she accidentally knocked over a pot while playing on the floor with the wooden cooking utensils. Lannera snapped from her daze when he grabbed her arm and yanked her to her feet, his other hand on its way to her face.

"Don't ever strike my daughter," she had practically growled as she rose to her feet, her height putting her at eye level with Delsin.

Something in her had commanded him and he'd backed away, grumbling about Nev being a brat – but he didn't strike her that day or any other, until that final smack on the cheek, the sting of which she could still feel when she thought of it.

In hindsight, she couldn't help but wonder if, even after she was gone, her mother had somehow prevented Delsin from doing more harm than he'd managed throughout her raising.

But otherwise, the shell of a woman she remembered was certainly no match to Nina's version. How was it possible for her to have been so strong and formidable, only to be reduced to a woman who watched the walls day in and day out, eventually taking her own life?

Not even Delsin was that powerful.

"Nina, I can't make sense of this," she said, breaking the silence.

Compared to the night before, their progress seemed slow as they made their way south through the forest, yet their pace was steady, the light of the fireflies lending clarity to their course.

The fog penetrating Nev's thoughts, however, remained unenlightened.

"How did my mother go from the warrior you describe to the broken woman I remember from Roden? It doesn't add up. And how did she end up in Roden with Delsin anyway? She was far better than that the way you tell it."

Nina had moved ahead on Soot, leaving Nev to her thoughts, but slowed so she could keep pace when the questions reached her ears.

"Some of that I can answer, some of it I can't," Nina told her when Mica had hit a stride to match Soot's. "One thing I can tell you is she suffered terrible things, Nev, unimaginable things. And that caused her sadness."

"After I arrived in Roden, Lannera told me what took place after we parted in the mountains," she said, her voice becoming cautious. "I can only tell you what she told me, but I will do my best to relay it as she did, for it is her story, not mine.

"I think it best if I begin by telling you about the Fauho, because to understand the events, you must understand the history," she said.

As if asking permission to begin, Nina looked at Nev and waited until she gave a hesitant nod.

"For as long as time has been measured, the Aile have hunted and slaughtered the Fauho, their hatred so vehement they have built every aspect of their entire world on its foundation," Nina said.

"It is said the hunt was born when the Fauho vixen Syene seduced the Aile ruler Nisatus, and once she had made him love her, took his heart and disappeared into the night.

"At first thinking something had taken her from him, Nisatus sent his best hunters to find and bring back his love, but as time went by, he realized he had been tricked, and the hunt became one of revenge instead.

"For centuries, the elusive Fauho scattered, hiding from the Aile, until about a hundred years ago when Velox, the strongest and wisest of the Fauho, stepped from the shadows and called his people together.

"Velox accomplished what none ever had by bringing the Fauho together as one force, and, for the first time in their existence, the Fauho vowed to run no more.

"The Fauho proved a formidable enemy when following his lead, killing hundreds of Aile hunters in the only known battle fought between the two. It came to be known as the Battle of Futility, for it was a devastating war, and both took heavy losses in the fight – so heavy, in fact, the Aile and the Fauho soon realized there would be no victor.

"Both withdrew, not forging a truce, but neither side wanting to fully engage the other, either. In the years that followed, they actively avoided another battle, though they continued to strike out at one another whenever they crossed paths, taking the small victories where they could find them.

"Velox carried on his rule of the Fauho from deep within a mountain lair in the frozen north, and, while tension festered and grew between the Aile and Fauho, he worked to strengthen bonds within his own kind, teaching them the benefit of collaboration.

"Throughout, Alopex, his chosen son served by his side, learning of and preparing for the day when he would carry on his father's legacy in the eventual defeat of the Aile.

"When the Aile learned Velox was finally nearing the end of his days, they dispatched Lannera and her hunters. They hoped that by killing Alopex, they would stab at the heart of their enemy before they had a chance to recover from losing their leader."

"Did they kill Alopex?" Nev interjected, her curiosity burning.

She found it interesting that Nina seemed to have a softer perspective on the Fauho, as opposed to the way her shoulders tensed and even her lip curled whenever she talked of the Aile. And something about their plight as the hunted who stood together and rose up against the hunters had an appeal. It had honor and dignity... And it reminded her of how she had stood against Delsin.

Nev couldn't help but feel a little pride at Nina's initial answer, but the smile that began tugging at the corners of her mouth quickly dissolved.

"No, child, Alopex wasn't killed, and therein lies your mother's story," Nina said, sadness creeping into her voice. "The Fauho knew they were coming. By the time they entered the mountain and made their move, Alopex and his best fighters were ready."

Nina looked away, not making eye contact as she continued.

"Calvus was the only one who escaped. Buteo and Teesa were killed, and your mother was captured," she said in a voice that bore her empathy for Lannera.

"More than six long years they tried to get her to tell them Aileron's secrets. First with threats, then torture. Then Alopex himself took from her the one thing a woman has that should only be given freely..."

At that, Nina broke off, scanning Nev's face, but whether it was shock or an inability to connect with the revelation, Nev couldn't muster a reaction. Instead, she sat waiting for more.

"Alopex exploited her one weakness over and over again until the spark of her spirit was replaced by the emptiness of an animal who only survived.

"She was so strong in every other way, but after years of being worn down, I think it was that which finally broke her spirit," she said. "But even after she was broken, she still refused to give them what they wanted and for everything she lost, she kept true the secrets of Aileron."

Nev felt a bittersweet sickness move through her, a strange blend of pride, anger and sadness, for she understood enough just from her last few hours with Delsin to know what it felt like to have another control one's sense of self. To endure that and worse for years was more than she could fathom.

"Lannera herself couldn't recount how she finally got away, only that she did. To protect her loyalties through all the torture she endured, she had severed her connection to Aileron, and when she was free, she found herself aimless and alone.

"Somehow she made her way east of the mountains, and barely alive, until she collapsed in the plains north of Roden.

"It was there Delsin found her and, though she was weak and battered, he saw her beauty and wished to have her for himself. Even in her diminished state, a man like Delsin was no match for the likes of Lannera, and she saw in his greed an opportunity for a safe place to heal herself.

At first Lannera was Delsin's pride, a thing he displayed to the people of Roden like a jewel on his finger, but as time passed, and she refused to warm to him, he left her be in the burrow for fear people would see her distaste for him.

"Her absences were easily enough dismissed as the child inside her belly began to grow," she said, looking pointedly at Nev.

"But after your birth, when she continued to isolate herself, talk began to circulate that she was mad, and sympathy grew for poor Delsin. Three summers, later when Lannera called death to her, that sympathy took firm root in the simple minds of Roden."

Nina took a deep breath, then sighed as if the weight of eternity lay on her shoulders. Looking down at Soot's neck, she was silent a moment before she resumed speaking.

"When I arrived in Roden, I had no idea what Lannera had planned. I could see the state she was in, and, after hearing her story, I knew her pain was deeper than could be measured, but I never imagined she had called me so she could go.

"No one knew of your birth, child, not the Fauho or the Aile, and for you to have a chance at life, she knew it had to remain that way. I have often wondered if that wasn't the reason she took her own life, knowing that her presence could lead them to you."

The meaning that wove between the words was not lost on Nev, who sat stunned. Avec too, who had been silently listening from his perch atop Barge, hung his head.

Shame and grief set in as she realized her mother had died to keep secret the anger and hatred that defined the blood circulating through her veins.

Staring off in the opposite direction, Nina continued, unaware of the river of mute tears that ran down Nev's cheeks in response to her words.

"She asked me to keep watch over you from a distance and to be there if the time ever came, but it wasn't until she was gone that I realized why."

Her words tapered off, and, turning back, Nina gasped at the sight of Nev, engulfed in sobs.

Mica stopped walking and looked over at Soot, who followed his lead, narrowly providing room for Nina's hurried dismount.

"No, no, no, child! You stop that!" The woman practically clucked as she rushed to grab Nev's arm and pull her from her horse.

The woman pulled her close, as she fell into her arms, as if to squeeze away the pain.

Struggling against the sobs that had reached an uncontrollable tempo, "Evil," was the only word Nev could manage before the choking sobs seized control again.

Her hand stroking the back of Nev's head, Nina's words crooned against the tide of anguish.

"No, child, you're not evil. I promise you, you're not."

Nina pulled Nev to the ground and held her like a small child, while Avec and the horses stood round, watching with concern stretched between them like a barrier to the outside world.

Nina's hand absently continued to stroke Nev's hair as she spoke in a low, melodic tone.

"My girl, you alone decide what you are. Neither the Aile or the Fauho are *born* with hatred in them. That is something that is taught.

"Your mother knew that by hiding you in Roden, regardless of what you endured there, you would grow free to chose for yourself. She had no such choice, born by design and indoctrinated from her first breath. And as evil as his acts against Lannera were, Alopex, too, was cast into that role by decisions and currents that existed long before him.

"You must see, as your mother did, that you are more than just the pieces you are made of. I promise you, if your mother believed for one moment that you were evil, she herself would have seen to it that you never drew a breath. But instead she wanted more than anything else to keep you safe," Nina said, the conviction in her voice unmistakable.

"Her actions tell me she had weighed the consequences, and the value of your life was measured. Always know that for every physical truth that made your mother a woman, the hunter within her was stronger, and she was not one to make foolish decisions."

While her doubts were not entirely assuaged, Nev was soothed by Nina's words and, perhaps even more so, by the comfort of her loving touch.

The weight on her soul and the malevolent storm of thoughts that consumed her eventually gave way to sleep, her body stepping in to give reprieve where her mind could not.

As she drifted into nothingness, her only awareness was of the tendrils of compassion from her companions that wove together to cover her like a warm blanket.

"I am with you." Avec's thought floated through her like a wave of sunlight in an abyss, leaving her with a small, albeit distant hope that Nina was right.

●● Chapter Nine ●●

"Shhh! Wake up, child!"

Nev heard the muffled hiss near her ear, and at the same time, a hand wrapped over her mouth, keeping her head tight to the ground and stopping her from crying out.

The recognition of Nina's voice quickly replaced her surprise with a throb of steady panic as her eyes popped open and she looked around for a reason.

Lurching to a seated position, Nina's outstretched arm stopped her from rising fully.

Placing a finger in front of her lips, Nina rose to her feet and allowed Nev space to do the same.

The firefly was still awake, buzzing excitedly beside her cheek, but its contribution made little difference as she looked left, then right, and saw nothing.

Leaning over, Nina stretched to the balls of her feet to whisper in Nev's ear.

"There's someone nearby," she said quickly. Pressing something into Nev's hands, Nina was slipping off to the east between the trees before the words "Follow me" made the short trip from Nev's ear to her brain.

Looking down at her hand, Nev saw it was holding her knife, its blade no doubt still covered in Delsin's blood. She resisted the cringe that wanted to have at her and instead reached out for the hawk.

"What can you see?" Nev asked Avec, as she moved quickly to catch up with the spry woman ahead of her.

Avec was slow in his response and Nev detected that his jealousy of before had been replaced with that protective pity of his that tended to heat and froth the blood in her veins.

"*WHAT do you see!*" she said, this time snapping the question at him with unwarranted intensity.

The hawk's mind centered, and he simply responded with, *"Almost,"* showing her that he was flying just a short way from a break in the trees.

It was an adjustment looking through Avec's eyes. Without him having the aid of a firefly she could see night still surrounded them but his superior vision compensated for it with a sharpness that cut through the dark.

The sound reached her ears before Avec's eyes found the source.

A child's sharp cry of pain pierced the silence, only to be followed by a pleading wail that sent a chill through her and gave her feet speed she had never known before.

Nearing the clearing herself, the visual Avec sent her didn't match the horror conveyed to her ears.

Frantically searching the still meadow through his eyes, she spotted the dark shape of a horse carriage stopped along the edge of the treeline, not far from a wide, rough path that cut east through the trees.

The lack of chaos she'd expected to find almost brought her to a halt until the scream shattered the silence again.

As Avec closed the distance, Nev saw subtle movement around the carriage which she pinpointed to three figures.

In the driver's seat, a slender man wearing a stiff uniform shifted uncomfortably, his hands moving up to rub his ears as if the action would somehow block the noise. The driver's discomfort was a sharp contrast, however to the smirks of two like-attired men who, far larger than he, stood on either side of the carriage door.

Another ear-piercing scream cut through the silence, and one of the men shook his head and chuckled.

"This one's got some lungs on her, ain't she?" he threw toward the other man, picking at a loose thread on his coat as if he didn't expect an answer.

The other man met the expectation with a casual nod and a snort of concurrence while up above in the carriage seat, the thin, older man buried his head in his hands as if to drown out the cries.

With Nev almost to the clearing, Avec broke off from her and continued flying over the small road the carriage had obviously used to get there.

She was just crouching behind a tree near the carriage when Avec pulled her back to share what he had found.

Nev's heart sank as she recognized the splintered walls of the wooden cart that was pulled into the trees at the side of the path. The pock-faced man whose forfeited coins now belonged to her was standing with his back pressed against it, taking a break from the apple he was eating to dig between his teeth with filthy fingernails in search of a wayward bit of the fruit's skin.

When the sound of hands smacking against the inside of the cart were followed by a heart-wrenching plea, he withdrew his fingers from his mouth and slammed at the wood with the side of his fist.

"Shut up in there," he barked gruffly as he raised the apple back to his teeth.

Nev snapped the connection off herself this time, her mind pulling back to the scene in front of her as the next scream reached her ears, this one long and shallow. The scream faded into cries intermingled with grunts born of an inability to draw regular breath and almost simultaneously the men pulled away from the carriage, its swaying ruining their respite.

One last scream and a final plea were all Nev could take.

Darting into the clearing, she heard Nina's loud whisper from somewhere among the trees, begging her to stop but she couldn't, pulling her knife from its sheath while she ran.

Something deep inside her commanded her feet, and rage overtook her as she covered the distance faster than should have been possible. She moved so fast in fact, that they never saw her coming.

She first reached the man who had spoken but her knife swept across his throat without delay as she moved on to the second man.

Shock registering on his face as he watched his partner slump to the ground, the man managed a single, indistinguishable exclamation before her knife sank into his chest, and he, too, fell to the ground.

Looking up, Nev held her finger to her lips and the thin man in the carriage seat nodded as she reached for the door.

Before she could pull it open, she heard the heavy sound of something falling to the floor inside followed by a whimper, and the door was pushed open.

Stepping back, she readied her knife.

"Keep it down out here. I'm almost finished," ordered a demanding voice with a nasal inflection.

A coiffed head emerged through the opening with an air of entitlement that was quickly lost when Nev yanked the door from his hands, causing him to spill out on the ground in a cursing heap.

The small, graying man looked up at her in terror as she leaped over top of him and sunk her knife through his heart.

Climbing to her feet, Nev saw the man's robe had fallen open and his nakedness was smeared in blood that was not his own, a sad explanation for the cries she had heard.

Fury still coursing through her, she hesitated, taking a moment to prepare herself before climbing up to look inside the carriage.

As she had feared, her eyes met with the sight of a small figure huddled on its side between the two seats. Nev quickly snatched back when her gentle touch sent the figure into a series of whimpers.

Her heart broke as she took in the sight of the thin girl, who could have been no more than ten summers old, retracting into a tightly coiled ball against the back wall of the carriage, but more than anything, it was the child's eyes that sent shivers through her and awakened every ounce of rage she possessed.

"You are safe, little one," she heard her own voice whispering the instinctual comfort as she again reached out her hand. This time, the girl didn't recoil, instead launching from the floor to wrap herself around Nev in a choking embrace.

Holding tight to the small frame, Nev backed away from the carriage, noticing as she looked down to secure her footing that the child's bare legs were smeared with blood under her thin tattered dress.

When she turned, she found a startled-looking Nina standing amidst the bodies.

In a grim acknowledgment, Nina's eyes met hers, and she issued a single nod of consent as she reached out for the child.

Almost before the girl was transferred completely to Nina's waiting arms, Nev had turned and started toward the small road, the purpose in her steps this time defined and calculated.

"He didn't hear," Avec told her, sharing sight of the cart driver where he had moved off to the side of the path and stood facing the woods.

The speed returned to Nev's feet, and even she was amazed at how quickly she covered the distance, coming to a stop only inches behind him, silent and unnoticed.

There was a feeling of exhilarating power moving through her as she took him in, the giant of a man who was completely unaware that he was not alone.

His smell curled through her nostrils, and she breathed deep, taking in first the scent of the oils that coated his filthy hair, the stale sweat that stiffened the fabric stretched across his girth and the sharp tang of the apple lingering on his breath. For a brief second, she thought she even detected the scent of the tiny flakes of dried skin that coated his broad shoulders.

He shifted, and moving his legs out to the side for balance, reached inside his pants to free himself.

The acrid mix of metal and fermentation that embodied the warm smell of his urine as it splashed against the leaf-coated ground made its way up to her flared nostrils, and she took one last, deep breath, committing the diagram of his essence to memory.

The stream of urine stopped abruptly, then rushed in an uncontrolled burst as her knife pressed against his grime covered neck and he realized her presence.

"I am Never," she hissed into his ear through her clenched teeth. "Think of me during your journey to the fires of eternity." She pressed her face deep into his ear and pulled his head back tight as she dragged her blade across his neck, the force of her anger pushing the blade beyond his throat, nearly to the bones of his spine.

She held him up long after he had gone, her breathing rapid and her heart racing faster than it ever had before as the scent of his life pouring out fed an insanity within her.

The ragged breaths that grew from her chest echoed in her ears, drowning out all else, and she threw her head back as if to take it all in.

For a brief second, she could almost remember the smell of her mother's blood-dampened cloak, and took strange comfort in the warmth of the blood that now coated her forearm as the redness of it spread to tint the light around her.

"Nev..." Avec's voice tried to enter her head, but she pushed him out, as she felt a visceral sound reach from the center of her stomach and launch from her parted lips in a primal growl that grew to a shriek.

"NEV!" This time the hawk's fear reached through and penetrating her consciousness, Avec opened his eyes to her, forcing her to look.

The shock of what she saw sent fear through her as well, for the woman she saw before her was a stranger.

Her eyes wild and lost and her nostrils flared wide, she saw herself standing between the trees, holding the bloody corpse of the cart man with no apparent strain against the weight that should have buckled her slender frame. But her eyes skipped over the contradictions, instead focusing on the face which she knew to be her own but barely recognized.

A milky hue had taken over the color of her skin which stretched across sharpened features, the soft contours of before given way to definition in her nose and higher cheekbones. Set in teardrop-shaped recesses above her cheeks, Nev's once-soft blue eyes now cut like shards of ice through the smokey eyelids that surrounded them.

But it was her hair that shocked her more than anything. White and gray locks had replaced the charcoal color of before, save for two thin, black lines that ran the length of the hair that fell on either side of her face.

Issuing a deep gasp, Nev felt her arms let go of the trader's weight, and she pulled out of Avec's mind, not wanting him to see the vulnerability of her shock.

The speed of her heartbeat was fading, replaced with a dull thud that reverberated through her chest and ears followed by an out of sync banging sound.

The mismatched rhythm was met by the crunch of the leaves beneath her feet, working together to create a thread of reality she could follow back to where she stood among the trees.

Her head snapped toward the wooden cart, where the two bays shifted nervously at the smell of blood in the air, and she made her way to stand below the slats along the sides.

"You are safe," was all she could think to say to the fingers that reached out to her from the darkness of the opening, for she already knew what lay within.

Though she had never driven a cart before, she took the seat and reins and gently reached out to the bays with her mind, asking them to move forward along the road.

Almost simultaneously the mares heaved sighs that ended in rumbling snorts of pleased agreement for her presence in their minds signaled the end of cruelty for them as well.

The distance was short, and the mares made good time of it, pulling to a stop beside the carriage in the clearing.

Nev had been gone long enough for Nina and the carriage driver to drag the bodies to the treeline, but the mares still detected the scent in the air, shifting nervously for a moment before they settled and dropped their heads to sniff at the lush grass beneath their hooves.

Hopping down from the high wooden seat, Nev moved quickly to the back of the cart and forced up the heavy iron hasp. Pausing, she called out softly to the women and children inside to let them know all was well, then she allowed the heavy door to swing wide.

A rush of putrid smells rushed out at her. Blood, urine, feces and sickness hitting her like evil spirits fleeing the cracked seal of a tomb.

The firefly did its job, casting ambient light throughout the box, but for once Nev wished instead for darkness as she forced herself to face the scene within. The sight of the hollow eyes that stared out at her opened voids in her heart that she would have given anything to close.

Of the twenty or so women and girls, it was the small blond girl she had seen when she looked inside the cart from Roden, who rose to her feet first, moving to stand in front of her broken little sister with a posture of defensive hope at the sight of Nev in the doorway.

Despite the wounds to her body, the girl still had a fire in her eyes that Nev grasped onto as she tried to block the scene in her peripheral vision.

"Can you start helping them out?" she asked of the girl, not wanting to break eye contact.

Nodding, the girl turned and reached first for her sister as Nev had expected. After a brief struggle to lift the child, she carried her to Nev, handing her over with a look of trust, followed by a nod as she turned back to the box and began helping a woman twice her size rise shakily to her feet.

Turning to find a spot to lay the child in the grass, Nev was startled when her eyes locked with Nina's. She had been so absorbed in the horror, she hadn't realized the woman was standing behind her.

Fighting back the tears that struggled to free themselves from her eyes, she defiantly thrust the broken girl into the woman's arms as if in challenge, but Nina said nothing as she looked down with sadness and gently stroked the little girl's hair back, pulling at a wisp that was caught between her cracked lips.

"We've started a fire. Bring them this way," she said simply then walked away with the child, stopping just inside the treeline, where Nev noticed for the first time a thin curl of smoke grew, moving toward the treetops.

The slender man appeared to stand where Nina had been, his arms stretched out with a tender caring to help a woman climb from the platform.

Something in the way he wordlessly wrapped his arm about the woman's waist and supported her slow steps as she made way to the treeline let Nev know he wasn't like the four men she'd just killed and she knew she'd been right to spare him.

One by one they emptied the wooden box of souls, some of them needing to be carried, but most able to make their own way, albeit with support, until they collapsed by the fire that had by that time grown large enough to cast warmth.

While the cart was unloaded, Avec flew out about a half a dozen times, each time returning with a plump rabbit in his claws, which he dropped in a pile beside the fire.

Once the cart was empty, Nev set about skinning the rabbits and placing them above the fire to cook, her hands, but more so her mind, glad for the menial task that served as a distraction from the scene around her.

Nina had rummaged through the bags to find water skins, which she and the carriage driver made several trips to fill in the nearby stream. They were now moving from person to person, giving sips of water and wet rags for cleaning.

Using a small knife Nina had produced for the purpose, Nev meticulously cut along the abdomen of a particularly plump hare, trying to ignore the stench that clung to her skin.

Inhaling deeply when she had first sat, she had noticed she could separate the tendrils of odor, identifying each source – blood, dirt, the trader, the women – it had proved a maddening exercise that she now wanted to shut off.

And she had tied her hair back in a braid as well, not wanting to be reminded of the change to it each time a lock slid over her shoulder in a fight to untuck itself from behind her ears.

In fact she was so intently focused on the tawny brown fur being tugged by her fingers that her grip instinctively tightened on her knife when a set of filthy toes appeared in the edge of her vision.

Relaxing when she took note of the smallness of them, her eyes followed them upward until they met with those of the blond girl.

After a flickering scan of the child's face, Nev looked back down at the rabbit and resumed her work, not entirely surprised when the thin pair of legs crossed and the child plopped down beside her.

"I'm Elasine," the girl said casually. "But I like Elsie better."

Nev was struck by the precocious life in the child's voice, given what she had endured, but she didn't let on to the absurdity of it.

"Hello Elsie," she replied, forcing herself to look up, even though she really would rather have been left alone with her futile efforts to forget what had happened.

"What's your name?" Elsie prodded.

Sighing, Nev again looked away from her chore to meet the eyes of the child.

"My name is Never, but I like Nev better," she said with a wink that surprised even her.

"I like your name. It's pretty, just like you," Elsie said with a wide grin, speaking fast as if Nev's acknowledgment had opened a floodgate of some kind.

Again Nev was shocked at how the girl seemed to have no sense of the seriousness around her and even appeared unaware of the deep gashes that ran along her back, visible through matching slices in the blood-stained fabric of her thin frock.

"Well, thank you, Elsie. That's very sweet of you," she responded as she juggled her observations against the words. "How is your sister?" she asked, separating the last bits of hide from the meat before her.

Elsie's tone became so serious that Nev glanced up briefly to be sure the source of the voice hadn't changed.

"She is alive, but she won't talk to me. She just stares," Elsie replied, her perplexed concern casting a shadow over them. Even Nev's firefly seemed to respond, growing dim for a moment like a candle short of air.

"Maybe she just needs some time," Nev said, not wanting to be careless with hope and at the same time wanting to lighten the conversation.

Forcing a happier tone, Nev asked Elsie where they were from, satisfied when the simple question sent the girl into a breathless ramble, giving Nev the certain impression she would know the child better than herself before the rabbits were cooked.

Elsie and her sister Ivy were from a city named Valen that, from the best Nev could gather, lay to the east of Roden by at least three days.

Details of the child's parents were sketchy, with most of her attention focused on Persimmon, the woman who looked after them. Her eyes grew faraway and dreamy when she spoke of all the songs they sang and games Persimmon played with them. It was one of those very games, Nev learned, that eventually separated them from "Percy," as they liked to call her.

Percy liked to teach them their lessons outdoors, Elsie said, and one day, while hunting for leaf patterns that matched the pictures in their books, the sisters had gotten bored and decided to hide from her.

They heard footsteps from deep within the bush where they hid and, as she always did during hiding games, Ivy giggled.

Not ready to give up the game, the two darted out of hiding to find a better spot, only to run into a "big, smelly man."

Though Elsie had a well developed vocabulary for her age, no doubt the product of Percy's tutelage, Nev noticed there was an innocence to her view of the world that could only have come from sheltered privilege.

But it wasn't necessarily changed by the horrible experiences she and her sister had endured. Instead, rather than blending toward an overall increased maturity, the result appeared to be a divide in the child's mind where the innocent and horrific coexisted, handing control back and forth between them.

The realization was a little startling but Nev skipped past it, dismissing it with the thought that perhaps in the future, the child could work toward reconciling the dichotomy.

"Well, Elsie, we're going to try to get you and Ivy back to Percy, all right?" Nev asked, turning her face to meet the child nose to nose.

Elsie's squeal of delight caused groans and shuffling noises throughout the camp, but it was the quick smack of her lips on Nev's that she found most disconcerting.

As Elsie bounced off in Ivy's direction to tell her the good news, Nev sat frozen, resisting the urge to wipe her mouth of the moisture left behind.

She hadn't even realized Avec had returned from hunting until another rabbit carcass fell from the air above her, riding a trail of the hawk's laughter all the way to where it landed in her lap.

Growling, she scruffed the limp body and tossed it onto the pile beside her in a huff.

"Oh, you're not so tough," the bird threw over his shoulder as he

climbed above the trees and into the rising morning sun on his way to fly a quick patrol of the area.

Nev waited until she was sure he was out of sight before she reached her fingers to her lips and gently wiped them clean. Smiling secretly to herself, she allowed a low chuckle and, for once, enjoyed the thought that the bird might be right.

●● Chapter Ten ●●

By the time morning was upon them, most of the work had been done, and the camp was starting to take shape. A count had revealed eighteen: three women, seven girls over the age of twelve and the rest of the girls mere children, the youngest of which was only four summers old.

Thankfully, the increased number of eyes and ears had made conversation with Nina impossible, because Nev honestly wasn't sure what to say.

She could no more explain her actions of the night before than she could explain why her hair changed color in an instant and, quite frankly, she didn't feel like trying at the moment.

And Nina seemed to understand, her easy partnership with the carriage driver, who they had learned was named Chit, keeping her plenty busy as they bustled around the camp serving teas, doctoring wounds and performing other menial but necessary tasks.

The quiet and humble Chit, as it turned out, was an accidental participant in the events of the night before. Forced into servitude over a debt he owed to the man in the carriage, he had practically begged for their forgiveness when he told them he'd had no idea he was driving the wealthy man in pursuit of evil doings.

They hadn't questioned his sincerity, for his hunger for atonement was apparent while he worked tirelessly to see to everyone's comfort, the weight of their pain born in his eyes as he moved with Nina, rushing to meet every need he could.

While the meal cooked over the fire, Nev had gone back to find Soot, Mica and Barge, and on their return she had cut some limbs to fashion into makeshift shelters.

As daylight overtook the night, her firefly burrowed into her hair, nesting between the cross sections of her braid and though she was curious to try and connect with it, she decided the night had been long enough and the venture was best held for another day.

Avec had delivered enough rabbits, which when combined with some roots Nina had shown her how to find, had made a decent meal for everyone.

On one side of the camp, Nina and Chit made makeshift beds for two woman and three children that needed more care than the others, but most everyone else was up and looking after themselves, or at the very least able to eat.

Some of the women and girls had even walked to the stream to bathe and rinse the filth from their clothes. With their hair drying in the morning sun and the grime and stench scrubbed away, they might have looked like an intentional group of travelers were it not for the morose air that clung to the camp.

Some of the children were like Elsie, bearing little evidence of their ordeal as they devised quiet games among themselves using rocks and sticks as implements in the absence of toys.

But there were those who, like Ivy, had been cut too deep.

The child whose screams had alerted Nev the night before was somewhere in the middle of the two.

The others said little Aster, at nine summers old, was the newest among them, having been sold to the trader by her grandparents in the village before Roden.

She was polite and spoke when she needed to, but there was a calm quiet to the girl that had struck a chord within Nev more than all the others. Between that and the fact that Aster held the position among the group that would have been hers had Delsin's plan worked, Nev felt a bond with the child.

Already, in the few short hours since they had been freed from the trader, Nev had noticed Aster slipping off by herself for moments of quiet, only to be pulled back in by someone who worried that she shouldn't be alone.

Spotting the child sitting off to the edge of the camp trying to respectfully wriggle free of one of the women who felt she needed holding, Nev made her way over to the girl.

"Aster, could you come and help me with something?" she

asked, smiling at the woman, who was smothering the miserable girl against her well endowed bosom.

Relieved, Aster looked up at the woman with a "thank you" before practically sprinting to Nev's side. Walking away from the camp, Nev stopped to kneel before the girl.

She knew that what she was about to propose might seem extreme, but something told her it would do the girl some good.

"Aster I have to clean up from what happened last night, do you want to help me?" she asked gently. "You don't have to if you don't want too."

Silent for a moment, Aster seemed to mull the thought over in her mind before she nodded confidently.

"If you find yourself upset or you need to go back to camp, you just let me know and that will be that, all right?"

Nodding again, this time Aster showed no hesitation, and Nev began to feel her intuition might have been more accurate than she thought.

Nev called Mica and Barge from where they and Soot grazed with the rest of the horses. Looking down at Aster walking beside her, she realized the girl was having a difficult time keeping up, though she was trying to hide it and even though it wasn't far, it was sure to be excruciating for the child.

Offering her a ride on Mica, she was pleased when the girl eagerly accepted. Hoisting her up, she situated her sideways on his back after she saw her wince in pain at her attempt to straddle him.

Stifling her pity so Aster wouldn't see, Nev smiled and patted her on the leg as they set out.

The carriage had been moved near the camp, and its cushioned seats were being used to accommodate some of the group, yet Aster kept her distance from it, staring at it with a mixture of fear and loathing that seemed far beyond her youthful face.

But the wooden cart had been left in the meadow, both its scent and sight unwanted in the camp, and the bodies of the men Nev had killed still lay inside the treeline, far too close.

Since it looked like the group would need a couple more days to regain their strength before moving, the bodies needed to be moved further out, and the cart would eventually be needed to transport everyone, though Nev planned to clean and modify it before that happened.

Looking up at the small girl on Mica's back, Nev wondered what must be going through her mind. Her long, reddish-brown hair tucked behind her ears, Aster stared toward the spot where the carriage had been, though how she knew the location was beyond Nev, as there were no traces of it left in the mid-day sun.

Following the treeline, Nev didn't have to look hard to find the bodies, for the flies had already discovered them.

"Aster I have to tie them all together, then I will have Barge over there pull them off so we can move them far away where we don't have to see them." Or *smell them,* she finished silently, scanning the girl's face for signs of emotion but finding none.

Leaving Aster and Mica, she walked through the underbrush to where they lay, surprised at the lack of blood that she had imagined would be everywhere.

Leaning down to roll the uniformed man whose throat she had cut, she discovered the answer in the red stained dirt beneath him that had been soaking up the blood that had seeped from his body through the night.

The men's uniforms were simple and black, tailored meticulously but with no insignia to identify them. Curious she bent to look closer at the man from carriage.

He was older, probably seventy summers or more. He wore a shiny, black robe trimmed in black fur under which he had nothing else. His slender body was wrought with wrinkles, showing he had once carried more weight, and his face was sharp, his nose like a beak above thin lips.

The wound in his chest seemed small in the light, almost making it hard to believe it had been fatal.

As Nev stared at him she found herself amazed that such a non-threatening figure could cause so much pain, but it was hard to muster the fierce anger she had felt the night before.

A rustling in the leaves drew her attention, and she turned to find Aster standing behind her, her face red with anger and eyes wild at the sight of the man who, just hours before had ignored her pleas for mercy.

Thinking she had made a mistake in bringing the her, Nev stepped back, but she stopped short of putting her hands on the child when her nose detected the smell something burning.

Following Aster's angry stare, she saw that thin tendrils of smoke were rising all around the man from the ground beneath him.

Her mouth open in disbelief, Nev stared frozen, watching as tiny flames appeared, and the man's clothes caught fire. Within seconds, the body was ablaze and Aster stood watching as it burned, her face frozen in a kind of hate that Nev understood all too well, for it was the same rage that had pushed her knife through skin and bone the night before.

With the fire burning quickly, Nev moved to one of the men timidly at first. Checking to make sure she wasn't agitating Aster, she dragged, then rolled him on top of the other burning man. With no reaction from the girl, who was still intently watching the flames, Nev did the same with the second man.

Moving back to stand with Aster, Nev gently reached out her hand to grasp the smaller one beside her together, they stood and watched the men burn.

"I'm sorry." Aster's small voice broke the silence as the flames gave way to burning cinders.

Kneeling, Nev took Aster's face in her hands. "Why in the world are you sorry, Aster?"

"Because I'm not supposed to burn things. That's why Grandfather and Grandmother sent me away," she said. Her face was again devoid of emotion, her rage having died out with the flames.

"Aster, you've nothing to be sorry for. You did a good thing here, and you saved me a lot of work," Nev smiled at the round face that hinted at a return smile.

"Those men are gone now and they will never, ever come back, do you understand me? He shouldn't have done what he did to you, and they shouldn't have let him. But you have seen with your own eyes that they can't ever hurt you again," Nev couldn't help the tears that trickled down her cheeks as she spoke, noticing their twins gathering in the brown eyes before her.

Suddenly bursting into tears, Aster grabbed Nev as tight as she could and cried, her tears soaking both of them as she let loose the pain that she had been trying so hard to pretend wasn't there.

Nev held Aster for what seemed like hours, until the girl finally calmed and sank into her arms like a baby soothed with warm milk.

Leaning against a tree, Nev held her while she slept, her own eyes growing heavy.

"Nev?" She felt Avec probing at her gently.

Sleepily, she let him in though she would have rather not.

"What is this child?" he asked, indicating he had seen the fire but kept his distance until the child was asleep.

"I don't know. She's just a little girl," she responded offhandedly, still trying to doze.

"Nev, she's not just a little girl. Little girls don't burn things with their minds like that. Promise me you'll talk to Nina about this," he asked, practically pleading. *"Promise me..."*

"Fine, I'll talk to Nina about it. Can I sleep now, just for a moment?" she asked.

Withdrawing, Avec sat in a tree branch above as Nev and the girl curled together, noticing that while Nev lapsed into deep regular breathing, Aster whimpered and her breath hastened, letting loose a series of short whines before she calmed against her protector.

Shaking his head, Avec found himself wishing he could talk to Nina himself.

When Nev woke, she could tell by the low position of the sun on the other side of the trees that several hours had passed. With only a few hours of daylight left, she wanted to get to work on the cart so it would be ready when they needed it.

Satisfied that Nev was safe and alert again, Avec flew off to do his patrol over the forest.

Stretching, she clambered to her feet and left Aster sleeping, moving to check the remnants of the men. The embers and coals had finally gone out, leaving behind a pile of ash in which she found a handful of buttons and some bone fragments, but little else. Spreading the pile one last time with a stick, Nev reached out to grab something that glittered in the sun.

Rolling her hand over, she realized it was a ring blackened by the fire. A rub along her breeches revealed a smooth silver carving of a fox, its body coiled, with tiny white pearls around it in a circle.

It must have been the old man's, she mused, concluding his two guards hardly seemed worthy of such a ring.

Thinking perhaps Aster would want it someday, or she might be able trade it for supplies along the journey, she tied it into the lace of her breeches, then tucked it inside her waistband.

Gently waking Aster, Nev lifted her back on Mica, who had grazed nearby with Barge while they slept, and began the walk to the cart on the opposite side of the clearing.

When they reached it, she helped Aster down and set about prying boards loose from the sides with her knife, not yet ready to face the stench of the inside.

It was difficult at times, with some boards fused together by weather and age, but others popped free from their moorings with ease.

As she would work one loose, Aster would carry it off and place it in a pile.

The work seemed to to do her good, though she already seemed like a different child altogether. Her smile came a little more frequently, diminishing the appearance of fragility she had worn before, and she even had a slight bounce to her step as she carried a board then rushed over to wait for another.

Smiling internally, Nev felt relief that maybe her idea had worked after all, though admittedly making the girl look at the man who had hurt her had carried the risk of going the other way and doing further damage.

In a short time, Nev had pulled all but the lower boards from both sides of the cart and the huge door from the rear, leaving the roof intact, but opening up the sides to the light of the sun.

Scowling, she viewed the inside, noting blood stains on the floor, human waste in the corner and remnants of dried food scattered across the floor, no doubt the remains of food scraps the trader had thrown to them like dogs in a cage.

"I can clean that," Aster said, her high pitched voice expressing an eagerness to help with Nev's conundrum.

Turning, Nev raised an eyebrow at the girl.

"Aster, the whole thing is wood. If you start a fire, it will burn it to the ground," she replied, perhaps a bit more dismissively than she had intended.

But Aster was unfazed, laughing at Nev's doubt.

"If I promise not to burn it down, will you let me try?" she asked.

Thinking she must be insane to even consider it, Nev nodded and stepped back to watch as Aster climbed onto the platform, moving to stand in the center.

Closing her eyes, a small smile played across the girl's face as she rubbed her hands together, and a white glow began to form between them.

When it had grown large enough that she had to lay her palms flat, she opened her eyes and leaned down, letting the small ball of fire roll onto the floor. Putting one foot forward, she applied all her weight on the ball until it began to flatten, then moved her other foot to stand squarely upon it.

Nev watched in amazement as the flames pushed out from beneath the weight of her body, moving in all directions at once to cover the surfaces within the cart.

Aster stood watching from the center of it all, turning her head from one side to the other as she monitored the white flames licking across the wood, consuming everything in their path.

Satisfied that nothing was left on the surfaces of the wood, Aster stepped back, relieving the pressure on the ball. When it had returned to its original shape, she reached down and scooped it into her palms, bringing them together as it shrunk and disappeared as quickly as it had formed.

Turning to Nev, still frozen in awe, Aster clapped her hands together and giggled, her pride beaming from her in a match to the glow of the fire.

Speechless, Nev forced a smile and moved over to help her down from the cart.

She hurriedly tied the pile of lumber together and ran a rope around Barge's broad shoulders, her shock making her feel clumsy.

When she was finished, she grabbed Aster and lifted her up on top of Mica, taking a moment to smile reassuringly.

"You're a pretty amazing little girl, you know that?" she managed, making a mental note to distract Aster once they got back to camp and head straight for Nina, the promise she had made to Avec burning with a new found urgency.

As much as she hated to admit it, it seemed for the second time in a day, the bird appeared to be right.

●● Chapter Eleven ●●

Things were quiet in the camp, some of the group stepping forward to help fashion an evening meal from more roots, leftover rabbit meat and herbs Nina had foraged earlier in the day.

Passing a reluctant Aster off to some of the older girls, Nev went in search of Nina, her steps quick with the desire to share her experience with the child.

She found her sleeping by a tree outside of camp, the events of the day and the night before having finally taken hold. Nev chuckled when she noticed Nina had one of the decorative pillows tucked behind her head, and she took note that the woman had indeed changed since they left Roden.

Back in the village she had seemed to be eighty summers or so, but here, even with the lines of exhaustion clearly etched across her face, she seemed closer to sixty, give or take a few summers.

It was certainly strange, but what about Nina wasn't strange?

Crouching down to investigate the depth of her slumber, guilt overcame her urge to wake the woman and she stood to leave.

"What is it, girl?" Nina's voice stopped her in her tracks as she tried to slip away quietly.

"Not now, Nina. You go back to sleep. I can talk to you later," she said, the guilt firmly taking hold as she realized she hadn't been quiet enough.

"I know how much sleep I need. Why don't you come over here and let me know what's got you in a twist," Nina said, patting the ground beside her.

It was funny that with everything that had happened – her apparent aptitude for killing, incredibly fast reflexes she hadn't know she had, heightened senses and most notably her changed appearance, to name a few – it was Aster that plagued her most.

The girl didn't upset her, and in all reality, it hadn't sent her mind to questions when she burned the bodies, it was more the fact that she was so casual about her control of fire and that she had obviously explored her abilities quite thoroughly. That and the fact that if she had such powerful capabilities, how had she come to be so horribly victimized by the old man?

Settling in beside Nina, she leaned back against the tree and started explaining everything that had happened with the child, starting with her idea to let Aster see her dispose of the body of the man who brutalized her and ending with the flames that had cleansed the cart on her command.

As she explained, Avec landed above them in the tree and reached out to Nev to add to the telling.

"She whines in her sleep like a dreaming dog," he said, describing the child's fitful slumber of the afternoon as she slept in Nev's arms.

Any caution about keeping her connection to Avec a secret from the woman had been unequivocally erased by the events of the last few days, and in hindsight, seemed to have been a silly concern given everything else that had happened.

Not knowing what bearing it could have, she conveyed the hawk's observation to Nina, who nodded in receipt.

At the end of her tale, Nev waited, watching Nina for a response.

Sitting up, Nina reached behind her and pulled free the hidden pins that held her hair. Working her fingers through to let it fall loose around her shoulders, Nev watched, realizing it was the first time she had ever seen the full length of the woman's hair.

Like spun strands from a spider's web, her hair had a glimmering gold hue, lightened by the streaks of white that wove throughout.

Her fingers combed through it as she pondered the information, and when she had it smoothed, they went to work forming a tight braid that she again twisted and pinned to the back of her head.

"Does the child seem to know what she is?" she finally asked, turning to look at Nev.

"I don't think so," Nev responded. "She just does these things, and while she appears to have practiced at it, she doesn't seem to see herself as anything in particular. Otherwise, I would think she would have told me, but she certainly doesn't appear to have any hidden intentions."

Nina leaned back again against her pillow, closing her eyes long enough that Nev almost got up to leave, thinking she had fallen back asleep, until her eyes popped open again.

"Do you think she can handle being asked some questions?" Nina asked, her concern for what the child had endured evident in her tone.

"I think so," Nev said. "Not much seems to upset her."

"Go get her and let me talk to her then," Nina said. Throwing in a reassuring smile, she reached out and patted Nev's leg. "I just want to talk to her, girl, but don't you worry yourself, I don't think its as bad as you fear."

With that, Nev stood. She watched as Nina leaned back, stuffing the pillow between her head and the rough bark of the tree, closing her eyes. Were it not for the warm trace from her hand that remained on Nev's leg, she might have thought she'd been talking to herself with the seamless way the woman settled into the exact pose she'd found her in moments before.

"Well *she* certainly didn't seem like she's scared of Aster," she sent to Avec as she walked back up the low incline that led to the camp. She couldn't resist the twinge to her words that sent a fairly clear "I told you so" his way.

"When has Nina ever seemed scared?" he shot back, obviously catching onto her smugness, and, nowhere near ready to dismiss the child he found so unsettling.

He made a good point, Nev thought, and, though she was stubbornly unwilling to show it in her expression, internally, she bridled her optimism.

Aster was sitting near a group of older girls, watching as they chatted and passed around a needle and thread Nev had loaned them to mend their tattered clothes.

Watching the child from a distance, Nev still found herself resistant to seeing anything sinister or threatening in her small, bent frame.

Quite the contrary, the curve to the girls tiny shoulders and the way she tucked her skinny little legs under her gave the impression she'd sooner curl into a ball and disappear than strike out at anyone. And, as Nev was starting to realize more and more, she reminded her of herself, or at the very least, she presented a tangible manifestation of how she had felt most of her life.

Aster spotted her before she could call her, jumping up and running to her with a speed Nev hadn't imagined she was capable of, especially in light of her ordeal.

"I was looking for you, but I couldn't find you." she said, looking up at Nev, her voice rising slightly at the end of her words.

"I was with Nina in the woods," Nev replied, bending down to make their height more equal. "She wants to talk to you. I can take you to her if you want."

Aster nodded and grabbed Nev's hand, following as she led the way back to the tree where she had left Nina.

"Is she mad at me about the fire?" she asked, causing a sound strangely reminiscent of a cluck from overhead as Avec coasted past.

"He doesn't like me," Aster said with a sad twist in her voice, her head hanging over her marching feet as she worked to keep up with Nev's longer strides.

Nev opened her mouth to respond, but found she only managed a short gargled sound as she realized she didn't know what to say.

"Yes, I know..." she instead sent to Avec, extremely relieved to see Nina's figure appearing in front of them.

When she heard them approaching, Nina opened her eyes and sat forward, wearing that cheerful face of hers that had unraveled so many of Nev's worst days and nights over the course of her childhood – an effect Nev was pleased to note was not lessened in the strangeness of the moment.

Greeting them, Nina turned to Nev with a knowing smile.

"Would you mind if I spend a couple minutes alone with Aster?" she asked, though both women knew the question was asked with only one answer in mind.

"Of course, Nina," Nev responded on cue. Leaning down, she brushed the hair back from Aster's eyes and smiled as comfortingly as she could.

"I'm going to go check on the horses. You'll have fun with Nina, she's my closest friend," she said with a wink.

Aster smiled and nodded, turning back to Nina as Nev walked away.

Pausing just before the pair fell out of view, Nev looked back, taking in the sight of little Aster sitting cross-legged in front of the woman, who was leaning forward as if soaking in her words.

The child's hands were moving in the air while she talked, and a small peal of laughter from Nina gave the sign that all was going well.

She felt a small twinge of jealousy at the realization that even though she hadn't known it consciously, back in Roden Nina's sole focus had been her and she hadn't ever had to move out of the way for anyone else.

And the realization extended beyond Nina as she connected to the thought that Avec must have been feeling much the same the last few days as their lives had grown more and more cluttered with other people and disruptions.

Hugging him with her mind, she felt him almost fall from the air above at the rush of emotion.

"I'm sorry I haven't been thinking of you as I should have the last few days," she told him as he regained his composure.

"You've nothing to apologize for," he said in return. *"I'm just glad you're safe, that's all that has ever mattered to me."*

Finding a cool spot on the grass at the edge of the clearing, Nev settled to the ground and lay back, enjoying the way the glowing evening sun changed the color of the trees. Avec nestled close to her, curling between the crook of her neck and the arm she had tucked under her head for support. She didn't doubt his words were deeply sincere, for as long as they had been connected to one another, she had worn his concern like her own skin, always aware and never separated from it.

Life outside Roden sure was different, she mused, wondering, if the pace continued as it had, how long she would be able to keep up. Living with Delsin had been hard, terrifying in its own right, and living outside Roden had certainly proven challenging too, but there was something satisfying about it.

Even she was startled as she counted back, to discover only two days had passed since the night they fled the village, yet it felt like a lifetime.

Looking over toward the camp, she could see the silhouettes of two girls playing a jumping game with sticks, and a sense of pride gathered in her throat as she thought of those same girls only hours before being tossed around inside the wooden box as it moved toward some dark horror.

Yes, she thought, the risk involved was certainly worth the taking and without a doubt held more value than the risks she had taken just to live a minimal life in the burrow. As uncertain as her current path was, it felt incredibly more promising than anything else she had ever known.

"So do you think your future lies in Aileron?" Avec asked, tied into her thoughts like a living, breathing part of her mind.

The question struck Nev with a weight she couldn't have anticipated. Traveling to Aileron had been thrust upon her before she had even fully understood its meaning, and the recent chaos hadn't exactly given pause for her to examine it. But with the question raised, she found she had no answer.

"I don't think so," she said finally, ignoring the way Avec peeked through the eyelid closest to her as if he had expected that response.

She felt no bond to her mother's people and, truthfully, saw no reason to go there. From everything Nina had told her, she felt more disgust for them than anything else, and if she really was the child of Alopex, then she could hardly envision a warm welcome for herself in Aileron.

She seethed at the thought of Alopex. Regardless of what Nina said, she might be able to understand her mother's choices, but not his.

Alopex' actions made him no better than the trader whose throat she had cut and it seemed grossly unfair that his cruelty twenty summers before continued to spread itself so thick through her life. From the loss of her mother and the agonizing years with Delsin all the way to the view she held of the sky at that very moment. He was to blame for all of it.

The feeling of something crawling in her hair jolted her for a moment, until she realized her firefly was stirring, waking with the sinking sun.

Avec had obviously noticed too judging by the way he tucked his head under his wing and feigned sleep.

Reaching out, Nev gently joined her mind with the tiny bird's, confused at first by the webs of gray and white fiber that appeared to have them trapped until it dawned on her she was looking at her own hair from deep within.

He was certainly much calmer when he was sleepy, she noticed, enjoying the sweetness with which he greeted his day. Sucking in a deep breath, he stretched his wings out to the sides and exhaled, vigorously shaking his head.

"Hello," she queried gently, making sure to fill her mind with positive feelings so he wouldn't be afraid.

He almost seemed to blush in embarrassment when he realized she was with him, nervously straightening the feathers along the edge of his wing before he responded.

"Hello," he answered timidly.

"My name is Nev. Do you have a name?" she asked quickly, expecting him to burst into his normal, high-energy self at any moment.

He thought for a moment, tilting his head, as if in so doing he might make the answer roll from one side to the other where he could grasp it.

"I do not, but there is one I would like. May I choose?" he asked, startling her with his proper tone of admiration.

"Certainly. What would you like me to call you?" she responded, trying hard not to laugh for fear it would hurt his feelings.

Puffing up his chest, the little bird proudly and solemnly lifted his head, speaking with all the pomp of one issuing a proclamation of monumental importance.

"I wish to be called ... Wybert," he said with dramatic pause.

The tiny bird bristled and glared, his feathers puffing when Avec snorted loudly and let loose a screech of amusement. It was a combination of noises she hadn't thought physically possible for the hawk, and Nev struggled to keep from bursting into laughter herself, glad that the little bird couldn't see her face.

Shooting the most sinister look she could at Avec, Nev choked on a deep breath and managed to reply "That's a lovely name," before smacking her hand in front of her mouth to block the laughter that threatened to burst out.

Thankfully, her recognition seemed to do the trick, and Wybert jutted out his beak again, his shoulders squared.

"Well, Wybert, the sun is nearly set, and I imagine you're ready to fly after such a long sleep," she said, still struggling against the smile that kept spreading across her face. Instead, she grazed the tip of his beak with a tiny mental kiss.

"I am very glad we got to speak and I'm even more glad you are with me. I would be lost without you." The compliment sent the little bird's mind in a whirl that she darted out of the way of as he took on a blinding glow and dove beak-first from her hair.

When he had assumed his normal position to the side of her eye, he reached out his beak to her skin with a return kiss that made him buzz with such fervor his features were momentarily blurred.

Holding Wybert's eye and smiling, Nev quietly slipped her hand across to the crook of her arm, where Avec still nested and clamped it over his entire head, locking his beak shut and muffling his laughter, only letting go when she feared she might suffocate him.

She was thankful when a rustle in the leaves startled all of them, and Avec took the distraction as an opportunity to fly off, his laughter marking his path through the trees.

"Wybert... Wybert?"

Shaking her head, Nev turned to see Aster, her face beaming widely as her pace quickened.

"Nev come eat with us. Nina is getting it ready," the girl said enthusiastically, reaching out her hand in an invitation Nev accepted with a smile, climbing to her feet with the girl's help.

"Did you have fun with Nina?" she asked, careful to keep her question casual.

"Oh, yes. We talked about my grandparents and about when I was a little girl," she said with an air of indignation that showed she was clearly of the opinion she wasn't a little girl anymore. "She wasn't mad at me at all. She just wanted to talk. I like Nina.

She's funny," she said.

Nev agreed and let the girl lead her to where Nina sat waiting near the fire with a serving of food for each of them.

It was clear fairly quickly that the talk had not left Nina with the same ease of mind it had Aster, but finding no way to broach the subject with the child sitting beside them, Nev followed Nina's example and focused on her food with as pleasant a face as she could manage.

Once they had finished, Nina gave her a quick glance then disappeared into the woods. In a hurry to follow, Nev tracked down the woman with the large bosom and shuffled a less-than-pleased but begrudgingly-cooperative Aster off with her and slipped into the woods.

She found Nina easily enough, though she had moved a good distance away from the camp, presumably so there would be no chance of them being overheard. Sitting on one of several rocks that protruded from the ground, Nina gestured for Nev to join her.

"I'm afraid I don't know much more than before," Nina admitted, almost as if she were disappointed. "I do agree with you, she doesn't have an ounce of meanness in her. But at the same time, I'm not entirely convinced she isn't a danger.

"It doesn't sound like her grandparents were very interested in her and she says they sent her away because of her fires. Other than that, she seems to know very little about how she came to be with them, what happened to her parents, or where her powers come from," Nina said. "Do you remember I told you most of what people call magic is just not understanding the way things work?"

Nev nodded.

"Well, that's the case here. The child isn't magic, and she isn't possessed by evil spirits – if it occurred to you to worry about those things. Aster is mixed with human and something else, and those gifts are natural abilities that she has, no different than breathing," Nina said with absolute certainty. "The only questions I can't answer is what she's mixed with and what kind of trouble that could cause, or if she has enough control over those fires of hers to keep from hurting somebody."

Nev pondered the observations realizing that Aster was indeed like her, and that was probably why she felt such kinship toward the child, with similar circumstance bringing similar characteristics out in each of them.

"I want you to keep the child close to you and help her where you can, but more than anything, try to act as a buffer between her and others," Nina said, looking almost pleadingly at Nev.

"Until we know how much control she has, we need to keep a close eye on her so nothing goes wrong... These women and girls have been through enough already. We don't need to add to it."

Nodding, Nev looked out through the trees, still marveling at the effect of the firefly and the way the light grew dark, then bright dependent on her mood.

"Oh, I talked to my firefly this evening," Nev said, unable to resist a giggle that she had to work to stifle. "He asked to be called *Wybert*."

Nina looked at her and broke into laughter. "Wybert?"

Nev noticed out of the corner of her eye when the little bird perked up at mention of his new name, gaining control before he realized why they were laughing.

Angling her eyes toward Wybert with slightly dramatic flair for Nina's benefit, Nev brought her finger to her lips quickly, then tucked it out of view again.

Nina smiled and nodded.

"I knew a Wybert once a long time ago. He was a very fierce warrior," she said with a wink.

"Oh!" Nev exclaimed when the sky grew so suddenly bright she instinctively brought up her hand to shield her eyes.

Nina exploded into laughter, reveling in the success of her prank with so much joy Nev decided to overlook the slight, taking a relieved breath when Wybert settled back to normal and she could again see detail around her.

Nev decided to shift the focus to a slightly more serious direction in the event Nina got the idea to flatter Wybert again for the fun of it.

"When do you think we should move again?" she asked, blinking to clear the reflex tears still gathered in her eyes.

Taking a deep breath to regain her composure, Nina too wiped tears from her eyes and sighed before responding.

"I think they will be up to the trip by the day after tomorrow," she said, back to her level self.

"Where will they all go?" Nev asked.

Other than Aster and Elsie, she hadn't interacted much with the group and knew nothing about them. Nina, on the other hand, had been talking with them and caring for them throughout the night and day since they had made camp.

"Surprisingly, most of them have homes to return to," Nina answered, her voice filling with disgust. "It seems it was actually rare for the trader to pay for women and girls, preferring instead to save his coins and steal them when he saw the opportunity. There are only two others who, like you and Aster, were sold, and others have invited them into their homes."

"This experience has left them with a strange, but deep bond," she concluded.

"And Aster?" Nev asked timidly.

Nina paused, causing concern to build in Nev's throat.

Reaching over to place her hand on Nev's leg, Nina smiled. "You have a big heart, child, don't ever think any less. We will figure that out when the time comes, but for now just keep giving her your attention, for that can do no harm."

It wasn't an answer, but Nev hadn't exactly expected one either. It was a heavy dilemma and she knew it. It wasn't as if she had anything to offer the girl. Not a home or even, for that matter, certainty of a next meal, and she had no idea what lay ahead.

But she also knew that Aster, like herself, needed something she wasn't going to find in a little village like Roden.

Sighing, she had to agree with Nina, the decision was one that could wait, even if it was just for a day.

"Are you growing younger, Nina?" The question popped out of her mouth before she had completely decided if she should ask it.

Laughing, Nina wore the same grin Nev had always known and looked at her with those sparkling blue eyes of hers.

"I thought you'd never ask," she said, smacking her leg. "No, child, I'm just getting closer to the real me. Once we left Roden, and you learned the truth, there was no reason for me to continue with the illusion of old age. It was something I did just because it made me seem less threatening to people there. If there's one thing I've learned in all my travels, it's that most people don't question someone that reminds them of their grandmother."

"You know, I think there's a plant out there to cure every woe and fit every need," with that, Nina launched into a lesson in plants and the miraculous things they could accomplish, including the illusion of aging.

Nev leaned back to listen, fascinated as always by the woman's stories of how she had discovered this and that and her recounts of tests gone awry before finding her way.

For a little while Nev almost felt like she was back in Nina's burrow and briefly missed sitting at the low table on a pillow listening to an adventure story over a cup of tea.

But as she listened, her nostalgia was quickly replaced with the realization that the comfort of those moments had never been about the tea or the pillows, and was just as easily found sitting on a rock in a strange forest as in a familiar dirt burrow.

●● Chapter Twelve ●●

The night and following day passed quickly, bringing Nina's predictions to fruition, and by the next evening the makeshift beds were emptied – their occupants able to sit for their meal.

Nev was amazed at the resiliency of the human body and in the case of the younger children, the mind.

Life had blossomed in the small camp with each passing hour welcoming the sounds of play and the bustle of activity.

There was little doubt they all bore the scars of their experiences, some injured physically but all scarred in spirit.

It was not uncommon to see emotional outbursts or someone engaged in activity suddenly stare off into space, growing quiet for a moment before snapping back to whatever they had been doing, but overall, the fervor of life was growing stronger and Nev was beginning to feel confident that they would make it back to their lives.

Ivy was the exception.

The girl still had not spoken a word in the two days they had been there and just sat like stone, staring off into the woods.

When Nev looked at the child, she still saw the broken doll she had seen that night in Roden when she had her first glimpse through Avec's eyes. Ivy and Elsie had been with the trader nearly a full year before they arrived in the clearing and from the older sister's accounts of that time, Ivy had been a first choice for his customers.

With the loose blond curls that hung down her back and delicate features, the little girl had no doubt appealed to the trader's unsavory clientele as the epitome of innocence, though it was ironically that very innocence they had shattered. But more than that, Nev feared Ivy might have been broken beyond repair, for her eyes maintained their hollow appearance, having gone well beyond pain and fear to a bottomless empty.

Nev couldn't help but wonder if that was how Lannera had looked as she stared at the walls of the burrow, stuck in the horrors of her own mind. Remembering the indifference Delsin had shown for her and the ease with which he had planned to send her to the same fate, Nev was amazed that such wanton depravity existed in the world.

Watching Elsie press torn pieces of meat to Ivy's little lips as she chewed her own meal from a tree stump at the edge of the camp, Nev found herself hoping that something would reach inside and soothe the child, but her intuition told her that whatever Ivy had been was forever lost.

Elsie, on the other hand, had gone the opposite direction of Ivy, displaying a maturity level far beneath what should have been appropriate for her age. The few times she had tried to interact with the others, her ill-timed laughter, exuberant energy and inability to see when others wanted to be left alone had gotten her the cold shoulder several times and put her at odds with everyone else. As a result, Elsie had withdrawn to remain at Ivy's side, obviously resentful, but with no apparent understanding of why she wasn't well received.

Nev couldn't help but see a difficult road ahead for both girls and questioned if their beloved Percy, or anyone for that matter, would ever be able to undo the damage that had been done.

Aster, however, was different than all the others. While they mended and some showed improvement, she seemed to actually flourish. She seemed to be growing chattier, quicker to smile and appeared to be genuinely enjoying herself.

As much as Nev would have liked to place credit on letting the girl face her monster in the clearing that day, which she had no doubt had indeed helped the girl purge the event, she still knew better than to credit that as the sole reason.

Rather, Aster seemed to be thriving on her interactions with Nev, Nina and even Chit, and Nev suspected the reason was it was the first compassion the child had experienced in a very long time, if not her entire life. Even as she sat pondering the girl's improved spirit, she was off helping Chit gather wood to keep the fire going through the night, her giggles drifting back to the camp from time to time as he told her silly jokes.

Thankfully, there had been no more fire incidents since Aster had cleaned out the cart and with the exception of her random, sometimes eerie insights, she had been downright normal.

Even Nev was feeling rather normal herself. No one in the camp seemed to look at her as odd, even with her strangely colored hair and new dramatic features, for they had never known her any other way.

They seemed, in fact, to see her as a leader of sorts and while Nina was seen as the one who had the answers or gave direction, Nev felt like they saw her as a protector. It was an interesting twist of things for her, and one she wasn't quite sure how to handle, for she knew she had no idea what she was doing and the responsibility they gave made her nervous.

In all honesty, she mused as she rose to her feet and dusted the crumbs from her breeches, she was ready for them to go on their way and had an overwhelming desire for the quiet and simplicity of before, a feeling she knew without a doubt Avec shared for she had noticed the more alive the group became, the more time he spent out flying by himself.

Making her way past the women and girls scattered across the ground where they sat picking at their food, Nev moved in the direction of the clearing, seeking its peace and quite, for she found even the low hum of the evening meal was nudging against her restless spirit.

Nina joined her as she reached the edge of camp and they walked together through the trees.

"You seem edgy girl," the woman broke the silence that stretched between them.

"Sometimes they overwhelm me," Nev replied, surprising herself at the succinct explanation she gave.

Nodding in understanding, Nina's shorter legs kept pace with hers. "That they do. Those ladies have challenges before them that we cannot help them with girl," she said as if she understood exactly what was going through Nev's mind. "You have done more than your part and the rest must be up to them."

Not responding, Nev accepted her words and allowed them to comfort her.

"I have something for you," Nina said, coming to a stop as they reached the edge of the woods.

Turning, Nev looked down, realizing for the first time that the woman had a small, tightly wrapped bundle in her hands.

"I had been keeping it for you since Lannera... Well, I was waiting for the right time and I think it's here," she said thrusting the bundle into her hands.

Wrapped in plain white cloth, a simple piece of twine was tied around the flexible mass. The realization it enclosed something that had belonged to her mother made her hand shake a little as she pulled on of the ends and let the knot fall away.

Gently pulling back the cloth, Nev's fingers came in contact with the softest black leather she had ever felt. Lined with thick but soft white fur, it was a garment of some kind, she realized as she moved to unfold it, allowing her hand to slide once more across it's surface before it spread open, amazed at it's delicate feel on her skin.

Her eyes flickered up briefly to meet with Nina's as she held the vest before her, marveling in its perfection. There were no obvious stitches holding its parts together and it had virtually no weight in her hands yet it had a feeling of strength to it like no other garment she had ever seen.

Turning it to examine the back, she found herself perplexed by the small swath of leather that joined the shoulders until the reason dawned on her.

"Wings?" was all she could manage as she stared at the oversized openings.

"Let me guess, you've been flapping around without a shirt on," Nina said laughing as she crossed her arms over her chest as Nev felt heat rising to her cheeks that were already enlarged by a smile.

Letting the cloth and string fall to the ground, Nev tucked the vest between her knees for safe keeping and grabbed the bottom hem of her tunic, bringing a surprised snort from Nina, who hurried to turn her head, the heat rising in her cheeks this time.

Within seconds, she was sliding the vest over her head, amazed at the glorious feel of the fur against her skin as it fell into place like it was made for her.

"It's... incredible," Nev uttered in awe as she looked down and pressed her flat palm to her abdomen.

Turning with regained composure, Nina reached out and gently nudged Nev with the tip of her hand, guiding her to turn. With her back toward Nina, Nev looked down over her shoulder to see the woman's hands working to undo a lace on the back.

"You're a little thinner than Lannera was. This was custom made for her and designed to last a lifetime, but lucky for you, they always leave a little room in case you eat too much," she said with a wink as she tugged the laces tight and retied them.

It hardly felt like she was wearing anything at all, she realized as she swung her arms around testing it out. The evening air felt cool against her exposed skin but the areas covered by the vest were warm as if by the rays of the sun.

"There are special sleeves that are worn under it for the cold, but I didn't think you'd need them tonight," Nina said, stepping back to scan its fit with an approving eye. "You're every bit as beautiful as she was child," she said, her loving smile sending warmth through Nev.

Feeling giddy like a child, Nev reached out for Avec to tell him, looking down at the vest so he could see from where he sat half snoozing, half guarding the path through the forest.

"Nice," was all he said through his relaxed fog as he took to the air on his way to come join them.

"Try the fit with your wings," Nina said casually, startling Nev as she absently stroked the leather with her hands. The woman's statement cast an uncomfortable shadow over her happiness and she suddenly felt like an imposter.

"Nina I told you, I can't fly," she said, unable to hide the sadness and humiliation in her voice.

Stretching her hand out to place it on Nev's shoulder, Nina squeezed reassuringly.

"Just give it a try girl," was all she said.

Connecting with Avec, Nev allowed herself to share in his

weightlessness as he coasted across the clearing. Realizing she was with him, the hawk expressed a small tingle of excitement, suddenly diverting his course and banking upward.

Gasping, the exhilaration struck Nev full on and she closed her eyes, welcoming the tingles that woke throughout her body. Focusing with the hawk, she worked to pool the energy between her shoulders, delighting in the warmth that radiated beneath her skin.

Willing them free, she felt her skin stretch as her wings emerged, stretching faster this time than ever before, catching even Avec off guard as he reached the top of the trees and pushed past.

Stretching them out to their full expanse, Nev opened her eyes and looked at Nina, her humility returning with the feeling of being exposed for the first time.

But Nina wasn't looking at her with critical eyes, nor was there an ounce of judgment on her face. Instead, the woman looked upon her with a face of shocked pride.

"What is it?" Nev asked hesitantly, confused for surely Nina had known what to expect, but before Nina could respond, she felt similar shock coming from Avec as he circled back and entered the clearing.

Avec's only response was to share his view with her and as the sight sent her reeling, she instantly understood.

Tall and lithe, the figure she saw standing in the dimming light of the evening sun was not that of the girlish and awkward Nev, instead it was a beautiful but imposing young woman.

The fragile powdery blueish wings she had in Roden were gone and stretched out behind her instead were strong, cold gray wings with blackened tips presenting an image that was anything but fragile.

But more than the change in her wings, it was the complete picture that was startling.

Throughout the last few days Nev had managed for the most part to forget the change to her hair by keeping it tied back, but knocked loose by her stretching wings, it was unmistakable now as it moved in the breeze around her. And the blend of her milky skin tones with the gray of her hair, when cast in the shadow of her wings, made for an intimidating combination.

Nev was glad Nina and Avec seemed to remain speechless, and lingered for a moment, taking in the sight of herself before she broke the connection and silence simultaneously.

"What is happening to me Nina?" she finally asked the question she had avoided since the night that had changed her in so many ways.

Nina didn't respond at first, obviously unable to pull her eyes away until she visibly gained control and took a deep breath, shaking her head.

"I have been pondering the same question for two days now and I am sorry to say I can't entirely answer child," she finally responded in a low voice that was almost apologetic.

"Never before has there been a mixing of Aile and Fauho blood and no one, including me, has any idea what that means."

Nina raised her eyes from the ground to meet Nev's, offering her a smile even though she was obviously still distracted by the sight that stood before her.

"I only know about the Aile because of my time with Alcedo and there are things I can teach you about that side of yourself but I know very little about the Fauho, so in that regard, I am of little help," she said.

"One of the few things I can tell you is that the Fauho are said to be a passionate people, far more so than the Aile, who have actively sought to shed their emotion in favor of strategy and skill."

Pausing, Nina reached out her hand and placed it on Nev's shoulder, giving her a little squeeze.

"I believe it is that very passion that has awakened the Fauho blood in you, for I watched you change in the woods as you listened to Aster's screams. I cannot tell you what comes with that change, but I would like to be with you through it if you'll have me," she finished, waiting for an answer.

Nina's words held disappointment for Nev, who realized for the first time that at some point in their experiences of recent days, her initial resentment toward the woman for holding so many secrets about her had transformed into an expectation of wisdom.

To now hear that she, like Nev, had questions for which she lacked answers was a frightening realization but at the same time, her commitment to helping Nev find those answers gave comfort.

"I think I need you now more than ever Nina," she responded with the most honesty she had ever felt in her life, for she knew it to be true.

Flexing her wings behind her, Nev couldn't help but laugh as Nina abruptly clamped her mouth closed at the sudden gust of wind that assaulted her.

"*They are stronger,*" Avec said, with a hint of admiration as he landed backward on her shoulder so he could see them up close.

"*We should try them,*" he said, his eagerness almost goading.

Nina, having caught her breath, smiled as if she had heard him and stepped back a few paces, nodding her head.

With a little reluctance, Nev tilted her head and caught Avec's eye, nodding herself at the reassurance and excitement she found there. As if he'd been waiting, Avec launched from the side of her shoulder, taking to the air with a speed she had only seen him use in the hunt.

Closing her eyes, she linked to him and felt the surge of thrill as the ground rushed beneath him.

Stretching her wings as far as they could extend, she began curling them inward and marveled at the quickness with which they responded as they began to beat rhythmically and she felt the ground fall away.

Her confidence grew as she realized weightlessness and found herself hoping that the differences she was feeling would lead to success.

"*You're doing it!*" Avec practically shrieked at her from where he circled above. Breaking out of the vortex he had created, he cut left and swooped down, tickling her stomach with such suddenness that she giggled and her eyes popped open.

Panic struck as she looked around and realized she was nearly above the treetops and she pumped her wings harder, instinctively bracing for the rush of air that would signal the prelude to impact, but instead the ground grew further away.

Heart racing, she pumped her wings harder, and laughed as she looked down on the forest below, picking out the spec that was Nina at the edge of the clearing.

"You can't keep going up, you'll get lost in the clouds," the hawk said laughing as he showed her how to angle her body and extend her wings so she could coast, tilting again to level out and cut through the air.

Following his lead, Nev found herself clumsily stretching her arms out the sides to steady herself as she tried to dive, then bank as he had, finally gaining enough control to turn abruptly, right before she grazed the pointed top of a pine tree that jumped out in front of her.

Giggling again at the near miss, Nev pumped her wings and rose higher, then dove again, this time mastering the swoop and turn well above the trees.

Angling back up, she willed her wings to beat faster, wanting more, but like legs wearing out in the final stretch toward home, they balked as if there were a hidden weight pressing down on them and she realized fatigue was gripping the muscles.

Fear seized her heart as she willed them to stretch and found them unable. Suddenly aware of how high she was, she reached out to Avec, who had already sensed something was amiss.

"I can't move them," she said as they locked in place fully extended, cramps shooting through her back that were accompanied by a pain equal to none she had never known. Crying out, she felt herself tumbling and knew the distance to the ground was not one she was going to survive.

"NEV!" the hawk called out to her in a panic. *"Pay attention! Angle yourself and curve!"* he shouted out to her, intruding on her mind to show her how as he rushed to fly just below her.

Closing her eyes tight, she blocked out the sight of the rushing ground and tilted, pushing past the pain that encompassed her entire body as she felt her wings reverberate at the changed resistance. The pain lessened slightly as she angled more, and out of reflex she lifted up toward the sky a little, her aversion to the ground below making her seek height.

The change shot another rush of pain through her that this time was almost crippling and would have caused her to curl into a ball had the air not been pushing her body from below.

"*NO!*" Avec barked at her.

"*You must angle like you're diving into the ground and we're going to circle to slow your fall,*" he shouted through her pain.

In contradiction to every instinct in her body, Nev did as she was told and pointed her nose to the ground, hoping that when she met it, it would at least be a fast demise.

Nudging her with his mind, Avec directed her into a right turn and directed her to ease her body level with the ground, tilt, then back into a dive as she went, alternating through the pattern.

It was working, she realized, as she could feel her fall slowing to a controlled descent that was still much faster than she would have preferred, but definitely more controlled nonetheless.

Opening her eyes, she breathed deep to steady her heart as she saw the tops of the trees rising up to meet them.

She had almost regained her composure and was following Avec into another turn when a frantic squeal   pierced her right ear and she saw Wybert flash in front of her right eye. His eyes bigger than his body, he became a little white streak as he flew backward and she felt the insanely invasive sensation of him whirring in terror as he crawled into her ear canal and lodged himself against the tender flesh, reduced to a shaking lump.

Resisting the urge to shake her head, Nev tried to pull her focus back to the ground that rose up before her, bracing for the impact that was coming.

She was able to twist and lift her head at the last crucial second, her left shoulder digging into the dirt until its density became too much and she flipped end over end, coming to land flat on her back, her wings still locked out to the sides.

Unable to breath, she lay with her mouth open and her eyes staring into the sky as she tried to cough, sucking in too much air when her lungs finally allowed it. Ragged breaths took over and she lay still, afraid to move even when she saw Nina come into view, rushing to kneel beside her.

Pain was screaming through her body by the time she felt the woman's hands against her skin as her fingers pressed and investigated in search of injuries.

"My wings..." she managed groaning in pain as Nina moved out of sight to check.

Agony wracked through her when she felt Nina's hands tugging her left wing, then heard one popping sound followed by another. Screaming with the pain, she could barely hear Nina shushing her as everything went dark.

●● Chapter Thirteen ●●

Nev woke to a weight on her chest and the metallic taste of blood in her mouth followed by momentary panic until she remembered she had already hit the ground. Opening her eyes just a sliver at first, she slammed them shut again when she saw Avec's face, his eyes staring intently into hers, his beak to the side of her nose, waiting and watching for signs of life.

His call to Nina rang shrill through her ears as he turned his head from side to side, rubbing it against her face in relief.

Trying to expel the feathers that had invaded her mouth, Nev turned her head the other way and spat with a lot less force than she had intended, managing to only send a small tuft of air through her lips.

'Welcome back girl!" she heard Nina's voice, turning her head slowly to see the woman looking down at her with a wide smile on her face.

Managing a groan, Nev grasped the ground beside her and Nina helped support her as she shifted, trying to get up. The effort sent fingers of pain through her as she leaned back against Nina's hands for a second to breathe before pushing forward again, this time making it to a seated position.

Looking around her, she noticed the light had fallen but it wasn't completely dark yet, indicating she hadn't been out that long.

Nina was staring at her, as if waiting to give her the first words, but when she didn't speak fast enough, the woman launched into explanation of how she had to reset the joints in her wings, causing Nev to glance behind her in search of them only to find they had retracted while she lay unconscious.

"If you were more practiced that wouldn't have happened," Nina said, patting her on the shoulder when she started to protest, her pride kicking in. "Child you did nothing wrong, they are like any muscle in your body. They must be used to grow strong and if they're not, they will tire, just as your legs would if you tried to run all day."

"You did well!" Avec chimed in from where he was perched on her knee. He was beaming with pride, judging by the regal tilt to his head.

Reaching up a finger, Nev tried to scratch at her ear, plagued by an insane itch until she recoiled in guilt at Wybert's cries as he retreated deeper inside, begging her to stop.

As soon as she pulled her finger free, he zoomed out into the dusk, visibly shaken as Nev's vision started to take on the illumination caused by his presence.

Words tumbling together in a mass of confusion that obviously reflected his thoughts, the little bird zigged and zagged in front of her as if he truly believed she could understand him.

"Wybert calm down, we're fine," she said, sending him all the comfort she could muster through her exhaustion, which thankfully had him in a diminished enough state that she could communicate with him.

"What happened?" he buzzed, slowing down enough to form the question but clearly not satisfied with her pacification.

Quickly she summarized as she might have for a child, explaining that she'd been flying and something had gone wrong but they had made it to the ground, not in much mood to give him the full story and not sure he would understand even if she did.

The explanation seemed to suffice, though Wybert was genuinely perturbed by her account.

"You mustn't do dangerous things! We could die!" he said, practically shouting at her in the most respectful way he could manage, the huffing of his chest a tell to his inner frustration.

Trying not to laugh, more because it hurt than for any other reason, Nev assured the little bird that she would be more careful, thankful when he zoomed into his normal position, the evening gloom lifting a little as he began to calm.

The exchange did little to improve Avec's perspective on the firefly though it did serve to give him yet another chortling laugh at the tiny bird's expense, but Wybert didn't seem to notice, still absorbed in his harrowing adventure.

Turning back to Nina, Nev asked if anything had broken, still amazed that she had not been alert for the retraction of her wings and feeling at a disadvantage since she hadn't gotten to confirm their state for herself.

"No, but the stress and overexertion did dislocate some of the bones," Nina replied. "It's going to hurt, but you'll need to stretch them and work them as often as you can to help strengthen them again."

Groaning, Nev lay back down in the grass, for she could only imagine how bad the pain was going to be given how she was feeling at that moment. Her shoulder and upper arm had lost a layer of skin somewhere in the not-so-soft landing and her back, head and just about everything was starting to shift from sharp pain to dull throbbing.

Her mother's vest, however, was dusty but unscathed she noticed, sitting back up to look it over as it finally struck her... she had flown! And while Avec was with her throughout, she hadn't been utterly dependent on her connection to him this time.

Saying as much to Nina, she and the bird were both taken aback by the woman's answer.

"Of course you don't need him to fly girl! I assume he was the one that opened your mind to the concept and prompted the emergence of your wings, but you would have discovered it eventually," she said dismissively, seeming not to notice their shared shock as she continued.

"The Aile don't waste their time talking to animals or birds and human minds aren't open enough. They only use their mental connections to communicate with each other, which they have perfected for the hunt. I think the only reason you learned to communicate with the creatures around you is because back in Roden, they were the only ones receptive to you.

But had you been raised in Aileron, you would have never spoke to anything other than your own kind."

She went on to to explain that Alcedo, sometimes feeling isolated at the loss of his brothers and sister, had reached out to animals, but she said he rarely found it rewarding and never felt it was replacement for the lost connection to his own kind.

"I believe the bond the two of you have is unique, even when compared to Alcedo, who's abilities were superior to most Aile, for that was the exceptional talent that got him assigned to hunt with your mother," she told them, her eyes flickering down to the raptor on Nev's knee. "And I think you have adapted its application quite well, taking it in a direction the Aile would never dream of Nev, but I believe it's really nothing more than a coincidence that you and the hawk found each other and have the sky in common."

Nev found herself not wanting to believe what Nina was saying even though she had just seen it for herself. In all her attempts at flying back in Roden, she had clung so tightly to the bird out of the belief she couldn't fly without that connection and yet today she had.

But there was no doubt he had saved her by guiding her back from the sky and she surely would have died had he not shown her how to slow her fall.

Noticing Avec had grown still on her knee, she sent him reassurance, hoping his distant look was tied to similar thoughts.

"I would have never survived that fall today without you," she sent, knowing without a doubt that whether or not he was the key to her ability, he was crucial to her success.

He seemed to accept her offering, and though the distance that had grown between them since leaving Roden did at times take its toll, they both knew that regardless of how their connection came to be, it went well beyond circumstance.

Turning to Nina, Nev felt the opportunity was right to ask a question that had been weighing on her.

"Is that how I was called to Aileron? Did someone connect with me while I dreamed?" she asked.

Nina pondered the question for a moment before responding, giving Nev the distinct impression she had already mulled it over herself and rather than searching for the answer, was trying to think of how to convey a conclusion she had reached long before the question was posed.

"Yes girl, I believe it is. The Aile use the connection to call their hunters home and to communicate special messages. Alcedo would always grow sad when the calls went out, knowing he couldn't answer," she said.

"Tell me one thing, were you called by name?"

Nev nodded, briefly explaining the drifting voice that had called her but stopped short of explaining the intimate feelings that had accompanied the dream.

Nina looked almost disappointed as she shook her head.

"I had hoped you picked up on a call to hunters, but someone in Aile has learned of your existence," she said, her lack of answers obvious in the perplexed furrows that stretched across her brow. But more than anything, Nev sensed concern underlying the woman's words.

"You have been called there but for what and by whom I cannot tell you. Lannera had many secrets. She must have told someone about you," she said, but Nev could tell even Nina wasn't convinced.

There was silence between them for a moment as Nev pondered how to convey the thoughts she had been turning around in her head, thoughts that had grown in her over the past few days.

"How long till winter?" she finally blurted out awkwardly.

Surprised, Nina looked up at her. "Maybe three months, why?"

"I want to find the Fauho," She said, the words that followed spilling out rapidly, having been contained within her brain too long. "I have no interest in the Aile and I don't see why I should go there if we don't know who has called me there or why. Besides, it's not as if I can expect a warm welcome with the blood of their enemy running in my veins."

Her next words came out sounding far less intimidating than they had when she plotted them in her own head.

"The only thing I have in common with the Aile is I share their hatred of the Fauho and I want to finish what my mother started and failed at. Alopex should pay for what he did to her."

Nina sat silent, looking off toward the trees as if she could see through them to the other side. The silence stretched on so long, that Nev grew nervous, fearing she had finally found the one thing that would turn the woman away from her.

By the time Nina turned back to face her, even Avec began to shift awkwardly and was on the verge of flying off to escape the uncomfortable air that had descended on their little group.

"Girl, I would do you a disservice if I didn't tell you that you're not ready to take on the Fauho, we don't even know what you really are beyond naming the parts," she said, her tone more harsh than Nev had ever heard it before as she continued. "You have only had one successful flight that nearly killed you and you would be dead if that bird hadn't gotten you down and now you want to go and challenge the very people who destroyed your mother?"

The words stung as they pelted against Nev, but the hurt quickly transformed to defensive anger.

"I'm not a child Nina! You saw what I did to those men and to Delsin, I am not afraid to kill," Nev instantly regretted lashing out, but couldn't seem to stop herself as she kept shouting, her voice getting louder and her words more cruel.

"You're just afraid because you're a weak woman that never did anymore with your life than get lucky enough to fall in love with someone a hundred times stronger than you could ever be!"

The hurt that swept across Nina's face cut through Nev's anger like a heated blade that left a burning trail behind as it moved from her stomach through her chest, lodging in her throat like a ball of poisoned fire she couldn't expel.

Even Avec looked at her in shame and disbelief, turning his back to her as he launched into the night sky and disappeared without a sound, leaving her alone to face her deed.

"Nina, I..." before she could finish, Nina's hand raised toward her face, but rather than striking her as she deserved, the woman's fingertips gently rested on her lips, blocking her words.

"You are right, you're not a child Nev and you haven't been for a long time, at least until just now," she said in barely more than a whisper, tears gathering in her eyes.

"I am afraid and if you were wise, you would be too. But you are also right, I have lived my life in the shadow of those far stronger than I, so if this is what you must do than I will go with you, even if it kills us both. But know this, you have shown tonight that you would hurt those who love you most in pursuit of your own interests and that, my child, is something you should fear more than anything else."

Even if Nev could have found the words, she wouldn't have had opportunity, for Nina was disappearing into the trees by the time she realized she was all alone in the clearing.

"Nina, I'm sorry," she whispered to nothing and to no one, wiping angrily at her cheeks as the guilty tears started to flow.

Curling up on her side, Nev's tears fell like wasted and unnoticed wishes into the grass, emptiness welling up inside her.

Suddenly and for the first time, Nev realized that Nina's support was something to be earned and she had just trampled on it as if it were meaningless. All her life she had been reaping the benefit of a promise that was never hers and she had grown comfortable in the security of Nina's commitment to her mother without even knowing it.

But somewhere along the way, Nina came to actually love her, the promise evolving into something well beyond Lannera and her provision – only she didn't deserve it.

Nev lay in the grass steeped in self loathing for what seemed like an eternity until finally sleep overtook her. The sleep was fitful and the dreams moved through her brain like one storm after another in a rapid succession of turmoil after turmoil, but she slept deeply.

Watching her toss and turn in the grass, crying out occasionally, Avec stayed nearby, for even though she probably should have been left alone and certainly deserved a dose of misery, he couldn't leave her unprotected.

It was moments like these that made him question his bond to the girl, for his life would certainly follow a more natural course if he just went his own way, but anytime such thoughts entered his head, he shut them down as quickly as they came. Trying as she could sometimes be, he knew without a doubt that he wouldn't be content with a simpler life if it meant she wasn't in it.

And, truth be told, he knew that he and Nina too would follow her into anything if she only asked, but it sure would help if she could gain some self control and start behaving more rationally, he thought.

Shaking his head, he settled into his branch and watched, his mind drifting to thoughts of their first flight together in search of something happier to get him through what was sure to be a long night.

She had been quick and daring, taking to it naturally as he had hoped she would and she would no doubt be even more successful as soon as she learned to shut off her brain, which had proven to be her biggest obstacle.

Running through the experience in his mind, he found himself creating lessons for their next flight and coming up with creative ways to help her understand how to move into the resistance of the air pushing on her wings instead of responding to her natural instincts to pull away as she had when she injured herself.

Avec was so deeply engrossed in his thoughts that he almost missed the flicker of movement that grazed his peripheral vision, yet when he tilted his head to get a better view, there was nothing there.

Unable to dismiss a growing sense of unease, he launched from his branch sweeping around the edge of the clearing in an effort to set his mind at ease but found no comfort in returning to his branch without confirmation.

Something had been there, he told himself, sure that he had not been imagining it, for his very life depended on having the ability to detect even the smallest morsel wriggling beneath the grass.

His feathers ruffling for a second, he allowed them to smooth flat, hoping the exercise would somehow sooth his ragged nerves as he looked down at Nev again only to discover she was no longer alone.

Curled with her, lay Aster, her little body melded against Nev's sleeping as comfortable as if she'd been there all along.

Only she hadn't and he knew it. Avec felt every nerve in his body respond simultaneously to the wave of angry suspicion that swept over him.

Never in his time with humans, had any one person set his instincts on fire like that child did and it infuriated him that she had somehow slipped by him, though he couldn't figure out a plausible explanation as to how.

For some unknown reason, she made Nev happy, one of the few things that allowed him to overlook his own proprietary sense for the girl as in the case of Nina, but something wasn't right about that child and nothing was going to convince him otherwise,

His suspicion lingered the rest of the night while he watched over the sleeping pair, and though it never truly left him, it did ease a little when Nev began stirring just before dawn.

●● Chapter Fourteen ●●

Aster's breathing started to drift into Nev's consciousness, but it was the little girl's arm, flung limp across her face that woke her with a start. Jolting upright and pushing back at the same time, Nev realized the stiff pain in her muscles about the same time she identified Aster as the source of the disturbing smack.

Avec sailed to her side with speed, not sure what had caused her to bolt from her sleep as she had until she shared the foggy recollection with him and put him at ease.

Her arms coiled around her knees, Nev sat with her head hanging as the events of the night came back to her one piece at a time.

"I didn't mean to hurt her," she told Avec and herself, her heart aching with shame and grief for the pain she had caused Nina with her hateful words.

"I know Nev, and I believe she does too, but that doesn't make it go away," the hawk told her in an effort to reassure her realistically.

Fresh tears trickled, carving clean paths down her already stained cheeks and she buried her head in her arms.

"I accused her of the very thing I'm guilty of myself," she finally said, as if relieved to admit it but still burdened by the truth's existence. "As I was falling asleep, I realized that I am only strong because of you and Nina and those around me. Because you are all strong. But when I was sitting here alone, I suddenly knew that I am small and weak without you, and she's right, I'm not ready to take on Alopex and probably never will be."

Stunned, Avec wasn't sure how to respond. Part of what Nev said was absolutely true, but part of it was pure self pity and most importantly, he knew none of it was going to do her any good.

Thoughtfully, he spoke with all the care he could muster.

'There is nothing wrong with needing others and drawing strength from them Nev, for without those bonds you are right, life is empty and futile. Nina needs it and so do you," he said, his voice taking on an urgency with his next words, for it was critical that she hear them.

'But you must be realistic about challenging Alopex. Your mother was trained at fighting and had the support of people like herself and even she failed. That is not to say you can't accomplish what you set out for if you work at it, but you will certainly not succeed through anger and misdirected emotion. That, I believe, is what Nina was trying to tell you."

Nev sat for a moment, the words sinking in as she fought against her pride in an effort to hear them clearly and shaking her head, she marveled at her own childish stupidity.

"I want this Avec and more than I can put into words. I know that I need to destroy him for all the pain he has caused. I can't and won't turn back from that," she said, the stubbornness creeping back into her voice, though her posture showed she'd been humbled. "But I also accept that I have much to learn and I can't do it alone. Will you help me?"

Lighting on Nev's folded arms, Avec used his beak to part her hair so he could look her in the eyes as he spoke. *"That is something you never have to ask of me, because even at your worst, I will be here to help you."*

"I will help you too," Aster's small voice volunteered, piercing the silence of their conversation.

Freezing, Nev and Avec stared at one another in shock before slowly turning toward the girl who returned their looks with confusion.

"What's wrong?" she said, reaching up to rub sleep from her eyes.

"Aster, were you eavesdropping?" Nev asked.

"I wasn't sneaking, you woke me up with your talking," the child said in an apologetic voice that showed fear at the thought she might be in trouble. Fully awake now, the skin around her eyes was turning pink as if tears were about to flow. Her shoulders had stiffened.

"Aster I'm not angry, but I need to know, is this the first time you have heard us talk to one another?"

Nev was beyond perplexed by that point, searching her memory in an effort to recall all the times she had spoken to Avec in the child's presence. Only it wasn't necessary because in her haste to redeem herself, Aster began recounting everything she had heard with amazing precision.

"... And there was the time when I went to talk to Nina in the woods, when he said he didn't like me ..." Nev's mind was reeling as she realized that there was far more to Aster than she had ever imagined.

Taking a deep breath, she reached out and gently tickled at the girl's mind, recoiling in shock when Aster giggled in response. Letting loose another deep breath, Nev reached out again, this time asking a question.

"Red," the child blurted the color of her hair, smiling in wait of affirmation.

Looking at Avec, Nev shook her head in wonder, stopping herself just before she asked him his thoughts out of habit.

But the reflex gave her an idea.

Focusing, she put a barrier between herself and Aster, not unlike the times she closed the hawk out, and reached the other way toward Avec.

"Aster what color are my breeches?" she asked silently, turning to give Avec a satisfied smile when the child did not respond.

But her smugness was premature as she heard, "Brown" come from behind her.

Mouthing the word *"block"* to Avec where the girl couldn't see, she waited until he nodded, then closed Aster out and reached for Avec, feeling his acceptance.

"Aster, what color is Barge?"

"Aster?"

Pleased she winked at Avec and let her guard down, opening her mind.

"What color is Barge, Aster?"

"Why are you asking me all these questions? Barge is brown," Aster said, becoming aware that something was afoot.

"Well it appears we can speak without anyone hearing us," Nev sent to Avec, forcing herself to smile at the girl.

This time with her voice, Nev pressed the girl, hoping to gain a better understanding of what was going on, but Aster could provide no answers. She seemed unaware that what she was capable of was anything other than ordinary.

Looking at Avec in frustration, the bird nodded to let her know he had blocked his mind.

"Well if we both block her, she can't hear, but if one of us leaves an opening, she can hear everything," Nev said, running through it as much for her own good as his.

Sensing his nervousness, she tried to calm him as best she could. *"I don't understand this child either Avec and I trust your instincts, but this time I need you to trust me when I tell you she is not going to harm us. I can't tell you how I know that, only that I do."*

"I trust you, I just can't shake the feeling she gives me," he said. *"There are very few things that get to me like this, but she's one of them, without a doubt."*

"Then we shall agree to watch her closely, how about that?" she asked, glad to feel the strength of their bond and happy to offer him a compromise, for even she continually found Aster's surprises unsettling.

"Agreed," Avec responded.

Avec took to the sky and turning back to Aster, Nev held her arm out, which the girl gladly wrapped around herself, leaning against her on the grass.

"I'm sorry if I made you think I was angry, you just surprised me Aster. I have never met anyone else who can hear the hawk or talk to me like you can," she said, resting her chin on Aster's head. "I just wish I knew more about you."

Aster sat silent for a moment, then shifted to look up at Nev with pleading eyes.

"I know why the hawk doesn't like me," she said as if she had a guilty secret she wanted to purge. "If I show you, will you promise not to make me leave like Grandmother and Grandfather did?"

Nev looked at Aster, the realization dawning on her that she couldn't make that promise. The sun was rising in the sky which meant the camp would be stirring and everyone would be heading out on their way home, including Aster.

"You can't stay with me," she said abruptly and without the sensitivity the words required. When tears and disbelief sprung across the girl's face, Nev clutched her closer, wishing she could say it differently but knowing it was true.

"Nev you can't send me with them, I don't have a home to go to and even if they took me in, they aren't like me. They will make me leave too," Aster said through sobs.

"Aster, Nina and I are going on a long and dangerous journey that would be very hard for a young girl. I can't guarantee that you would be safe with us, and what if something happens to us? Then you'd still be all alone but far away from everything you know," she said, hoping the girl could understand. "I know you think things are bad for you now, but I promise you it could be a lot worse."

Shaking her head vigorously, Aster refused to hear her.

Her voice growing remarkably adult, Aster sniffed to clear her nose and looked Nev in the eyes.

"You don't understand Nev. If I was just a girl, my mother wouldn't have run away and left me with my grandparents, and they wouldn't have sold me to that man because they were scared of me and I wouldn't be here with you right now."

Gathering her feet beneath her, Aster pushed back off the ground and rose, standing before Nev with a look of hesitant determination. For a brief moment, Nev almost thought she might be about to attack her until she saw the girl's lower lip quivering.

Nev reached out to comfort the girl but pulled her hand back in surprise when Aster stepped out of reach. She closed her eyes tight forcing tears through her squeezed lids, took a deep breath and disappeared from view.

Shocked, Nev's eyes began darting around in search of the girl and she jumped to her feet, half backing, half turning but finding nothing before her.

"I'm here Nev," Aster's voice quietly drifted into her mind.

'Where?' Nev sent back, pivoting to look around.

Something brushed against her leg, and, looking down, Nev inhaled sharply at the sight of a small fox standing beside her. Thin and rangy, with ragged light brown fur tinged with red, the creature was awkwardly formed, its black tipped ears far too large for its slender frame.

But it was the eyes that drew her in, forlorn and surrounded by the moisture of tears, she knew them instantly to be Aster's, having stared so many times before into their bronze depths.

"Aster?" she asked, because though her mind still queried, her instincts knew the answer.

Sitting on its angular haunches, the fox wrapped itself in a tail that appeared to overwhelm its body and lifted its chin up to better meet her gaze.

Tentatively, Nev reached her hand out to touch the animal but the action was interrupted when a shriek spread through the clearing, its piercing urgency hurting her ears as a mass of claws and feathers came between her and the fox.

Crouching, the animal looked up and issued a hissing sound in the direction of the bird, but did nothing to fight back, instead, pressing itself tight against the ground.

Nev's protests were drowned out by Avec's cries of alarm and she was forced back by his fiercely flapping wings. Shouting at him, she found herself unable to penetrate his mind in his frenzied and relentless attack. She launched forward, falling over top of the fox to shield it, crying out in pain as his claws ripped into the skin of her back.

"Stop!" she screamed out pain gripping her when his claws entangled themselves in her hair, pulling chunks of flesh away with the strands as he struggled to free himself for another attack.

Beneath her, the fox trembled, whimpering in the safety of the alcove created by her body.

"Stop it bird! What's gotten into you?" She heard Nina's voice seizing control of the chaos and carefully raised her head to find the woman holding Avec tight, unfazed by the blood dripping from her hands and wrist where his beak and claws continued to fight in a struggle to get free of her grasp.

"Don't make me snap your neck like a chicken you fool bird!" Nina snapped, struggling against him with quick, jagged breath.

She didn't loosen her grip as the words seemed to reach through to him and he ceased his struggles, turning to Nev with wide questioning eyes.

"What is wrong..." she started, but finished with a drawn out gasp of astonishment as Nev pulled back, revealing the quivering fox she had been shielding beneath her.

The sight sent the raptor into a new fit of panic, his claws gashing deep into Nina's forearm, his eyes focused beads of insanity that cut almost as severely.

The renewed attack forced Nina to divert her attention back to Avec with a startled exclamation.

"Get me that cloth and twine over there girl and hurry!" she said, struggling to keep her grip on him as he fought against her with a strength disproportionate to his size.

Looking in the direction Nina indicated with a thrust of her head, Nev saw the wrappings that had held her mother's vest just hours before and scrambled the short distance to grab them, returning to Nina's side.

While she continued fighting to keep his claws and beak from doing further damage, Nina instructed Nev to cover Avec's head with the fabric then had her tie a loop around his neck and wrap the other end of string around his legs. The resulting configuration worked almost instantly when the bird, blinded to the object of his insanity, found if he struggled, he was only fighting against his own resistance.

Trying to catch her breath, Nina thrust the bundled bird into Nev's arms with a look of frustration and turned to look upon the fox, which remained motionless against the ground.

"Have you taken in another stray?" she said curtly, making it obvious she was still stinging from their exchange and though she was trying to hide it, she was also clearly shaken by her fight with the hawk.

"It's Aster," Nev said without hesitation, all capacity for strategic thought stripped away.

Turning back to shoot a look of surprise at her, Nina raised an eyebrow which Nev answered with a nod of her head, absently stroking Avec's back in an attempt to counter the racing heartbeat she could feel against the crook of her arm.

Bending down in front of the fox, Nina reached out a hand to touch the tip of the creature's ear, almost as if she were checking to make sure it was real.

The fox stood slowly, looking to check that Avec was still restrained, then walked the few short paces that brought her to stand between Nina's bent knees. Reaching down, Nina forced Aster's chin up gently so she could look into her eyes.

"Well, well. I guess that is you in there, isn't it little one?" she said, a wry smile forming on her face as she turned to Nev. "This certainly explains a lot about why her family cast her out and the strange sense that we have all had about her, particularly the hawk, who would naturally sense the presence of a fellow predator."

"How is this possible Nina?" Nev said, still treading lightly until she could find an opportunity to apologize and try to repair the damage between them. "She can connect with me and Avec too."

Nina seemed surprised at the revelation but not overly so.

"I can't tell you what she is exactly and I'd bet she can't either," she said. "But she is like many creatures in the world that humans live beside without even knowing they exist, not unlike the fireflies or the Aile. The Aile are organized and civilized more so even than mankind, but that is not typical. Most of the unusual creatures out there lead primitive and solitary lives far from view of the humans who misunderstand and fear them.

"Occasionally those species who have human traits will mix with a human and little ones like our girl here crop up. And I'm guessing your human family didn't take well to your unusual traits, did they child?" she directed her question back at Aster, her finger reaching to stroke the fur between her eyes.

The morning sun had risen high enough in the sky that a hazy fog was enveloping them and soon it would be full light a fact that impressed upon Nev a sense of urgency to resolve the dilemma the child presented.

"She wants to go with us," she said, not sure if she should

explain the inner turmoil the request had given her, hoping Nina would just understand. Avec, however, wriggled in her arm, showing his distaste for the idea.

Nina's brow furrowed and she looked at Nev then allowed her eyes to return to Aster, not speaking for a long moment while she studied the fox.

"I don't see how we have much choice," she finally said, earning a surprised sound from all including Nev, who suddenly had a mixed feeling of joy and trepidation.

"But how can we keep her safe? What if she can't handle the difficulties? She is only a little girl, Nina, she belongs in a home with meals and a bed and all those things we don't have," she said, unable to control the whiny edge that crept into her voice.

Patting the fox on the head, Nina rose and turned to face Nev.

"And she's never going to find those things in a village full of ignorant humans. It's far more likely she will end up cast out into the world exposed to dangers with no one there to help, or care what happens to her, Nev. Why do you think your mother called on me to watch over you?

"As much as I wish Aster could have a normal life like the one you describe, realistically she was never going to get that. At least now she has us."

Through her words, Nina had named and resolved the conflict that existed in Nev's mind. It was her simple and to the point way that Nev had always admired and this occasion was no exception. Nev hadn't told the girl no because she didn't care for her, it was actually the complete opposite and Nina was right, every hardship the girl had experienced up to this point centered on who, and, what she was, something they were better equipped than most to appreciate.

Nodding in agreement, Nev looked down at Aster and smiled.

"Are you sure you understand what this means?" she spoke in the direction of the fox, fairly certain there was no need to retrace all the arguments she had made before.

"Yes, Nev, thank you, you won't be sorry, I promise," she responded eagerly with her mind while Nina looked between them.

Chuckling, Nev leaned down toward Aster, making sure to hold Avec tight so he wouldn't fall.

"No more secrets Aster. And that starts with always speaking so Nina can hear you too unless you have no other choice, all right?" she asked out loud, eliciting a nod from the fury head.

Nev glanced up momentarily to look at Nina, surprised to find the fox had disappeared when she turned her head back.

Stretching back up to again stand beside Nina, she shook her head, barely managing the words, "I don't think I'm ever going to get used to that," before she felt Aster's arms wrap around her middle from behind, catching her off guard.

"Thank you, Nev!" the girl said through tears of happiness, moving next to hug Nina before Nev could respond.

Nina stroked the back of the child's head for a moment, then pulled her chin upward with her fingertips so she could look her in the eye.

"We are glad to have you with us, Aster but remember you must always listen and remember that we will only ask things of you for all of our safety," nodding, Aster smiled the biggest smile Nev had ever seen, giving boost to the feeling they were doing right by her.

"Now go wake Chit. We need to eat and get everybody ready to go," Nina said, returning the girl's smile with a heartfelt one of her own.

"Thank you!" Aster said again, darting over to give Nev one more hug before she ran off toward the camp, her joy showing in the lightness of her steps.

Avec had stopped struggling, his heart rate slowing to an almost normal pace, judging by the occasional pulsing she could still feel against the skin of her forearm.

"Aster is gone now so I am going to let you go, but I think if you go nuts again, Nina will make good on her word to snap your neck," she said so the the woman could hear, winking in her direction while her fingers set to work unraveling the binding that held the hawk's legs.

Once she set his legs free, she slipped the loop of string over his head and gently lifted the hood, finding a disheveled version of her friend beneath. Pushing his head up, Avec shook his entire body as if to also shake the feeling of captivity and glared at Nev, launching from her arm with an abruptness that made his hostility clearly known.

Watching as he wobbled a little in the air, still trying to regain his composure, Nev diverted her eyes back to Nina, knowing he would need some time alone to settle his nerves and sooth his wounded pride.

"I don't think telling you I'm sorry is enough, Nina," she said without hesitating, the words tumbling together in a rush of guilt. "Those things I said to you were wrong and cruel and I would give anything if I could take it back. I have great respect for you and I value your guidance. I just said those things because my pride was hurt, but I had no right."

Moving closer to the woman who was listening carefully, Nev timidly reached out her arms and wrapped them around the smaller set of shoulders, glad when she felt her embrace accepted.

"Please forgive me," she whispered. "I was wrong when I said you weren't strong, I am the one who needs you, not the other way around and I know that."

Carefully moving her hand away from the abrasions on Nev's shoulder, Nina rubbed then patted her back, holding her close for a moment before stepping back to look her in the eyes.

"Of course I forgive you, girl, but you'll do well to remember that the reason it is easiest to hurt the ones who love you is because they have something invested in you. Your tantrums won't get you anywhere with the rest of the world because they don't care. Keep that in mind next time you think to strike out," she said, her point driving home with amazing precision.

"The way I figure it, you have about a month, maybe a little more until we reach the mountains and in that time you've got a lot of work to do if you hope to have a chance. Let's go get these women moving and then we'll start on our own way."

There was a new edge to Nina that she had never seen, Nev realized as she watched the woman walk away. The message was clear that the woman had thrown up guards between them to protect herself and the awareness of the gap left Nev with a sense of loneliness. But she also knew she had no one to blame but herself this time.

Nev called to the bay mares and set to the task of hitching them to the cart, the work in the warming sun coming as a welcome contrast to the heavy night.

● Chapter Fifteen ●●

"I can't go back," Nev heard Chit saying emphatically as she made her way from the creek where she had just finished washing the dirt from her arms and face.

It had only taken Nev a short time to get the cart hitched and ready, her greatest challenge in persuading the mares to assume their positions in front of the wagon that held so many negative associations for them. It had taken some effort, but she had finally managed to convince them how important they were to getting the women and girls back home.

Now on her way to let everyone know it was time to load up, she was surprised to stumble upon what was obviously a private conversation judging by the way Chit and Nina had secluded themselves away from of everyone else.

"Chit, you have been of great help with these women and children but whatever obligation you feel you have has been long since settled. You can't go with us," Nina said, her stern but caring voice drifting to where Nev had stopped in her tracks behind a small cluster of trees.

"Nina you don't understand! I can't go back home pulling the empty cart of my employer. I'll be hanged or worse!" he said, his voice rising to an insistent tone that reflected his fear. "Don't misunderstand me, that girl of yours did a good deed with her knife, but I have no intention of swinging from a rope for something I didn't do.

"That man she killed was an extremely wealthy nobleman from Sarter," Chit said, his voice tapering as if he would rather avoid the topic altogether. "From what I gathered, we were en route to some kind of meeting three days west of here when we crossed paths with that trader outside of Roden and they arranged to meet here so Cravey could indulge in his disgusting appetites."

Chit's voice was full of unmistakable panic.

'I promise you, his absence will be missed Nina, and I have no interest in finding out what will happen if I turn up without him."

Nina put her head in her hands and sighed deeply. "Chit, please tell me that man was not on his way to the Council of Lords."

Nev didn't hear a response but thought she saw Chit nod his head. She was certain when Nina again sighed and leaned against a tree, growing silent.

Though she had no idea what the Council of Lords was, Nev could surmise its meaning from the little she remembered of the lessons Nina had taught her.

Leresan, the land that contained Roden along with scores of similar small villages, a scattering of towns and about half a dozen cities, had been without a ruler for nearly two-hundred years since Prince Daughtry had gone mad and hung himself in the bell tower of his palace, leaving behind no heirs to take his throne.

In the absence of a monarch, nobles and the wealthy had managed to keep things stable since with no central seat of power and each looked after their respective regions, usually maintaining control within their family lines. Remarkably there hadn't been much fighting between the nobles, most content to handle disagreements and property disputes as business dealings with a lot of buying and trading conducted between rulers.

One of the few exceptions was Sarter, now an aged man who had chosen to name his region and its capital city after himself. Sarter was always looking to gain more land and coveted the resources of the neighboring region of Kasen, which was ruled by Rylen and within which Roden was situated.

So greedy was Sarter, in fact, that he had tried to take Kasen by force several times, with three significant conflicts resulting in the past 70 years, the most recent having been a battle 25 years before.

In all three conflicts, residents of Kasen had risen up to fight off Sarter's advances, happy with the rule of Rylen and not willing to accept Sarter as a leader.

That was a history Nev knew all too well, for Delsin had fought in that final conflict, giving him common ground with Edric and the other village men, many of whom had fought in the first two. Each time the people of Kasen were successful in pushing him back and Sarter finally seemed to have given up, with peace falling between the two and a resumption of simple life in the small villages.

Within that climate of calm, the new generation had grown with very little understanding of anything beyond their immediate lives.

But Nina had always theorized that Sarter wasn't finished and would do anything to posses Kasen. Probably because she had traveled so extensively and had in-person perspectives on much of the goings on, Nina was a passionate study of politics and would listen for news of who had acquired what and the dynamics between rulers – all of which she incorporated into the lessons she gave Nev.

But Nev had always fallen a little short of sharing her passion and had learned the basics but retained little else, making her think perhaps this Council of Lords was one of those things she had missed or forgotten.

Her ears perked as Nina began speaking again, surprised to hear a rant of frustration from the woman who was usually so steady and calm even in the face of crisis.

"So you're telling me she killed one of Sarter's top men while he was on his way to the Council of Lords? Oh this is wonderful, just wonderful!

"As if it weren't enough she wants to take on one of the most fierce men in existence, she has turned the village of Roden against us which will eventually trickle throughout Kasen, and now she has likely set off a war by killing the emissary of the most unstable leader this side of Leresan, because there's no doubt Sarter will use the death to blame the other lords, regardless of the truth."

Guilt enveloped her while she listened, but it quickly turned to shock when Nina practically fell into Chit's arms and sobbed like the weight of humanity lay on her very shoulders.

It was a side of Nina she had never seen before a fact that rattled Nev so much, she backed away quietly, giving them the privacy she knew she should have respected in the first place.

Making her way to the camp, it dawned on her how much Nina had sacrificed for her and that despite all that, she had failed to see her as a person with her own set of issues and concerns that extended beyond the role she filled in Nev's life. The accidental encounter made it apparent Nina and Chit had grown close in a way she hadn't noticed because she'd been so self involved.

Even if she could, she didn't think she would take back the events that led to the loss of their homes or the death of Sarter's man, or for that matter, her vow to make Alopex pay for the pain he had caused her and her mother. But picturing Nina's emotional breakdown, it occurred to her that the promise Nina had made her mother all those years ago had come full circle and the debt was paid, if not swung in the other direction entirely. And it was past time for her to start acting like it.

The smells of food and burned wood were strong in the camp and taking in the sight, Nev was struck by how industrious the group had been in such a short period of time. Chairs had been fashioned from pieces of fallen logs and rough shelters formed from long sticks propped against one another and covered in leafy branches. The children had even forged toys using sticks, vines, rocks and whatever else they could scrounge, the ones most prized having scraps of cloth or ribbon salvaged from the remnants of the pretty dresses some of them had once had.

Their tattered and matted hair had given way to clean, freshly brushed and even braided locks, dresses and tunics were mended and skin was scrubbed clean – all in an effort to regain some semblance of pride despite the circumstance. And though a fog still clung to the group, smiles and laughter had even found their way back in.

It was utterly amazing when compared to the state they had been in just two days before and Nev couldn't help but feel a sense of pride that she had played a part in that.

Her approach drew attention, bringing the hum of activity to a lull, and eyes began to focus on her giving hint to everyone's excitement at returning home. The group had mapped out a course with Chit and Nina's help, determining a route much like the trader's, albeit more direct.

The large bosomed woman had the furthest to go to reach home. Named Bronwyn, the farmer's wife had been snatched while tending crops near her home in the marshlands east of Valen. Competent and rugged in nature, she had committed to taking charge, promising to see everyone home with Elsie and Ivy marking the last stop on the route before she returned to her own family. She had even insisted on taking in three of the girls because they had nowhere to go.

Bronwyn had emerged in the camp as an organizer and nurturer with a protective side, qualities which gave Nev comfort that everyone would be in good hands.

Nev gave her the nod to start moving everyone to the clearing and watched in admiration as the woman began barking orders, sending girls this way and that to fetch what they planned to take with them.

"Bronwyn, have them take whatever can be of use from the carriage," Nev said as an afterthought, stepping over to dismantle the cushioned seats and begin pulling the tough fabric shell from the upper sides. Moving over to help, Bronwyn looked at Nev curiously, but didn't question, coaxing a couple of older girls to help.

In short time they had removed all the parts that could be useful including the harness rigging, and were in the process of removing the wheels when Nina and Chit approached. But rather than explain, Nev just shot a smile in their direction and kept working, sending Nina off to pack up some food supplies and engaging Chit to help with the last and most stubborn wheel.

The cloth, cut in sections, was placed in the box cart so the pieces could be used as coverings along the trip and the cushions would help with some of those passengers suffering physical injuries.

Hunting for somewhere to place the extra harnesses, Nev discovered the splintered slab of wood that served as the driver's seat lifted, exposing beneath it a compartment where the trader had stored a bag of apples, a stale, crusty chunk of bread and a bag of coins. Stowing the harnesses within, Nev pulled out the coin bag, staring at it in hatred.

Looking around at all the lives that were represented within it, she found herself momentarily halted by a wave of nausea that swept through her. Surely filling it had been the rancid man's proud accomplishment – it even smelled of him she realized, the stale odors of his essence reawakening the feel of his weight sagging in her arms – which, unlike filling the bag, was truly an accomplishment deserving of pride.

Tinged with filth, it's irregular shape was heavy in her hands, no doubt a sign of the value it contained, but by comparison to the women and girls around her that stood waiting to climb in the cart and rediscover life, it seemed worthless.

Nev walked to where Bronwyn was strapping the last of the extra wheels to the roof of the cart and wordlessly pressed the bag into the woman's surprised hands, knowing that while the coins might help with the trip and even leave the woman with extra, they could never be enough to make up for what had been done.

"I found some apples under the seat. If you divide them carefully, there should be some for everyone" she said, intentionally diverting focus from the coins.

Tears gathering in her eyes, Bronwyn nodded her head and unexpectedly pulled Nev into an awkward, pillowy embrace, leaving little room to breathe but thankfully, it also left no room for words either. Instantly understanding Aster's aversion to the woman's affection, Nev tried to hide her discomfort until Bronwyn appeared satisfied and pulled away, tucking the coins into a sling-style satchel that encircled the waist of her simple skirt as she moved off to help get everyone situated.

Aster trailed behind Chit as he carried little Ivy, hoisting her up to the platform of the cart where Nina waited. Nev's heart lurched every time she laid eyes on the still unresponsive child and though something told her the breakage was too severe, she held out hope Ivy would find comfort with Percy and allow herself to be coaxed back to life.

Elsie too would no doubt have a difficult path ahead of her, having regressed emotionally to the point the other girls now completely shunned her. They seemed unable to stomach the abrasive and annoying girl she had evolved into in such a short period of time.

With all but three situated in the cart, Nev walked back to the front, checking the harnesses on the mares one last time. Cleaned and open to the warm summer air, the crowded cart was hardly recognizable. The mares especially, standing in wait with an air of determination and a new-found bend of pride in their necks, didn't look anything like the broken down nags that had pulled it before.

Rubbing the forehead of the mare closest to her, Nev sent her thanks and admiration for the strength the pair had displayed, relaying Bronwyn's plans to reward them with a life of easy grazing when they reached their destination. Tossing her head with a snort, the mare acknowledged the message, the gratitude she felt toward Nev ringing through clearly.

Patting her on the shoulder one last time, Nev ran her hand down the reins, guiding them in a straight line back to the wooden seat where she looped them around a hook placed there for their keeping.

Helping Bronwyn climb up to the seat, Nev rested her hands on the edge of the rough wood.

"They know the way, so you shouldn't need to do much. Just keep watch and let them have their heads and they will get you there," she said, looking up at the woman who seemed a bit uncertain at the idea of giving control over to the mares, but nodded just the same.

Squeezing Bronwyn's hand, Nev wandered back to the cart, reaching out to clasp the hands of girls saying goodbye. Spotting Elsie leaning over the side, she reached out and gave the girl a hug. "Take good care of Ivy, she needs you," she whispered in the girl's ear. "You will be singing and playing with Percy again before you know it Elsie."

She felt Elsie's hair moving against her own and squeezed tight a final time before releasing her hold and allowing the girl to pull back and disappear behind the low wall.

Moving off to stand with Nina, Chit and Aster, who had already moved back to watch the cart leave, Nev felt a pang of emptiness at their leaving. But at the same time, she was glad to see them on their way, she thought as the mares began moving across the clearing toward the small path that would guide them from the woods.

Turning to Nina as the wheels creaked out of sight and they were suddenly alone, Nev felt comforted to see similar emotions reflected on the woman's face.

"Well, I guess it's time for us to get moving too," she said, breaking the silence. Nodding in response, Nina reached out and squeezed Nev's arm in a loving gesture before walking back toward the camp with Aster skipping along beside her, excited to get started on their own journey.

Chit lingered, waiting until they were out of earshot to speak.

Meeting Nev's eyes, he hesitated as if he wasn't sure what to say. Other than the conversation she had accidentally overheard a short time before and a few functional dialogs over the past days, Nev realized for the first time that she had never actually had a true conversation with the man that stood before her.

The longer she looked at him, the more she realized his age was not as advanced as she might have thought, but rather his thinness and gaunt features showed the strain of hardship and pain, evidenced in his hesitant almost withdrawn mannerisms.

"I think I owe you thanks for a second time," he said, his hand reaching nervously to smooth his ruffled graying hair.

Meeting his eyes, Nev waited, for it was obvious he had more to say.

Clearing his throat, Chit looked away as if ashamed and spoke in a soft voice.

"My wife died in the winter. For twenty years, we sold items of antiquity to the wealthy out of a rented shop in Sarter and always did very well until her sickness set in. It came on so quickly and with such force, that rather than work, I stayed with her trying to make her comfortable," he said, an unexpected surge of emotion in his voice catching Nev by surprise. "She made it four months, her last day the most agonizing of all before death finally claimed her."

Looking over toward the edge of the clearing where the carriage had once sat with his employer inside, anger filled his eyes.

"Accompanied by his paid protector's, he was banging on my door moments after she drew her last breath, demanding the rent I owed him. I had nothing left, the money was all gone and when he gave me the option of working as his driver, it wasn't really a choice."

Nev could see the pain the man was struggling against, but then again it wasn't exactly a revelation because her intuition had told her that first night that he was a good man.

"I am so very sorry about your wife, and I am sorry that you ended up here and in this mess," she said, stopping him with a hand on his arm. "But you don't owe me an explanation Chit, I know that you are a good man and I know you would have stopped him if you could have. You have no debt to repay here."

Shaking his head, it was clear the man could not absolve himself so easily.

"Nev I can't get her screams out of my head. They live in the quiet moments, playing through my head again and again, growing unbearable if I try to sleep or even sit for a moment."

Until now, even though she had noted his obvious need to make up for his part in what had happened, she hadn't known the depth of how the ordeal had affected Chit. The awareness gave her a sense of compassion for the man, for though the event hadn't changed him visibly like it had her, its impact was undeniable.

"Chit, you are not responsible for what happened and I can't make the screams go away for you anymore than I can for myself, but I can tell you that somehow Aster has found peace and we must too," she told him, shifting her head in an attempt to draw in his gaze. "She survived and she is taking on life with an optimism even I find hard to understand, but we must follow her example. I am glad to have you with us and I know that Aster and Nina are too."

She couldn't help but smile when a small spark flickered in his eye at mention of Nina's name.

Taking a deep breath, Chit met Nev's eyes directly for the first time in the conversation.

"Thank you Nev, for welcoming me. I know that I am worn out and I haven't much to offer, but I will do everything in my power to be of assistance to all of you. You have my word," he said almost reverently and in a tone that left no doubt to his sincerity.

Nev accepted his promise with a smile. Moving her hand to his shoulder, she guided him in the direction of the camp.

They found Nina standing in front of the hollowed out carriage that had been left sitting on its axles in the dirt. There was little left of its finery but a wooden frame and base, the covering that once enclosed it having been peeled away. Turning toward them, Nina's expression made it clear that she was at a loss in terms of what to do with it.

An idea forming in her brain, Nev called to Aster, who was busy nearby dismantling the makeshift shelters.

"Can you get rid of this without burning down the forest?" she asked, ignoring Chit's look of surprise when Aster pumped her head up and down eagerly at the chance to use her skills again.

Stepping back, Nev watched as Aster walked in a circle around the carriage, tendrils of smoke rising up from the path her feet made in the dirt.

She found it amusing to see the looks of amazement on Chit and Nina's faces, for even though she had described the child's abilities to Nina, it was the first time either of them had seen her at work.

Long, thin red flames grew out of the circle of smoke, moving in at an angle toward the shell of the carriage. They grew up to wrap around and obscure it from view.

Aster stood by, her eyes focused on the fire, keeping it under control Nev assumed based on her look of concentration.

It seemed as if hardly any time passed before the circle of flames consumed the carriage, drawing inward until it disappeared completely leaving them watching a single flame that flickered and went out in the center of the circle where the carriage had been.

"Well done Aster," Nina was the first to comment, Chit still standing frozen staring at the blackened circle.

"How did she..." he stammered, moving closer as if he thought it some kind of trick.

"There are some things about us that you are probably going to find surprising the longer we're together but I'll let Nina explain," Nev told him with a grin, trying not to laugh when she imagined how he would react to her wings or Aster's disappearing-reappearing as a fox routine.

Calling to the horses, Nev looked around, and satisfied that the camp had been stripped down to the greatest degree possible, loaded her arms with bags and set off for the clearing.

Swinging the bags over Barge's back, she reached out for the two blacks in an effort to determine which would be most suitable for Aster to ride. She laughed when the smaller of the two stretched out one leg and bowed, showing his willingness to carry the girl.

High-bred and beautiful, the muscular pair was larger than Mica and Soot, though still no comparison to Barge, with long feathery manes and tufts of hair behind their hooves that gave them a fancy air, but their heads were level and they were glad at the chance to carry riders rather than pull the carriage.

As she tied the final strap to secure the bags to Barge, Nev broke down and called to Avec, fearful of what his state of mind might be. She had left him alone for the morning, knowing his pride was injured badly from what had happened. And though she knew he had heard the final decision to allow Aster along, she was sure he wasn't pleased.

Her intuition was correct, because he didn't answer at first, his mind finally allowing her in after what seemed to be an excruciating wait.

"We are getting ready to leave. Chit is coming with us too. I think Nina likes him," she said, trying to keep things light.

Avec didn't respond with words but let her know he would be keeping pace from the sky, obviously not ready to face the others yet, particularly Aster. Breaking off, Nev gave him his space knowing that even though she would have enjoyed his company it was best for her to leave him be until he was ready.

As the others walked up, Nev pointed Aster and Chit to their horses and listened with quiet approval as Aster connected with the small stallion, introducing herself and launching into a conversation that seemed more like an inquisition designed to find out as much as she could about him.

But the horse didn't seem to mind, performing his bow again to let Aster climb aboard.

"How did she make him do that?" Chit asked, watching with an expression of incredulity as his own horse snorted and did the same for him.

Clambering on, Chit looked down at the ground in utter amazement when his horse straightened and stood again, tossing his head for effect.

Nina and Nev laughed, climbing onto their horses with far less ceremony.

Looking from side to side of his horse's neck, Chit looked up with concern on his face, suddenly realizing he had no measure with which to control the animal.

"Where are the reins?" he asked in a near whisper as if afraid to startle his horse.

In response, the horse started moving forward, causing Chit to grip tightly with his legs and snatch a thick handful of mane, bringing about another snort from the animal.

The question, particularly when coupled with the man's complete helpless, but unnecessary fear, set Nina and Nev into a fresh peal of laughter, rendering them incapable of answering.

"You don't need any of that stuff Chit, they know what to do," It was Aster who finally spoke in an attempt to ease what was beginning to look like panic on the man's face.

With an approving nod from Nev, who was still trying to contain her laughter, Aster continued.

"Nev and me can talk to them Chit. They know where we want to go and have agreed to take us, so we don't need to do anything but ride," she said as if she were talking to a child.

"Your horse's name is Baryt, mine is Drusy. They say you used to call them Pitch and Sludge, but they forgive you," Aster said, causing snorts from Nina and Nev followed by an outburst of laughter when Chit stared at the child in shock.

Stuttering, Chit looked meekly down at Baryt's neck and apologized, visibly jolting when the horse tossed, then bobbed his head in response.

Looking at Nina and Nev for help, the man found none. Their laughter following behind them, they had already started moving forward with Aster, leaving him alone with Baryt who had bent his neck to look back in wait of a signal that Chit was ready.

On his go ahead, Baryt bolted, trotting to catch up and forcing Chit to grab handfuls of the horse's mane to keep from being bounced to the ground.

Brain pounding against the inside of his skull, his backside becoming intimately acquainted with Baryt's spine, it occurred to Chit that by comparison to whatever he had just gotten himself into, a hanging might very well seem like fun.

●● Chapter Sixteen ●●

Two weeks between them and the clearing, the foursome was starting to feel like a tight-knit family, one of the side effects of hours spent on a horse with nothing to do but talk, joke, irritate one another and talk some more.

Though they had been heading south in the direction of Aileron, they were now going north-west toward the mountains, but luckily the change in direction had occurred at an early enough point that they hadn't lost too much ground.

Outside the dense forest they had entered hill country that was still dotted with trees, though not near as many as before.

They rode and camped close to tree groupings whenever possible to avoid attracting attention in the open, for though they were intentionally avoiding villages and populated areas, there was always the possibility of crossing paths with the occasional traveler.

Their chosen route was desolate enough that they decided to forgo night travel, thinking it safer to spend their most vulnerable time, that of sleep, under cover of darkness. It left little time for interaction with Wybert, but the firefly seemed content enough just being near Nev, even if she was sleeping.

The horses seemed to prefer the gently rolling hills to the forest of before and were far from sorry to no longer be weaving through tight trees and carefully stepping over broken stumps and buried roots.

Avec was still tense, avoiding Aster as much as possible, but each day he seemed to stay a little closer for a little longer than the day before and had even taken a nap or two nestled between the bags on Barge's back. Likewise, Aster avoided him with similar trepidation and tended to be more subdued when he was nearby, for she had no interest in a repeat of what had occurred back in the clearing.

The tension was wearing on Nev, but she bit her tongue knowing they would have to come to terms with it on their own, their natural distrust for one another running deeper than thought and programed into them in ways that no amount of logic was going to undo.

Chit, on the other hand, opened up more and more as he gained a comfort level with his new companions. The man had seen more tragedy than any one person should, yet remarkably maintained a level head, using his hardships to gain understanding, a quality that Nev could do nothing less than admire.

Telling his stories, they all listened enthralled at the resilience he had shown and as it turned out, Chit was far more than just a worn out shop-keep.

It was almost expected of him, as the son of a soldier himself, he told. He joined Sarter's army when he was sixteen summers old and worked his way through the ranks, rising mostly by default when soldiers would grow sick or die, or just decide they were fed up and go home, as happened often enough because even Sarter's own people had little care for him or his agenda. But Chit found it to be an honest living as long as he never looked at the politics behind anything, and having been prepped for it by his father who drummed the warriors mentality into him from the time he could talk, it seemed a natural fit.

By the time the second conflict arose between Sarter and Kasen, or more accurately by the second time Sarter tried to take Kasen by force, Chit was commanding the largest unit in the army.

Advancing deeper into the heart of Kasan, Chit's unit commandeered several homes in the small, north Kasan village of Parlen and he wasn't there long before the miller's daughter caught his eye, her parent's home one of several serving as quarters for Chit and his men.

After the initiative failed – not by fault of the army, but because the one thing Sarter could never understand was that a people who rejected his rule could never be defeated – Chit passed back through Parlen.

When Ellana accepted his offer of marriage, he happily settled in to the village, trading the soldiers life for one of peace.

They had one child, a son, who took ill and died unexpectedly at seven summers, devastating them both. The pain of losing their child made life in the quiet village unbearable and to save themselves from pending madness, they struck out, wandering aimlessly throughout Leresan in search of relief from the agony that haunted them.

At the beginning of their travels he described them as empty and mindless, pushing on through their pain, but as time passed, they began to awaken to the nuances of the small villages they passed through, picking up curious items and various odds and ends until one day their collection had grown so large, they had filled their wagon to the brim.

Unwilling to discard their collection, they decided to open a store, settling in the city of Sarter and stocking it with all but a few of their more precious keepsakes. In time, people began to bring them things to consign and the business grew to turn enough of a profit to provide for their basic needs.

It allowed them 20 years of comfort together until Ellana grew ill.

Chit said he sold off everything he could and had enough to cover their expenses for a short time, but the money ran out and with Ellana growing more and more sick, he couldn't bring himself to leave her side for fear she would need him, or worse yet, die alone.

Nev found the notion of unfaltering dedication to be a novel, yet romantic idea. While it was well beyond anything she could relate to in her life, Chit and Nina had both experienced it, so it must exist. Aster too seemed to share her fascination with the concept and with each passing hour seemed to bond more to the man, seeing him as something of a hero. She had no idea that he held himself responsible for not helping her during the single most horrific moment of her life.

The dynamic presented a strange irony that Nev tried to dismiss as quickly as she detected it, knowing that to be revered by the girl only compounded Chit's feeling that he had failed her, succeeding in making him feel like a fraud.

But thankfully he never let on to Aster, interacting with her so well that if Nev hadn't known the inside story, she wouldn't have guessed at it herself.

Nina too seemed to warm to Chit at an increasing rate, his presence bringing out a side of the woman that Nev had never seen before. Smiling and happy most of the time, the biggest clue lay in the fact Nina had started wearing her hair loose through the mornings until the afternoon sun would heat to such a point that she had to twist it up again to get relief.

But there were other indications too, like the way Soot and Baryt always seemed to end up side by side, the reemergence of her quick smile and the dulcet tones, the way she would brush and straighten her tunic when she though no one was looking and especially the times she laughed at jokes that really weren't that funny.

Had it been any other woman, Nev might have thought her foolish, but in the case of Nina, she found it endearing – and thankfully it appeared Chit did as well.

In fact Chit had turned out to be a remarkably accepting man who, probably as a result of all his experiences, had a very adaptable personality – a trait that came in very handy the more he learned about his present company.

The first couple days after they left the clearing, Nina dedicated the time to filling Chit in on exactly what he had gotten himself into and he had taken it rather well, all things considered. For even though he had lived a full life with rich experiences, it had been a plainly human life, giving credence to Nina's description of how oblivious most people were to the depth of the world around them.

Nev appreciated the fact that in her telling, Nina skipped over the more emotional parts, not because she didn't trust Chit, but more because it just felt like those details were sacredly hers and closely tied to her pride. But of course she also understood that there were elements of her history that had to be given in order for him to understand other things, not the least of which was why two women and a child were on their way to a mountain fortress with the intent of killing the king of a race he had never heard of before.

So Nina, in the most gentle way possible, with consideration for the fact Aster too was listening, told the story of what Alopex had done to Lennera.

Chit seemed to take it all in stride, and though he appeared to realize there were layers of the story he was not being given, he was respectful enough not to press further.

Aster, however, seemed to wrap herself in the information, tying it about her like a chord of commonality that bound her to Nev even tighter than before.

But Nev still thought she could feel a change in the way they looked at her, because she had felt it all her life. Having a parent die was one of those things that always brought forth pity from others, but throughout the course of her life she had found it ironic that it also created a desire to place distance as if people thought it was something they could catch. As she heard Nina explain that she was a product of the worst violation imaginable and that Lennera had chosen to die rather than live a life with her, she couldn't completely squelch the feeling of being unwanted, no matter how hard she tried to believe it wasn't true.

Rather than become upset or lash out at her companions though, Nev turned her feelings inward, using them to keep alive her commitment to punish Alopex, for by his brutal treatment of her mother, he had made himself singly responsible for every bit of pain and sorrow she had ever felt.

She was finding it easier to control her anger and direct it appropriately, the exchange between her and Nina still as fresh as half healed burns on an overly curious child's fingers. Strangely, she found it soothing to stoke an inner fire of hate, taking all the little things that in the past might have led to an outburst and instead tossing them into the deep pool of her anger to watching the flames grow and roar within her heart. As it grew, that fire gave birth to a satisfying center of power that helped her feel she could not fail.

If Nina saw the change or sensed the heat at her core, she didn't let on, instead, pushing her harder than she'd ever been pushed before.

It began the day they left the clearing with Nina forcing her to exercise her wings.

She was reluctant to extend them, in part not wanting to feel like an oddity in front of Chit and Aster and because she knew it was going to hurt after all the injuries she gained from her first flight.

As it turned out, only one of her concerns had merit.

Aster had squealed in utter delight when she first saw them, her face turning instantly to one of awestruck worship when Nev, still seated on Mica, extended them to their full breadth. Similarly Chit had watched in utter amazement without even a hint of anything less than admiration in his expression.

The pain, however, was more excruciating than any she had ever experienced. The usual tingles of pleasure were no where to be found and in their place, fingers of agony reached into her back, echoing throughout her entire body.

"Stretch them girl, or the way you feel right now will be pleasant by comparison to tomorrow," Nina had barked at her.

And so it had gone at least twice a day since, with Nev extending her wings, flexing, stretching, slowly flapping and even contorting them to their limits, depending on whatever Nina's torture prerogative was at the moment.

As much as she hated to admit it, the pain had lessened and they did indeed feel stronger now than ever before, though she was reticent to give Nina the satisfaction of knowing it – a last bit of childishness she was willing to accept.

But of course Nina had picked up on the fact the exercises weren't hurting, not buying into winces feigned for her benefit, and had expanded the regimen to include what she coined "wind resistance conditioning." It involved Mica galloping with Nev on his back, flaring out her wings at Nina's command, then holding them against the pressure until she was told to relax them.

Mica seemed to look forward to and thoroughly enjoy the experience, leaving Nev more than a touch embarrassed on one occasion when she peeked in his mind and caught him fancying himself a winged stud.

For Nev, on the other hand, Nina's torturous wind simulation games tested and pushed her muscles in exactly the same manner her near-catastrophic first flight had, giving her a couple of days reminder of the pain she was trying to overcome. Yet she couldn't deny that it was working and her endurance was increasing exponentially, so well in fact, that she was anxiously awaiting her next opportunity to fly.

Patrolling from the air during her work sessions to be sure no one stumbled upon her, Avec watched with amusement, often complimenting Nina's thought process, and, though she was burning with the desire to snap at him, Nev tossed the glares she would have shot his way into her inner fire instead.

In all truth his input, as usual, was quite helpful, though some of the things Nina had her do were difficult for him to understand. As a bird, Avec's flying posture was always struck in such a way as to help him cut through the air with the least resistance possible and in fact his entire body to include his beak was designed with that in mind. Avec would never have positioned himself in such a way as to create undue wind pressure on his wings and in all reality, couldn't, because his body was inherently positioned in a way to work with them.

But the dynamics of flight were different for a human body, Nina told him one day when Nev conveyed his confusion.

Something as simple as the legs and torso moving from a horizontal position to vertical mid-flight would put tremendous pressure and strain on the wings, potentially causing injury or complete failure, she explained. It was part of what had tired Nev so quickly her first flight.

Nina said the shape of the human body wasn't necessarily suited to flight. It could be accomplished, but there was no magic to being Aile that was going to bridge the gap for Nev. Rather, it was going to take good old fashioned conditioning and hard work. Just having wings didn't mean a thing could fly efficiently, or at all for that matter, Nina told them both, explaining there were plenty of flightless birds out there that hatched with wings but still couldn't get off the ground.

The explanation was something of an epiphany for Nev and even more so for Avec, neither of them having ever considered the differences before – they had just equated wings with flight. But in reflection, it made a lot of sense and it did go a long way to explaining Nev's failures. Sure, back in Roden she had gotten off the ground, but without the proper conditioning and strength, it made sense it wasn't going to last long, hence all the crashing.

So with new-found drive, she opened her wings time and time again, subjecting them to countless hours of exhausting work, in the hope she might exceed Nina's promise that a difference would be felt quickly enough, even though the end results would take weeks or months.

But months was something she didn't have, and flying was just one of the challenges before her.

Hand to hand combat was an area where, in another surprising twist of luck, Chit was rather well versed. His body well past its prime and stricken with aches, failing strength and abused by lack of care during the previous year, the old soldier didn't have the capacity to actually implement the skills of fighting anymore, but that didn't mean he had forgotten.

Whenever the group would stop for meals or to rest the horses, Chit would demonstrate techniques, then coach Nev through them. He drilled her on what to do if she were thrown to the ground, running her through dozens of scenarios from being held by the neck to having her arms pinned, showing her how to fall so she wasn't injured or breathless and how to roll rather than pitch headlong – not just showing her how to dominate, but how to be dominated – and survive it.

He even taught her to use measures she would have thought of as dishonorable.

"Always trust your heart and show mercy where deserved, but remember, the only thing that really matters in a fight is being the one who stands at the end of it," he would repeat, encouraging her to use her elbows as weapons, to dig into the bones at the base of the neck or between ribs with her fingers, anything to gain the advantage and control the momentum.

While he himself wasn't able to engage her, he would go through each move in slow motion, repeating it time and time again before pairing her with Aster or Nina, neither of which were any match for her physically.

More than just her appearance, she now found her reflexes were quicker than they'd ever been, which put her well past what they were capable of. Even more than that, she had a new level of speed in her movements, increased flexibility and a strength she'd never known before.

But she also found those things did not make her invincible. Quite the contrary, relying on them got her into more tight places than not, and Chit would not allow her the crutch. As soon as he saw her depending on strength alone, Chit would pull her opponent aside and whisper instructions to them that when they executed, inevitably resulted in her defeat. And each of those earned her a reprimand.

"Think Nev, THINK! Use your brain, muscle has nothing to do with it!" he would shout at her. "What will you do if your opponent is bigger and stronger?"

Bruises covered bruises and abrasions from rolling on the ground were hardened into scabs with new ones appearing from each lesson, but she became less and less aware of them everyday.

And her muscles seemed to be learning as much if not more than her brain with the repetition.

She felt coiled and tight but fast and fluid a the same time, sometimes even amazing herself at how quickly an arm would move to block a blow or how her entire body would spring forward and roll even before the idea had struck her as appropriate.

They were about three weeks from reaching the Fauho, with the mountain village where Nina had met Lennera even closer and Nev was feeling the pressure of time closing in on her. Anticipation mingled with nervousness at the nearing goal and she found herself trying to keep the two bound together within her, fearing that if she allowed them to split, the nervousness would win out.

Instead, she dove into the pain in the hope it would bring her closer to the freedom that she knew would only be hers when Alopex was forced to face her and confronted with the results of his deeds. Even though the others worked tirelessly to help her prepare, she knew the driving force within her was something she carried alone.

But for the first time in her life, Nev found herself anything but alone. The strange collection of souls that accompanied her gave her comfort and emboldened her in ways she could never have envisioned back in Roden when she was looking toward a future empty of promise.

And the irony was not lost on her that in pursuit of killing the only family member she had left, she had found a new family that fulfilled her life more than anything ever had.

●●Chapter Seventeen●●

Yes, she could definitely feel the new strength in her wings as she pumped them in unison, rising higher and higher with each lift and fall of their curved expanse.

Laughing above her, Avec watched her ascension with happy satisfaction, waiting for her to join him.

"Come on, slow one," he said playfully, soaring in a self made convection while he waited.

Laughing herself, Nev soaked up the feeling as she sped up, easily meeting him.

"Let's go," he said approvingly, his anticipation clear, his words like an accelerant to fire.

All of Nina's lessons clicked in her brain at once and her body molded to the air as if it knew what to do without being told.

Using the force created by her wings, she dove forward, simultaneously tightening the muscles in her abdomen to aid in lifting her legs behind her.

Once her position was correct, she found herself cutting through the air effortlessly, her movement creating a platform of air beneath her that eased the strain on her muscles and worked almost as a cradle holding her exactly as she needed to be.

"Air has as much weight and strength as stone, a lesson you have learned the hard way. But it is your greatest ally if you can learn to use it as you would the ground beneath your feet," the woman's voice echoed in her mind, coaching her as she went.

Oh how had the earthbound woman known such truth? She wondered as she tucked her wings against her back and arms across her chest, allowing herself to roll as if down hill.

She laughed uninhibited when the controlled fall made her stomach rise up to her chest, sending tickles through her before she eased her wings back out and pushed forward, curving around to weave parallel with the ground again.

"Show off!" Avec shouted her direction, doing his own tumbling roll in response.

Laughing like children, they drew side by side, the hawk pushing slightly in front of her to lead the way through the austere sky.

"This is the most wonderful feeling in the world Avec!"

"Yes it is. There was a time when I feared you would never join me in it, that we wouldn't get to share the sky ... but we have done it Nev."

Coasting blissfully, his sentiment was so rich in feeling Nev found herself drawn to look his direction, wondering if hawks could shed tears.

Perhaps, perhaps not, she thought when she felt moisture gather in her own eyes, though if anyone had been there to notice, she surely would have blamed the air rushing against her face.

"I wouldn't want to be in the sky if you weren't with me," she blurted unabashed.

But as soon as the words were out, she dove upward, not regretting them but also not wanting to be there when they registered on his face.

Giggling at the advantage the heartfelt sentiments gained her, she rushed faster and faster back the way they had come as he curled around in the air and tried to catch up.

Yes, this was bliss. Pure, unadulterated bliss that she could find no comparison for in any corner of her memory bank of experience.

Finally Avec was closing on her, but she allowed him to fall in beside her rather than outpace him again, as she knew she could.

Slowing to an effortless coast with her wings locked out at their full lengths, she tested their strength by allowing her legs to lower just a bit.

The strain was instantaneous but thankfully not painful and she pumped her wings rapidly and dove forward a little to help her legs lift back above the air current beneath them.

"I can't believe I never realized before how much of a difference that would make," she said, still amazed that it had taken Nina for her to realize that which now seemed so simple.

"Well don't be too hard on yourself, I was just as frustrated as

you were and all I knew was nothing was working," Avec responded.

"I thought it was in your head. I guess it never occurred to me that your body was working against you so badly because I've never had those challenges. My parts just go where my wings take them."

It certainly was profound, Nev thought as she tilted her wings to the right, banking into a wide sweep only to rise up higher again.

Once level, she again pumped her wings to gather speed, then tucked her arms to her sides and wove nose first in a line through the air, much like she imagined a fish must moving along the surface of the water.

The resulting giggle was involuntary.

"You're enjoying this too much fledgling," the hawk said, though she could feel what surely equated to a happy grin accompanying the words.

"We should return before you begin to tire, Nev, we need to build up to it or we'll have a repeat of what happened last time."

She worked not to express her disappointment, because she knew if he could, he would have spent the rest of his days in the sky with her, but he was being prudent and regrettably, he was right.

Looking down below, something she had resisted doing since they took to the air, she could see a tendril of smoke curling up above the small patch of trees they had chosen for their evening home. Nina and Aster were no doubt still watching from where they had left them in the nearby open and the smoke gave indication that Chit was probably waiting for something to cook over his newly built fire.

"Once we get you safely down, I'll go catch some fish," Avec said, responding to her thoughts, his own appetite showing itself with near audible drooling.

If the bird had a weakness, it lay in his voracious hunger.

"I know you're all tired of eating rabbit and I found a decent sized stream not too far away that was full of plump morsels."

Nodding, she couldn't resist cutting one more swath through the air, turning away from the the direction of camp and gathering as much speed as she could before listening to the twinge of fatigue that was growing louder.

Banking back, she felt a momentary surge of fear at the thought of getting back to the ground. It was the perpetual rub to flying, at least as she had experienced it. For as it turned out, height was nothing to fear, instead it was the ground that tended to hurt the most and the distance between the two now stretched before her like a gauntlet of everything that defined terror.

"You are going to be fine. You follow me and I will take you down in controlled circles. I think that's how you should do it until you get the hang of landing," Avec told her.

Nodding, she didn't question him in the slightest, putting all her energy instead into stifling the panic that was growing despite her efforts to turn it off with logic.

"Nev, you will be fine," he reassured her, for of course he felt her fear too having shared her pain every time she hit the ground.

Flapping her wings to keep her momentum, she fell in line behind him and mirrored the gradual downward curve that would get her back.

Avec made wide, sweeping circles that were more like coasting than flying, guiding her in a spiral so loose she might not have realized they were descending if she hadn't already known it.

It was so controlled, in fact, she began to relax and enjoy the rhythm of it, fear being replaced with confidence as the ground rose up.

Trees and rocks began to grow before her and the hills stretched up through the grass, giving definition to the scene before her, but she stayed with him as the spiral tightened gradually.

"We're very close," he said, pointing out the obvious.

"It's time to start dropping your legs. You can either continue in a circle until your feet touch the ground and then run out of it until you slow, or you can try flapping your wings to control and stop yourself, then just land. It's up to you."

Things had gone remarkably well, but Nev wanted to keep it that way and had no pride involved in her deciding to keep the circles going until she could hit the ground and run.

"That's a good decision. Just be prepared to flap your wings to keep from falling until you get your pace right," he said, cutting

up a little so he could watch.

Just feet away, Nev wasn't sure what he meant but figured it would come to her soon enough as she curled her toes up and traced the balls of her feet for impact.

As slow as she seemed to be going in the air, the momentum propelling her forward was still more than her feet were ready for as she scrambled to get the timing right.

But it wasn't going to happen.

Pitching forward, she realized what Avec had meant right about the time she tucked her wings rather than flap them.

But thankfully as her mind went blank, her muscles remembered and it was instead it was Chit's teaching that kicked in, her chin tucking to her chest as she curled into a forward moving ball.

Rolling first her shoulder, then her back against the ground, she sprang to her feet on the other side, standing in amazement with her hands before her as if to block an invisible enemy until the realization set in that she had already beaten her foe.

And then she just couldn't help herself.

Jogging her feet up and down, she hopped in the air and stretched her wings for affect.

She was still laughing when Nina came running to smother her in a huge hug, that ended up more around her neck than normal as she maneuvered her arms trying to avoid her wings.

"Good job girl! I was hoping I wouldn't have to spend the rest of the night doctoring more of your wounds," Nina said.

Avec too arrived, landing on her shoulder to rest his head against hers briefly.

"Well done fledgling," he told her, coating his pride in humor.

"Nina it was the most amazing thing ever!" Nev began babbling as she allowed her wings to retract.

She was unable to contain herself as she recounted the feeling of finally and successfully finding her way in the air, remembering to thank the woman profusely for all her tips and even torture.

Laughing, Nina waited for her to finish, a broad smile on her face as she listened patiently.

"It will only get better child, but remember your limitations. You can not push yourself beyond what your body is ready for or you will pay dearly," she said, rubbing Nev's shoulder reassuringly.

Reaching out spontaneously, Nina clasped her in a hug that sent Avec back to the air to prevent being toppled from her shoulder.

"Your mother would be so proud girl, you looked magnificent up there," she whispered, pulling their heads close while she stroked the back of Nev's hair.

Pushing back to hold Nev at arm's length, Nina looked her over, then pulled her back into the embrace.

"You're special child. In all the years I spent with Alcedo I never saw him move through the air with such grace and comfort. I may have been wrong about your bird, because either he compliments you tremendously or you have natural abilities I never imagined," she said, drawing back again. She met Nev's gaze, which by that time was growing damp at the compliments and affection.

"Don't use it as an excuse to stop working, but have no doubts you are special. Do you understand me?"

Just as Nev nodded her head, a shriek of terror from Aster shattered the moment. It was quickly followed by wails of pleading agony.

"*D-R-U-S-Yyyyyy!*" her cry trailed out through the air, stopping Nina and Nev dead.

Turning, they ran toward the trees, Nev leaving Nina behind as she moved with every ounce of speed she could muster.

Her fear overcame her sense as she broke between the trees to where the child was, only to have her eyes met with more figures than she could quickly count.

"NEV, NO!" she heard, her hand stopping as it met with the handle of her knife. Her eyes searched until they located Chit, his neck enveloped by the bicep of a brutish looking man whose other hand held a knife to her friend's throat.

Drusy, off to the left, was frantically pulling back against ropes that snaked around his neck and shoulders while three men struggled to hold him. The object of his resistance was clearly Aster, futilely wriggling and kicking at a towering figure of a man that held her off the ground a short distance away.

A man in the center of the activity turned toward Nev, his eyes taking her in from top to bottom in obvious disbelief.

Frozen in place, she found herself in similar shock.

With hair a darker black than she had ever seen before and eyes that verged on yellow set above a broad jaw and defined features, he stood slightly taller than her and had to be the most perfectly formed person and easily the most handsome man she'd ever seen.

Unlike the other men – she had by that point counted seven – he was muscular but in a lean way that gave her the impression he probably had speed where they did not.

And he carried no weapons, but something about him told her he didn't need one.

As he pivoted and stood facing her, she couldn't miss the fact his movements too showed a confidence that identified him as the leader, even though there was nothing about his plain clothing that gave any indication he was above them.

In fact, by comparison to the obvious physical strength the other men had on him, he didn't fit in at all, but the intelligence in his eyes marked him easily as superior.

His eyes flickered away from Nev only at the arrival of Nina, who came to an abrupt halt a few feet behind her when she realized they were not alone.

A hush seemed to fall over the gathering with no one speaking, the only noise coming from Aster's sniffles, muffled by the huge arm that held her tight. Even Drusy had quieted with Nev's arrival.

Looking over to the horse, she met his eye briefly and silently asked him to stay calm until she told him otherwise.

The stranger said nothing, but Nev noticed he smirked slightly when Drusy tossed his head and dropped it in agreed submission to the ropes.

Locking eyes with her again, the stranger still said nothing, though a small smile formed at the corners of his mouth.

"Who are you?" she demanded, tightening her grip on the handle of her knife, though she made no move to brandish it.

He noticed just the same however, and Nev quickly realized even the slightest twitch of her muscles registered in his eyes, giving away the fact he was no stranger to the fight.

"I believe the better question, oh strange beauty, is who are you and why are you camping in these lands with stolen horses?" he said.

Nev couldn't put her finger on it, but something in his voice ran counter to the arrogant stance his legs took as he folded his arms across his chest and continued.

"Horses, that incidentally, were stolen from a man who hasn't been heard from in weeks," he finished. The corner of his mouth curled in a definite half smile before he straightened it back into a stern line.

Inside, she was kicking herself for the one thing they hadn't thought of when they left the clearing. Of course Drusy and Baryt would be easily recognized as horses that were obviously worth more money than any farmer or villager could ever hope to earn in a lifetime. They were built distinctly different than the horses common in the region – horses built for working and pulling and days of riding.

Horses like Smoot, Mica and Barge.

The arrogant Cravey must have had them imported to Sarter from some exotic place so they would be uniquely his, she thought, careful not to give indication of the realization to the man who was taking in every breath she drew.

"We found them wandering," she answered defiantly, gesturing back in the direction they'd traveled.

He smiled openly this time, holding her eyes a moment before responding. The smile was beginning to make her feel as if he knew her intimately, and that was working at her nerves.

"And this stray horse that you just found wandering the hills is so thankful for your kindness he bows his head in your presence, eh?" he asked sarcastically.

Ill timed as it was, Avec shrieked overhead, bringing an even broader lilt to the man's smile.

"I don't know what to tell you, I have a gift with horses," she responded curtly. She was tiring of whatever the man's game was.

"Well I have little doubt of that beautiful lady. If I were a horse, I imagine I too would hang my head and follow you anywhere," he said, brazenly winking at her. "But since these horses clearly don't belong to you and I am tasked with finding out what happened to their owner, I'm afraid it will be you following me today."

Glaring, Nev tightened her hand on her knife again.

"We're not going anywhere with you," she growled in response until she caught Chit's eye and saw him shake his head subtly.

Glancing over at Chit, the man was still wearing his smile when his eyes came back to her.

"You'd do well to listen to him my dear. Hopefully we can get this whole misunderstanding worked out quickly and you can be on your way again," he said, his eyes skipping over her companions.

Stepping forward, he held out his hand to her and she reluctantly accepted. Her expression remained stoic when he gripped as he would the hand of an equal, but when he added a small squeeze to her fingertips before he let go, it sent a jolt through her and she snatched her hand back glaring.

"Forgive me, I meant no offense. I'm Sirex," he said, the smirk returned to his face.

"None taken. I am Never," she said, her own face intentionally smug as she challenged him to react.

But he didn't, smiling a smile that this time actually seemed half-way sincere.

"Very well, Never, if you would be so kind as to gather your companions and follow us, we'll see if we can't settle this quickly," he said, stepping back as if to give her room to take action.

Scanning the group around her, Nev met with the eyes of Chit, Aster and finally Nina, realizing with frustration that her choice was to comply or single-handedly take on a fight that would probably result in one or all of her companions being hurt or killed.

But she refused to show her defeat, nodding sharply and turning her back to Sirex as Micah moved behind her.

Likewise, at her silent command, Smoot, and Baryt moved to stand next to Nina and Chit, while Drusy again strained in the direction of Aster.

Turning to Sirex, she ordered more than she asked.

"I would appreciate it if you would please have your men step aside so my companions can mount their horses."

He held her eyes for a moment, nodding to his men just about the time she found herself examining the dark brown that centered his pupils and reached out to meet the surrounding golden amber in a jagged ring.

Freed, Chit straightened his rumpled shirt and Aster huffed in indignant anger.

As if choreographed, the horses too showed their insolence, bringing amusement from Sirex who watched the four steeds bow before their riders and wait patiently to be mounted while Barge pawed at the ground in defiance.

A moment later, he didn't seem the least bit put off to have Nev looking down at him from Mica's back. Giving her another of those smiles that were becoming downright irritating, his own horse, a white mare with a slender but muscular build matching his own, appeared behind him.

"You certainly do seem to have a way with horses," he said with a wink, turning to effortlessly hop into the small thin saddle that awaited him.

She had been so distracted by the exchange, she barely noticed Sirex' men had mounted their own horses and moved in to surround her and the others.

Urging forward, she ignored their protests and stopped only when Micah was standing even with the white mare.

Looking straight ahead, Nev raised her jaw with as much insolence as she could muster.

"I will go with you because I don't seem to have much choice, but I'll be damned if I will follow you," she said, and Mica began moving forward another step as if on cue.

Sirex laughed, but as he caught up and rode silently beside her, she could have sworn that the expression she saw in her peripheral was one of respect.

●●Chapter Eighteen●●

The cottage was simple and small.

First to dismount in the grass that grew before the humble doorway, Nev found herself uneasy at its unassuming presentation, for surely given all the anxiety that had built up on the way to it, it must have hidden within its plain stone walls a monster of horrible proportion.

But the air was calm around it, an occasional breeze licking at the leaves of the trees that concealed it.

Off to the side, a small garden flourished and in the back, she could barely glimpse the movement of freshly laundered clothing lifting against the line from which it hung.

It hardly seemed the type of place to which one would be taken against their will.

The others had dismounted as well, Aster, Chit and Nina moving to stand with Nev, looking about in shared confusion at the serenity of the place.

Turning to find Sirex standing with his customary smirk, Nev rested her hand on Aster's shoulder.

"What is this place?" she demanded.

Smiling, he walked past her without answer, instructing them to wipe their feet on the rug before entering.

Doing as told, Nev looked back one last time to be sure the horses were all right, pleased to find Sirex's henchmen seemed afraid to touch them after the show of loyalty they had given back at the camp.

Passing through the doorway, Nev had to duck a little as she noticed Sirex and Chit had before her.

The doorway introduced an open room. Off to the right, a handwoven rug served as the only divider to a sitting area, cushioning the legs of two chairs and a small table between them that was near hidden by a pile of books and papers. In an adjacent corner, a neatly made bed sat empty next to another small table covered in a similar pile of books.

Search as she might, Nev's eyes found no monster waiting inside, instead coming to rest on a rounded woman sitting atop a stool in the kitchen.

Taking up more than half of the cottage with a stone hearth in front of a large fire opening in the wall and a huge table stretched before it, the kitchen was obviously the heart of the place.

She didn't look up when they entered and instead continued slicing carrots onto a tray in front of her.

Looking toward Sirex, Nev noticed his pleasant expression hadn't wavered, though he did have a sense of homage to his posture that hadn't been there before.

Separating the last chunk of carrot into two pieces with her knife, the woman finally lifted her head and pushed her white hair back from where it had stuck to her pink cheek.

"So, these are our horse thieves," she said, not really asking a question in a voice that seemed squeezed to a higher than expected pitch within her heavy frame.

"Yes Telasan, these are they," Sirex said. His smirk returned to give Nev the distinct impression the man found everything to be a joke.

But what struck her most was the sudden realization that the woman before them was Telasan, ruler of Harren, the largest of all the regions in Laresan and easily the most powerful. Though she had always assumed Telasan was a man, if any of the leaders of Leresan were in a position to take charge of them all, it was, well, the round woman before her now.

The way Nina had always told it, Harren had a stronger military, more wealth and more resources than any other region.

Hopping down from her stool with more quickness than her appearance seemed to justify, Telasan picked up the carrots and turned her back to them. She pushed the slices from the tray into a pot that was sitting on the hearth, then hooked its handle to a metal arm above the fire opening and pushed it in until it hung over the fire inside.

Turning back, she resumed her seat and propped her chin against her hands, elbows resting on the table in front of her.

"So what did you do with Cravey?" she asked, her eyes skimming the group until they came to rest on Nev.

When no one answered, she scratched her nose and looked again, this time directly at Nev.

"I asked what you did with Cravey," she asked, with an unmistakable air of authority.

Nev drew a sharp breath but wasn't able to stop Aster when she stepped forward to face Telasan. Her voice filled the room like a tumbling pile of bricks, lacking its usual softness.

"He hurt me but Nev saved me and killed him, then I burned his body to ashes, and I'm not sorry," she said, squaring her shoulders and jutting out her chin.

"And we didn't steal those horses, they want to be with us. Drusy is my friend and I won't let you take him from me."

Waiting for the blades to come out, Nev sucked in air and held, knowing that while there was probably no good way to have handled the situation, Aster had likely just discovered the worst.

But Sirex's booming laughter filled the room and Telasan's face softened, focusing down on the eighty pound child who was defiantly glaring at her.

"Who are you?" Telasan asked while Nev resisted the urge to move forward and shield the girl.

"I am Aster and Nev is, well, she's like my sister. I don't have a real family anymore. They are my family now," she said, pointing to Nina, Nev and Chit.

"Well that certainly explains why Cravey never made it to the council," Sirex said, moving closer to Telasan. There was a hint of approval in his eyes.

Stepping forward to put her hands on Aster's shoulders, Nev cleared her throat and spoke cautiously, still not certain where they stood with the woman before them.

"What he did to this child was unforgivable," she said in a level tone.

"I do not know what your feelings toward him might have been, but Aster speaks the truth and I stand behind my actions. I would do it again without a second thought, as I believe any decent person would."

Her words were met with a wall of silence that increased the tension in the room to an almost unbearable level before the woman answered.

"Nev is it?

"Well, Nev, you ask my feelings and I can tell you I never liked the man. I have long heard of his perversions and if it had been my place, I might have killed him myself long ago.

"But I'm afraid I cannot absolve you of your deed. I have already been blamed for Cravey's disappearance and now your act has made us targets," she said with seemingly genuine regret.

"I don't understand," Nev said boldly. "There is no body so no one ever has to know he's dead, and you have successfully held Sarter off for years. Why would you have fear of him now?"

She almost regretted the words, feeling foolish as Telasan and Sirex looked on her as they might a child.

Gesturing to the other stools around the table, Telasan told them all to sit, her explanation beginning before they had all settled into their seats.

"Word has it Sarter has found a new ally and the lords are all bracing for a renewed round of attacks. Not much is known about the company he's been keeping these days, but they are said to be stronger than any of the lords," she said.

Every year the regional leaders gathered for the Council of Lords to update one another and to work out trade agreements and treatise between each other. It was a tradition that went back to even before the death of Prince Daughtry, and Sarter was usually the only one to cause problems at the meeting.

"When Sarter's man Cravey didn't appear at the council, we were all relieved and talk turned to the rumors of his new alliance," she said.

"But after the council gathered, Sarter sent word that his man had disappeared. He blamed me and Rylen for doing something untoward to prevent him a representative at the table.

"It's no secret Sarter has always wanted to expand his territory and has his eye on the abandoned throne, but he'd been quiet for a long time until the rumors started flying this year leading up to the council.

"A strange man had become Sarter's closest advisor and it's rumored they've struck a deal to defeat the lords and give Sarter the Leresan throne. What he's agreed to give in return, no one's quite sure of.

"Honestly, based on the talk and Sarter's flair for drama, many among us half expected he would send Calvus to declare war on us right there at the council table," she said, shaking her head at the absurdity of the situation.

Her words sucked the air from the room and left Nev and Nina looking at each other in shock.

"Telasan, did you say Calvus?" Nina asked tentatively, hoping she had heard wrong.

"Yes, I think that's his name. That's the man who has taken up residence with Sarter," she said. "Why?"

Nina took over the conversation with Nev glad to bow out and sit silently, her head reeling.

"Telasan, if Sarter has indeed forged an alliance with Calvus, the lords must join and stand together. Even then, I am sorry to tell you the chances of succeeding will be slim, but without an alliance you have no chance," she said.

Nev noticed Sirex listening with rapt attention but his face showed indications that he already knew what Nina was saying.

She wasn't entirely sure what he was to Telasan, who she found herself liking the longer they talked, but there was something about him that nagged at her, she just couldn't quite put her finger on exactly what it was.

She found herself wishing Avec were there to help her understand, opening up her mind in case he was close enough to listen.

"What do you know of Calvus and why should I believe you?" Telasan demanded.

It was a question she knew Nina didn't want to answer and she waited, holding her breath. For once in Nina's life, Nev hoped she would make up a story rather than tell the truth because something told her that the truth wouldn't do them any good this time.

She wasn't entirely disappointed. While Nina didn't exactly lie, she did blur the lines a little.

"Calvus nearly killed me many years ago," she said.

But Nev's relief was short lived as Nina launched into an explanation of the Aile, leaving out only her relationship with Alcedo and Nev's lineage.

Sirex lifted an eyebrow but his eyes lacked the surprise that Telasan had at hearing of the Aile. The sardonic smile was completely gone from his face, sending Nev's intuition spinning.

He definitely knew more than he was telling Telasan.

Nev felt panic creeping into her throat and felt the overwhelming urge to stop Nina before she said anymore.

"As you can see from what Nina has said, it sounds like regardless of what happened to Cravey, Sarter is coming, so I see no reason for you to hold us," Nev interrupted, her statement so abrupt everyone in the room but Sirex looked at her as if she'd gone mad.

Telasan leveled her gaze on Nev.

"I think you all need to have a meal with me and spend the night," she said, her tone making it clear the polite invitation was anything but.

Nev stood and backed from the table, her eyes looking to Chit and Nina for support, but they, like everyone else, were just staring at her, having felt the shift in the room but not understanding why.

"But we really..." she stumbled, suddenly and acutely aware that the dynamic had turned for the worst.

Telasan didn't let her finish, rising from her own stool to plant her hands flat on the table and lean forward.

"Girl, you obviously don't understand what's happening here, so let me make it clear for you." Her plump features suddenly looked a lot less pleasant as her measured tone teetered toward anger.

"You four turn up on my land with the horses of my enemy's missing representative and you tell me he has joined with a race that is powerful enough to annihilate my people without a second thought. Now, while I have sympathy for your story and what this child here as suffered at the hands of Cravey, I get the distinct impression there's a lot you're not telling me," she said, her eyes glancing at Aster and Nina before coming back to Nev.

"Hear me now, because I don't like to repeat myself. I will stop at nothing when it comes to protecting my people. So until I get to the bottom of all of this, you're not going anywhere."

Her eyes flashing, Telasan looked at Nev so intensely, she found herself wanting to look away while the woman squeezed more words through clenched teeth.

"So I ask you one last time, will you have a meal with me or would you prefer to eat outside with my men?"

Nev noticed the smirk had returned to Sirex's face as she looked down at the floor, recognizing this was not the time to fight.

"We would be honored to share a meal with you Telasan. Thank you for your hospitality," she replied, her mind racing as the benign words spilled out.

Reaching out to Avec, she felt nothing in return and lifted her eyes to meet the softening eyes of the woman before her. Nev realized they were indeed not going anywhere, though for how long, she didn't know.

"Sirex, send birds to the other lords. Tell them what we have learned and to prepare. We may need to call an emergency council, so tell them I await their response. And make sure Sarter doesn't catch wind of it."

Sirex nodded and disappeared out the door while Telasan turned to a basket of vegetables that sat on the hearth.

"Nina, would you be so kind as to chop these for the stew?" she asked, her tone indicating she was done with the conversation.

Telasan put Nev, Nina and Aster to work, moving about the kitchen as if dinner were her only concern in the world, sending Chit out to help settle the horses into a barn she said was set further back in the trees away from the cottage.

As she tore herbs to add to the pot, Nev realized she had already forgiven the woman. She could understand the position she was in and her desire to protect her people.

Her real qualm lay with her concerns about Sirex, but unable to talk with Nina or Chit about it and still unable to get a response from Avec, she felt helpless.

The horses were content, Chit said on his return, thanking Telasan for the grain and hay she had offered. Glancing at Nev, it was clear he was still confused but he quickly accepted Telasan's invitation to sit and read while they finished preparing the meal.

Telasan was a traditional woman who, if given a choice, would prefer to focus on her domestic responsibilities. There had been a husband but he died twenty summers before, a fact she'd kept very private.

Even when he had been alive, he had merely served as the figurehead but it had always been she that ran Harren, glad to allow the illusion that he was leading the region.

Nina and Telasan seemed to hit it off well. Even Aster enjoyed her motherly ways, proudly helping to stir this and that.

A rustling in her hair let her know darkness had fallen outside but Sirex still had not returned by the time they sat at the table to eat.

Nev asked Wybert to stay put for a while, briefly wondering how Nina had kept her firefly out of view, but dismissed it as something to ask later.

The meal was the best Nev had eaten since leaving Roden and possibly even before that, though her concerns still made it difficult to fully enjoy.

Swallowing a mouthful of the savory stew, she hardened herself and asked one of the questions burning at the back of her mind.

"When will Sirex return?"

Telasan's head rose up from her bowl and the table grew still.

Smiling, she looked at Nev with curiosity in her eyes.

"You aren't near old enough for hair that gray girl. I had a cousin that turned gray early, though not nearly to the extent yours has. But you certainly wear it far better than us old ladies," she said, winking at Nina.

"Morning, maybe sooner. Once he sends the messages he will occupy himself somewhere. He keeps to himself most of the time. He's about your age I think," she said with a twinkle in her eye that was unmistakable. It was a twinkle in which Nev saw an opportunity to learn more.

A blush was a hard thing to fake, but she did her best, averting her eyes sheepishly.

"Where is he from? He seems … different somehow," she said, feigning a girlish giggle.

Nina caught herself sitting with her spoon suspended in shock and returned her attention to her food. Even Aster and Chit had quizzical expressions on their faces as they listened to the exchange without saying a word.

"Very observant Nev. Yes, he's from the north," Telasan said casually, her interest in creating a match obvious as she moved on to accentuate his finer points.

"He came looking for work a couple of years ago so I hired him to oversee my men. He's extremely intelligent and has been very reliable and dedicated. I don't have to worry about a thing when he's around."

Putting down her spoon, Telasan reached her hand out to clasp Nev's across the table.

"I know we got off to a bad start and I apologize if I seemed harsh," she said, her expression sincere.

"I'm an excellent judge of character and you appear to be good folks. I do hope that you can see yourselves as my guests.

"Hopefully within a few days we can get this all figured out and you can be on your way. Or perhaps you'll find someone or something to keep your interests here," she said with a wink.

Nev smiled in response.

"I understand your concern for your people and we appreciate your hospitality," she said.

And she meant it.

Nev had no doubt Telasan was sincere and the woman's warmth was comforting. But she also had no doubt she would be far less hospitable if she learned she had beneath her roof a member of the very race that threatened her people.

As they cleaned up from the meal, she realized her concern about Sirex was worse now than ever before. It was clear even Telasan didn't know much about him and Nev was of the sneaking suspicion that the mysterious man was concerned with something other than Harren's best interests, possibly even to the point of working counter to them.

Had anyone looked inside the cottage that night, they would have thought it a social visit amongst old friends.

Sitting sprawled on the rug, Chit showed Aster maps he had found amongst the pile of books in the sitting area and Nina and Telasan chatted cheerfully, comparing stories and memories, leaving Nev leaned quietly against the wall, content to mull and stew over their dilemma.

She didn't begrudge Nina the company she seemed to be enjoying, but the obvious differences in the way she was with Nev and the way she interacted with someone her own age had her feeling a little sour.

Reaching out, she checked on the horses only to find them happily munching hay in the barn, far too distracted for conversation, not that they were very good at it anyway. Horses were one of the animals she appreciated most for their beauty and loyalty, but even she had to admit their minds were pretty simple, with their priorities being food, water, companionship and safety. And while the priorities might shift depending on the day, she had never found intelligent conversation to be on the list.

Not like Avec, she thought, reaching out for him again only to find an empty spot where his mind usually was.

It had been several hours and given everything that was going on, she was definitely worried, but absent the ability to do anything, she found herself relying on faith that he was fine and had good reason for his absence.

It was clear that Telasan was lonely despite the tough self reliance she exhibited and Nev got the impression she might have kept them there just for the conversation even if there hadn't been tides of war moving in.

Aster was the first to fall asleep curled up against Chit on the rug, looking like a child half her age. Fighting sleep himself, it occurred to Nev that the man was completely at home with the girl snuggled into the crook of his arm.

When Nina and Telasan, too, started yawning, their hostess rose to find makings for extra beds.

Even though she offered her bed, Nev and Nina politely

declined.

Having spent so many nights on the ground fighting bugs and the elements, just the thought of blankets and a roof seemed like paradise to them.

It was unfortunate they couldn't have met the woman under different circumstances, she thought, accidentally startling Chit as she pried Aster from his arms and carried her to a pad of blankets she had made for her.

Pulling a thick colorful blanket over the child, she was overcome by a feeling of caring for her, even despite the little bit of slobber that gathered in the corner of her wide open mouth.

She felt herself understanding the desire for companionship she saw in Chit, Nina and Telasan, for at one time they'd all had full lives that were forever changed by the loss of someone they loved more than anything.

If anyone had a right to be angry, it was them and yet they weren't. Even little Aster didn't seem to have an ounce of hatred for the people who had sold her like a thing they no longer had use for.

Any pain she had at losing Lennera came from a lack of memories, but not the pain of living with them, and that, she suddenly understood was a very different thing.

Looking around the room at the sleeping figures of her companions before coming back to look at Aster's dreaming face, she knew the irony that had become her life.

Curling beneath her own blankets, her mind wouldn't allow her the reprieve of sleep just yet, forcing her to admit what she had been trying to deny every day since she had left Roden.

Losing Lennera hadn't been as tragic as she'd always thought.

And at one time, she couldn't have imagined defending herself against Delsin or striking out with nothing, thinking back then those things were only possible for the strong.

But weeks from home, the man who had tormented her all her life was hardly a second thought most days, and though she had thought herself vulnerable and weak growing up under Delsin's cruelty, the truth of the matter was, she'd probably been stronger then than she would ever be for the remainder of her life.

Because vulnerability didn't lie in weak muscles or the inability to fight, it lay in caring about something so much you couldn't bear to lose it.

Like the love she had found in her search for revenge.

Their current predicament gave her a sense of foreboding like none she'd ever had before and the responsibility she felt at having dragged them all into such a mess didn't make it any better.

As she finally drifted off to sleep, she found herself searching for fuel to throw into her inner fire but instead found only the damp of tears gathering in her soul, sizzling as they dripped down into the flames.

Slumber, however, was held proprietary to the stones of the cottage. In the woods a short distance away, sleep was a stranger and Sirex was nervous.

The news he had to give wasn't good and he wasn't looking forward to the delivery he couldn't avoid even if he'd wanted to.

Pacing back and forth in the darkness, he finally drew a deep breath and exhaled once before sitting on a large rock that jutted from the ground nearby. Staring up at the trees that concealed him from view, he took one more breath, savoring this one just a little longer than the first before closing his eyes.

"It has begun," he said.

His words met with silence and for a moment, he almost felt relief.

But he shouldn't have.

"Tell me..."

He knew better than to hesitate.

"War is upon us, but this time Leresan will be divided with us."

There was another pause, this one longer than the first.

"How long?"

He had known this question would come and was prepared, though it didn't make the answer fall any smoother.

"Soon. She had me send messages to the other lords tonight and they will rally fast."

The response was as resolute as he had imagined.

"We are ready."

Before his opportunity was lost, he got to the source of his nervousness.

"There is one more thing..."

"What is it?"

He hesitated now, wanting to speak, but there were no words. Instead, he opened up his mind and allowed the girl's image to surface in his memory.

Silence ended in a low hiss that grew into a sound he'd never heard before, one comparable only to the sound of pain wrought of unimaginable torture.

His head pounding, the single word that rang in his ears was unmistakable as he collapsed to the ground.

"Lenneraaa..."

●●Chapter Nineteen●●

Avec hated to wake her.

Reaching out to her for the first time in hours, he could feel that though her sleep was fitful, it was deep and she needed more, but he didn't dare risk talking to her any other time.

Blocking her out had been hard to do because he'd wanted so badly to see that she and the others were safe and knew she'd probably needed the reassurance as much as he did, but he hadn't wanted to risk it.

From the moment Nev had scooped him into her hands and began their bond, it had only been them, but ever since the day Aster intruded on their conversation Avec had started studying the child, honing his senses to detect when she was prying.

Though Nev had relaxed to the point of hardly noticing at all, Avec had discovered there was a presence when Aster was there, almost like the breathing of an extra person in the dark when one thought they were alone.

She was already so torn by the tension between him and the child that he hadn't said anything about his discovery to Nev but now he almost wished he had.

Because maybe then Sirex wouldn't have been able to listen.

So knowing no other way to protect her, he had stayed away, but now he had no choice.

"*Nev...*" he sent, not surprised she didn't answer.

He pressed at her mind over and over until finally he felt her stir.

"*Nev, wake up please, I don't have much time...*" he pleaded.

Her response was more of a groan than anything intelligible but it would do.

"*Sirex has given you up, Nev, can you hear me?*"

Somehow it got through and he felt her mind racing to meet him, groggy but growing alert quickly.

"Avec? Where have you been?"

"Listen carefully because he will be back soon. I'm staying close but we must be careful not to connect when he's around, he can hear us and I don't know if blocking him will work like it does with the girl," he told her, hoping the message was getting through the fog of sleep that still enveloped her.

It was.

Quickly as she could, Nev conveyed everything that had happened inside the cabin that night, from Telasan to news of the alliance that had been formed between Sarter and the Aile.

Hanging his head while he processed it, the hawk allowed his eyelids to flicker closed for a moment.

"Nev, he has told someone about you and I have a bad feeling about all this," he said, deciding against sharing the wave of intensity that had knocked Sirex from his seat when the unknown voice cried her mother's name.

He did, however, tell her of discovering Sirex in the woods, including how he'd been able to capitalize on the man's distraction enough to hear parts of the conversation.

Her lack of surprise alarmed him more than the information itself.

"Nev, we are about to be pulled into the middle of a war!" he said. *"And they know who you are somehow. You must find a way out of here."*

"I don't know how," she said. "Telasan's men are surrounding the outside and I can't fight them all Avec. Maybe two or three, but not seven," she intentionally left Sirex out of the count because somehow she knew he was the one she stood the least chance against.

"Who did he betray us to?"

Avec's speculation came back at her with no solutions, only questions. The only thing that was clear was Sirex wasn't human, but that did nothing to explain who or what he was connecting with.

But something wasn't adding up and she could feel it in his thoughts.

"What aren't you telling me Avec," she asked sharply.

He didn't respond right away.

"Can't you just trust me?" he asked softly.

"This isn't about trust. If I am to protect myself, I have a right to know Avec, *I need to know...*" her words were a mixture of pleading and demanding, but he could tell she wouldn't let it go no matter how much he tried to convince her.

"They've recognized your likeness to Lennera," he said, relenting with a defeated tone.

Nev grew silent, long enough that he reached out to be sure that she was still with him.

"I'm here," she responded. "That could be anyone though. Nina said my mother lived as a human for years so who knows how many knew her."

It was a weak argument, she knew, but one worth making.

"Nev whoever that was knew your mother enough to feel immeasurable pain at the mention of her. I think the longer you stay here the better your chances of finding out who it is and you better ask yourself if that's a meeting you want to have.

"Please find a way out, please..." he begged, allowing Nev to see his concern without shame.

But her head was heavy with thought and he could tell she couldn't hear him.

"I want to leave this place as much as you do Avec but something tells me it's not time yet and I can't risk their lives until I know I can get them out safely," she said, as he felt her withdrawing.

"Find ways to communicate with me when you can, I need to know you're there," she sent before she closed the connection.

Settling back into her blankets, her mind was swirling so fast she felt dizzied by it.

He didn't understand, he couldn't understand how much responsibility she felt for the others, or how she lacked the confidence.

Something inside was warning her against rejecting Telasan's hospitality a second time.

And even if she tried to go, she actually questioned if the others would believe her enough to follow.

The pressure of the situation was bearing down on her, moving through her system like a drug and the only thing she could think of was sleep.

Avec stayed where she'd left him, watching down over the cottage as he felt her drift off again.

He understood better than she thought, though the sentiment did him little good without her there to share it with.

Avec's night was sleepless and troubled as he waited and watched.

For Nev too, that first night at the cottage was long, with morning coming after what seemed like an eternity, but the days to follow moved at an even slower pace, like the blinking of a dry eye.

It had been four days and it seemed all they did was eat, then begin preparation for the next meal while they waited for the birds to return with news.

For Nev the time was a mixture of agonizing stasis and welcome reprieve all bundled into one relaxed anxiety.

Time almost stopped in the woods surrounding the little cottage, yet she felt it thudding in her center like a drum beating louder every moment that passed.

Unable to practice flying and shut off from Avec, she may as well been struck blind, her frustration compounding exponentially with absolutely nothing she could do about it.

Telasan showed no concern about them straying from the cottage, so the first day she had ventured out, pushing the boundaries just to see where they lay.

Nestled in a small wood, the hills surrounding the cottage were a continuation of the tree peppered land they had traveled through since leaving the forest.

As long as she stayed within the center that started at the cottage she was surrounded by calm. However the austere pleasantness of the place was proved an illusion through her exploration, discovering it was more like the peaceful eye of a maelstrom. Regardless of which way she wandered, Telasan's men were nowhere and everywhere. If she stood quiet long enough, she could spot them, standing, sitting or riding quietly through the trees.

Avec was always there, flitting through the trees above her head or keeping watch from a nearby branch when she stopped to sit and think, but the silence between them kept him from feeling close, no matter how near he was.

Sirex remained a mystery and nothing had revealed itself by way of an explanation.

Quiet for the most part, the man kept to himself and was frequently absent, which was fine by her. He was the first man she had ever hated and looked forward to seeing all at the same time, making her prefer his protracted absences to his presence.

It was strange being so close to one that couldn't be trusted.

She wanted to despise him, almost feeling an obligation to do so, yet he was charming and flippant. Every time she fell for it and allowed herself to warm, she harshly reminded herself he was dangerous, shutting him off coldly.

Aster, though, had no such caution when it came to Sirex, shadowing him every time he returned from one of his mysterious absences. She would chat his ear off, following him as he made his rounds and he in return never shooed her, entertaining her questions and chatter with playful banter. Nev had even caught him giving the girl a ride on his shoulders one evening as they went to check the horses.

She tried to subtly steer Aster away from him, but it was increasingly clear the girl was developing a crush and even though she responded to direct pressure from Nev, as soon as her back was turned, she'd go seeking Sirex' attention again until Nev finally gave up and withdrew further.

Aside from the feeling the walls were bearing down on her, part of what drove Nev from the cottage and led her to spend so much of her time outside was the closeness that seemed to be growing between Telasan and Nina – and even Chit for that matter. With so much in common, they didn't appear to notice anyone else around, comparing stories and experiences into the late hours of the night as if they could talk for eternity and never tire.

Driven to sullenness, she hated to admit it, but she was jealous and missed her friend.

And while everyone behaved as if time had frozen and there

wasn't a care in the world, the drum beat louder and louder inside her. War was coming, yet they waited doing nothing, day after day.

But the beating followed her everywhere – in the pounding of Mica's hooves when she took him for a turn around the circle and in the way her arms swung from her sides while she walked to the cottage from the barn and in the contact her feet made across the floor on the way to the kitchen table where Telasan, Nina and Chit sat ashen faced with a strange man.

His clothes were tattered and torn, tinged with streaks of dried blood. Light brown hair that had once had a manicured shape was matted and filthy and the shag of an unintended beard grew out from his chin.

He was seated at the table leaning over a steaming cup, gripped between both hands; his posture, the stains of tribulation on his clothes and a hollow look in his shadowed eyes when he looked up as she entered the room, all came together to form a story of exhaustion and defeat.

Leaning against the stone hearth, even Sirex appeared shaken, which only made the beating grow louder in time with the heat that rose to her cheeks and the thudding in her ears.

"What is it?" she asked, swallowing hard in an effort to make it go away.

It was Nina who spoke when Telasan dropped her head.

"This is Rylen Nev," she said, reaching her hand to rub the back of the man beside her.

The beating was almost deafening, growing with each second she waited for understanding.

"Ry...?" she couldn't finish the word, working to register why the ruler of her homeland sat before her a broken man.

"I don't understand."

Nina cleared her throat, looking away briefly. As she spoke, Rylen stared deep into his cup.

"Kasen has fallen Nev. Sarter and the Aile started their assault three nights ago. They moved village to village slaughtering all who resisted. They never had a chance."

It didn't feel real. So much time she had spent with her mind on anything but the lives around her, yet to hear that all she had ever known had been stomped beneath the boot of an unstoppable force invoked a range of feelings she couldn't have anticipated.

She wasn't sure why she should even care, yet overcome with a wave of sentimental thought, she asked.

"Roden?"

It was Rylen who spoke, his voice hoarse and dry and filled with sorrow. His pain wrapped around him like a buffer that seemed to keep anyone in the room from reaching out to comfort him.

"Roden was taken, along with Valen and Parlen and all the others," he uttered bitterly. "They came through so fast there was no warning. They came in from the air and the ground, killing any who stood before them. We sent the women and children into hiding, most of them survived, but my men ... so many good men slaughtered like animals."

Nina shook her head, picking up for him when he lapsed into silence.

Nev was overcome by a wave of grinding pain. Elsie, Ivy, Bronwyn and the others would have still been traveling. Some of them may have made it home, but even their homes were in the path of the onslaught – they had sent them straight into it without knowing.

"The women ... did they make it?" she asked, hopeful yet afraid when she thought of them and how vulnerable they would have been.

Nina shook her head again.

"We don't know how they fared and there's nothing we can do for them. Rylen and a small group made it through but we can only assume they will be following close behind," she said as if to make it clear to Nev not to even think of going back to help.

"It must have been happening right behind us as we traveled this way and we never even knew," Nina said softly, though whether she was contemplating their fortune of timing or their misfortune to come, Nev couldn't be sure.

But what she did realize was that something in the news had quieted the beating drums and there was a calm in her blood, not unlike the end of throbbing heat once a splinter was pulled.

Finally there were answers.

Looking at Telasan, she could tell the woman was in shock at the state of Rylen and accepting defeat before she had even taken the fight.

"Telasan, is the location of your home well known?" she asked, trying to calculate how much time they had.

The woman barely raised her head and shook it so subtly she almost missed it.

Looking to Nina for help, she shrugged her shoulders in frustration.

Catching the cue, Nina squared her shoulders and straightened in her seat, looking to Chit before she spoke.

"Telasan, we have to start planning and we have to get word out to your people, how do we do that?" she asked, her voice taking on an air of authority. "We have to stop this before your people share the fate of Kasen."

Drawing a deep breath, Telasan lifted her head and stared at the wall behind Nev before she responded.

"We can send birds to the farther cities and the ones nearby can be warned by my men," she said, still staring at the wall.

Finally a flicker of life sparked into her eyes and she turned to Sirex where he still leaned behind her against the stones of the hearth.

"Sirex, pick some men to ride for whatever villages they can reach by midnight and tell them to call on village riders from each to go forth, then return here by morning," she was snapping to attention now, her mind growing more alert as she spoke.

"Send birds to the other lords and ask them to send all the men they can spare, then send birds to all the cities that lie beyond a day away. Make quick work of it, you're needed here."

Nodding, Sirex disappeared through the door.

"I'll be right back," Nev said, darting out the door before anyone could object, running toward the woods where she had last seen Avec.

Luckily, he was found easily enough, dozing on a low branch of a pine within view of the cottage. Waving, she caught his attention and pushed at his mind, glad to find he understood and was receiving her. Blocking all but him, she found she didn't really care if Sirex overheard.

Quickly, she shared the news with Avec.

"I need you to watch from the sky and alert us if you see anything. I can't tell you what to expect, but with the Aile involved, you need to watch the air too," she said.

The hawk looked down from his perch and seemed to give no more than a second's thought before sailing down to perch on her shoulder. Rubbing his head against her cheek, he tilted his head to the side and looked her in the eye.

"I will leave my mind open if you need me," he sent, his concern almost overpowering, he accepted his task obviously reluctant to let her out of his sight.

"Please be careful Avec," she said, mustering one last bit of affection before she gave full rein to her inner fire which was growing with each passing moment.

She stood a moment and watched as he took to the sky, then turned back toward the cottage, shooting a glare toward Sirex who was heading into the woods with one eyebrow raised in her direction.

Walking through the door, the room she entered was entirely different than the one she had just left.

No sooner had she crossed the threshold than she almost barreled into Aster running by with an armload of maps en route to the kitchen table where a hum of conversation had begun.

Rylen was an almost different man, the anger starting to surface as he explained how Sarter and the Aile had moved in.

Nev took a seat and watched as Telasan acquainted them all with the boundaries of her region and locations of concentrated populations, gaining input from Rylen on what to expect.

They were located in the center of the northern segment of Harren, predominately occupied by small villages and farms, but going further south there were three large cities and even more villages, Telasan said.

Her army was already positioned sporadically along the borders but Chit suggested she draw them inward toward a chosen location.

"If we just sit and wait we let them decide the course of things. We are not going to stop their advance and your borders are going to be compromised, so why leave your men to die needlessly? Let's move them where they can do more good," he told her, intently examining the map before him. His face took on a stony resolve Nev had never seen him wear before. When he next spoke, she understood why.

"You have too much land here to protect and your people are too scattered. We need to bring as much force as we can muster to our location and draw them to a place of our choosing," he said, not looking up.

"If we allow them to spread through your land you will never defeat them all. You can't command your troops at these distances and they will just systematically take your villages and cities one by one."

Skimming the map as if he were searching for something, Chit's finger slid across hills and rivers, coming to rest in a medium-size valley just north of the cottage by a little more than a days ride.

"Here," he said. "What is this place?"

Telasan barely glanced, her eyes coming up to lock with his.

"That is the Valley of Lights," she said. "No one goes there. It is said to be filled with spirits of the dead."

Looking back at the map, Chit nodded, the confidence in his choice undaunted by Telasan's concern.

"That is where we need to be," he said.

Rylen nodded in agreement.

"He's right Telasan. That valley offers us an ideal place to draw them in and take them by surprise," he said.

"The reason they were able to take us so quickly and completely lies in the fact we didn't know they were coming and we were spread out too thin.

"By the time word spread it was too late for my forces to be effective. If you let your people stand against them on their own, they will be cut down one at a time."

Placing her hands on the table, Telasan stood, her resolve similar to what she'd had the night she exchanged words with Nev.

"So be it. But nothing more will happen tonight and you need food and rest Rylen."

Moving toward the remnants of the evening meal that still hung over the shrinking fire, Telasan set about fixing Rylen a plate, which he accepted readily, looking like one who hadn't eaten in days, as he likely hadn't.

Speaking to no one in particular, Telasan straightened her spine and looked around the room.

"I will give my life if it's needed, but I will not give that greedy fool my people or my land."

Solemnly the group received the words. No one said anything in response because there wasn't really anything to say, instead looking at one another with eyes that carried an infantile but growing commitment to that which seemed to offer no alternatives.

The fervor of planning waned, giving way to near silence but for the occasional tap of a utensil against a dish or the table, the shuffle of feet or the scraping of a wooden stool legs against the floor.

Once fed, Rylen was ushered off to the bed to get some much needed rest, his eyelids made heavy by a special tea Nina had prepared to prevent him from resisting slumber.

With the weary lord drawn quickly into the tight embrace of an assisted sleep, a quiet moved in as Aster went out in search of Sirex and Telasan disappeared from the cottage with the look of one seeking the comfort of solitude.

Nev almost feared what seemed an obvious question that had occupied her mind as the afternoon had unfolded. Now with the weight of dusk pushing the light away outside and giving threat of yet another day at the place, she couldn't ignore it any longer.

Left in the kitchen with Nina and Chit, Nev found she could no longer abide the silence.

"Is this our fight?" she finally blurted.

They turned and looked at her with such critical eyes, she feared they thought her traitorous.

It was, she realized, the first time she had been alone with them since they had arrived at Telasan's and with the way they looked on her, she suddenly became aware of the unsettling realization that perhaps she no longer knew where she stood with her friends.

Absent a response from them, she forged ahead, feeling as if she were making up excuses for a bad deed like a child who had broken something special.

"We are not here by choice … and Harren is not our home," she said, the words making her feel guilty before she even said them, but she felt they needed to be said nonetheless for the pair seemed to have lost all perspective.

"You two seem to have forgotten we had an objective before we got hijacked and brought here. Telasan's a nice woman and she has huge trouble coming her way, but it's not our trouble," she said insistently.

"What of Alopex? Am I to forget about that?"

The pitch of her voice raised in such a way even she worried she was whining, and it was instantly clear they saw no legitimacy in her words, their eyes making her feel ashamed.

It was Nina who spoke first, thankfully, because the look on Chit's face told her she would have shriveled under his words had he set them free.

But she was angry, perhaps more so than Nev had ever seen her.

"Nev this is our fight more than the one you wish to pick with Alopex," she said, obviously metering her words to keep them level.

"Harren may not be our home, but if Sarter and the Aile succeed there will be nowhere in Leresan that we can go, and that is just the surface of the problem at hand. Has it occurred to you to ask why the Aile would take up the cause of a foolish human man when they have never involved themselves before?"

She hadn't and she instantly felt like a foolish child. Shaking her head, she wanted to avert her eyes but kept them on Nina, hard as it was.

Nina's voice became more gentle, her anger somewhat assuaged by the admission.

"Nev the Aile have no regard for humans. They see them as expendable fools that are barely more than animals. There are only two things that would motivate the Aile to forge an alliance with them," she said, pausing to choose her words.

"The first of those is their desire to root out and annihilate the Fauho. By using humans, they add thousands of eyes and ears to the hunt and make life unbearable for the Fauho, giving them nowhere to hide.

"The concept is not a new one for the Aile and was an underlying reason for Lennera's group being sent out to mingle with the humans."

The revelation filled Nev with the bitter feeling Nina had kept things from her.

"If you knew this was possible, why didn't you tell me before?" she asked, in a demanding tone.

Nina smiled a little as if to put her at ease, though it was going to take more than that and they both knew it.

"Nev at the time we discussed the Aile our focus was different and honestly, it never occurred to me that the idea was still being considered. When Alcedo shared the concept with me it had no bearing anymore. There had been a political divide over the idea but the majority of Aileron's high council had rejected it and chosen to use Lennera and the others the way they ultimately did. I tell you now, because something has obviously changed in Aileron."

Nev mulled it over and wondered which side of the issue her mother would have been on, or if she had cared at all.

She found she continually had to open her mind when it came to her mother and questions about how she might have thought or felt. Growing up Nev had always seen her mother through the lens of human conscience and objectives, attributing those ways to her. But the more she learned about the Aile, the more she realized, Lennera hadn't necessarily answered to the prescribed thoughts, emotions or values held by the world Nev understood, but instead had a completely foreign way of seeing things backed by a completely foreign set of values.

And that made guessing at Lennera's motivations or opinions near impossible.

Looking down at the floor, Nev almost asked Nina if she knew Lennera's position on the issue, but decided against it, not sure that it mattered anyway. Aile politics meant nothing to her, and besides, Lennera was dead, so what difference did it make.

Either way, she didn't see what any of that had to do with them and still wasn't convinced they needed to be drawn into the fight. She found herself wishing she had paid more attention when Nina had tried to teach her about political maneuvering and strategy, because she had a feeling she was missing something in the intricacies of it all, but had no idea what it was.

"You said there were two reasons the Aile would join with humans," she queried in a flat voice.

Nodding, Nina looked her in the eyes and waited a moment before proceeding.

"Rylen said they were looking for something when they went through Roden," she allowed a pause before she continued. "Nev, I think we all know they weren't just looking for something, they were looking for someone ... They were looking for you. And that means this is very much your fight."

Chit and Nina watched her for a reaction as the words sunk in, waiting.

"But no one knows I exist, how is that possible?" she asked. As much as her heart knew it was true, she didn't want to believe it.

"Nev, someone called to you after we left Roden and tried to lure you to Aileron and we still don't know why," Nina answered.

"When you didn't go there, I believe they set out looking for you and somehow they knew to start their search in Roden. It seems very likely that searching for you served as the catalyst that set all of this in motion. So you may not feel Telasan's problems are yours, but it appears in reality, you are actually the source of her problems.

"And you may be set on destroying Alopex, Nev, but his enemy wants something from you too and I don't think whatever it is, it will be something you want to give them," Nina's were stern and worried, a match to her emphatic tone.

It was too much to fathom. How had she managed to be caught at odds between two enemies out to destroy each other? And the thought that the lives of so many were somehow hinged on her was something she wasn't sure she could ever reconcile, even if she wanted to.

But it seemed pretty obvious that her desire to seek revenge on Alopex was not something she was in a position to pursue at the present.

As she reached the realization, she saw Nina and Chit's eyes move startled toward the door behind her, and before she could turn to follow their gaze, a deep voice filled the room.

"It seems you are about to learn the first rule of war girl ... *The enemy of your enemy is your friend*," the voice boomed, filling her ears to the exclusion of all other noise in the cottage.

Nev's senses went off all at once and long before her eyes found the source of the voice, a wave of heat overtook her body,.

Flanked by Sirex and holding Aster off the ground by her shirt like a mother dog would a pup, the white haired man that stood right inside the cottage door was not just physically imposing; he had an air about him that sent static through the room like a storm whose lightening set fires as it hung over a field.

His eyes were intent on Nev as if she were the only one in the room but she allowed her own eyes to skim over him, starting with the single black streak that carved a path from his temple to the back of his long hair then moving down his muscular build to stop at the child suspended above the floor in his hand.

She thought briefly that she saw a look of amusement in his face, but whatever she had seen disappeared as he spoke again, his voice taking possession of the room.

"Now would somebody please explain to me what you are doing with one of our children," he said in a gruff near-growl that sent an aftershock through the room as he looked down at Aster, setting her on the floor between them unceremoniously but with surprising gentleness.

Aster looked up to grin at the man, turning next to grin at Nev, clearly unafraid.

A broadly smiling Sirex stepped forward to stand in front of Nev though she was caught in the stranger's stare a full head above the black top of Sirex's head.

She forced herself to look to Sirex, searching through the gold of his eyes for some semblance of an explanation.

"Forgive me for my lack of manners, Nev, and allow me to make an introduction," he said. He bowed his head slightly and sarcastically, but she suddenly realized she didn't need to hear what he was about to say.

She knew the man standing behind him as sure as she knew the fire that raged in her center, for they were one and the same.

Lurching from her stool, she wove between Sirex and Aster, aiming dead center of the man's chest with all the force she had within her, propelling him against the wall.

Lifting her knife to press it against his throat, fury overtook her when his face, just inches from her own, gave way to pure amusement.

Nev awakened like she had the night she'd killed the trader.

She breathed deep, inhaling the musky essence that was him – drinking in the smell of his breath and the sweat on his skin that told her he'd spent days running across mildewed forest floors and crushing grass beneath his feet – the map of his essence blended with the familiar smells of the cottage.

And she knew him.

She knew him as surely as she knew the growing strength in her muscles that helped her lift him higher on the wall.

Behind her, she heard Sirex chuckle.

"*Alopex...*" She hissed looking deep into blue eyes that were a mirror to her own, her teeth clenched in a half effort to contain the hatred coursing through her veins.

The man beneath her knife smiled unflinching as she spoke his name.

"Now girl, is that any way to greet your father?"

●●Chapter Twenty●●

The smell of the small bead of blood that formed beneath the curve of her blade curled into her nostrils, carrying through to her brain where it became an intoxicating madness.

A snarling shriek crawled from her throat involuntarily and Nev pressed harder, delighting in the sight of a second and a third bead.

"My mother is dead because of you!" her whisper was a half growl as she ignored the flicker of emotion that moved through his eyes.

Her breath was quickening as the scent of his blood grew stronger and she knew nothing else.

There were no sounds, no sensations; nothing existed for her but the smell of Alopex' blood and she wanted more.

Then his laughter rang through her fog, cutting through like a sliver taken from a curtain.

"You are strong, girl, I'm impressed," he said, his voice drifting through the sliver.

"Will you kill me now or are you just having fun at my expense? Because I can stay here all night if that's what it takes for you to come to your senses."

She didn't answer him, instead pushing the knife a little harder, disappointed when the blue pools that stared back at her showed no discomfort.

His voice had a calming effect that began to chip away at the irrationality that had taken ownership of her.

"You should know that if you kill me it will only be because I allowed it. You're strong but you're not that strong," he said, his face spreading into a smile as she heard a chuckle behind her, no doubt from Sirex.

It just made her push harder and she was satisfied when she

finally saw Alopex wince a little, until she felt him enter her mind.

"Girl, you need me. You have no chance against the Aile without my help," his words moved through her mind like warm water, soothing as they went.

"If you wish to kill me later, I will make sure you get the chance, but for the sake of my people and these humans, sit down and hear what I have to say."

Something told her to listen, even though she wanted nothing more than to drive her knife into his throat and watch him bleed.

Nev brought her nose to his skin one last time, taking a deep, deep breath of him, enjoying when the scent pushed at the fragile sanity she had found and returned the intoxication to her.

"Name the parts that you smell," he was speaking to her again, drifting in through her fog.

She glared at him, but in her mind she went through labeling the map – the metallic warmth of blood ... the leather of his vest ... there was dirt... damp and moist dirt... and the unmistakable smell of pine, he had brushed up against a tree, the sap rubbing on his sleeve...

She began to feel strain in the hand that held Alopex suspended and her eyes pulled back from his, expanding out to take in his entire face and the space around him – the intoxication lifting.

"I give you my promise girl, I will give you an opportunity to kill me later, but let me help you now," he said. There was a gentleness to him that she wanted to ignore but couldn't and as much as she hated him and wanted to finish him right there, something told her he was telling the truth.

But her pride wasn't gone completely.

"Your life is mine, Alopex. And if you don't give it in defense of these humans first, I will claim it," she sent to him, staring deep into his eyes again. She added as much venom to her words as she could before lifting her blade from his flesh. Leaning down, she put her lips to his ear.

"I really hope you survive the fighting," she whispered her threat so only he could hear her.

As she loosened her hold on him and backed up a step, he

entered her mind again.

"My life is yours, Never, you have my promise."

There was a sincerity to his words that surprised her, though she quickly shuffled the tender feeling that followed them to the deep recesses of her brain before allowing it an opportunity to infect her.

Slowly the room began to return to life, though whether it had frozen in time or her perspective merely had, she wasn't sure.

Turning her back to Alopex without acknowledgment of his promise, Nev locked eyes with Nina, who sat like stone against the backside of the table. She may as well have connected with the woman, because her thoughts came through as clearly as if she were speaking them out loud.

She wanted to comfort Nev, and in a round about way, did so with a glance, but more than anything else, her eyes conveyed that she approved the truce.

Nev pushed past Aster, who still sat with her legs curled beneath her on the floor, her eyes seemingly larger than her head.

And fearing she would explode if she allowed contact with anyone, she next moved around Sirex, who stood looking at her with his perpetual smirk.

It wasn't until she found her seat and laid her knife on the table that the shaking started, beginning with her heart and spreading through her limbs like a wave. Her breath was unsteady and her head filled with an infinite number of bursting pinpoints.

She barely felt contained at all, as if nothing but a thin membrane stood between her and the world around her, threatening to expose her fragile insides with the slightest pressure. She knew that if she spoke it would be exposed, for her voice trembled even in her imagination and her racing heart told her she would stumble if she did anything other than sit as still as possible.

She felt eyes on her and looking to her right, found Chit waiting for the contact.

"Breathe Nev, breathe," he told her wordlessly, like he had a thousand times during their lessons.

And she heard him, drawing deep into her center the richest air she could find, taxing all the muscles of her stomach to pull it in.

Holding it for a moment, she released it only when she had no choice, making it exit with the same slow depth it had entered. She repeated the process again and again until finally calm began to lull the tremors and ease her thrashing heart.

And then she wanted to cry.

The sensation brought with it a self loathing that she capitalized on, screaming at the child inside of her that threatened tears.

So fierce was the battle, that she barely noticed the small hand that slid across her lap and the fingers that wriggled to grip her own where they sat locked in the shape of claws against her breeches.

Aster didn't say a word and leaned into Nev, melding against her side. Somehow, looking down at the top of the child's head, Nev found focus again.

The girl was warm, radiating like the surface of a rock that had basked in the sun for an afternoon, and in that warmth was pure love, for absent the doubts and politics and grudges of the adults that surrounded her, Aster knew only friends in the room.

Looking up, Aster smiled at Nev and rather than addressing what had just happened, took the path that only a child could.

"Does this mean we're sisters?" she queried, searching Nev's eyes with hope.

Though she had meant it in all sincerity, the girl's question broke through the heavy air in the room and brought forth peals of laughter from all sides.

The question took a minute to reach Nev's consciousness but it was enough to snap her back.

Alopex moved soundlessly across the floor, looking for welcome – which he got by way of a nod from Nina – before settling onto a stool at the table.

"In a round about way you are, child," his voice sounded out, ending the levity that had temporarily loosened the tight atmosphere.

Nev couldn't bring herself to look at him, instead focusing on the faint streaks of gold and brown that prevented Aster's hair from being completely red, but she was deprived of the distraction as the child straightened and turned to look at Alopex, along with everyone in the room.

With the agreement between them acting as a harness to her rage, Nev found herself not knowing how to act and focused on making her posture as nonchalant as possible in the interest of hiding her inner conflict now that she was forced to calmly face the man she wanted so badly to kill.

"The Fauho are a family within which many smaller families exist, so we are all brothers and sisters if you choose to look at it that way," Alopex said leaning down slightly to direct his words to Aster, who beamed with pride.

"If I knew who your parents were, I could tell you more, but you are one of us without a doubt child," he said, winking at her.

Rather than smiling, Aster's face fell, taking on the look of one about to be in trouble and her head dropped, whimpers quickly followed by sniffles as wet spots formed on the fabric of Nev's breeches.

Wrapping her arm around the girl's shoulders, Nev pulled her close.

"What is it Aster, what's wrong?"

Sniffling several times before she could speak, Aster couldn't seem to raise her head, instead, speaking through the curtain of hair that was blocking her face from view.

"I lost it," was all Nev could make out.

"Lost what Aster? What did you lose?"

The girl's next words came out in a series of wails punctuated by jagged sobs.

"Myyy...riiing ... I ... lost ...iiit," she said, crumbling into a mass of wet tears against Nev's leg.

"What...?"

And then it dawned on her.

Reaching inside the band of her breeches, Nev pulled out the drawstring, ignoring the strange looks.

She struggled to undo the knot that had grown tighter in the weeks since she had first tied it, sighing in relief when the small silver circlet was finally loose between her fingers.

"Aster, is this it?" she asked, poking the ring through the girl's hair so she could see it.

A little hand reached out and snatched it from her fingers and Aster's tear stained face lifted to show a smile like none Nev had seen her wear before.

"You found it!" she exclaimed, sliding it on her thumb where it rolled to the side, obviously to large for her small hand.

Proudly, she turned and marched toward Alopex, stretching the hand in front of her so he could see, her thumb curled under to prevent the ring from falling off.

"This was my father's. My mother gave it to me before she left me with my grandparents," she said, explaining as Alopex leaned down to examine the ring.

Anger crept into Aster's voice as she continued to speak. "That man took it from me... in the woods... he said if I was good he would give it back."

"I tried to be good. Even when he hurt me, I didn't burn him like I wanted to, but he never gave it back."

"I looked for it after Nev killed him, but I couldn't find it," she said, a small sniffle blending with her expression intent on conveying sincerity as if she were still afraid she would get in trouble.

"May I?" Alopex asked, reaching toward the ring.

Nodding, Aster pulled her hand back and slipped it from her thumb reverently, stretching her proudly open palm in his direction.

"My mother told my grandparents it was a gift from my father and that it was very important," she said.

"They always told me it was silly, but I took good care of it anyway."

Alopex examined the ring, his face expressionless as he handed it back to Aster with the same reverence she had shown. But Nev thought that beneath the mask she had detected a glimmer of surprise in his eyes, quickly disguised, but there nonetheless.

"Child, this is a very important ring indeed," he said with such seriousness Nev wondered if he was being dramatic for the girl's benefit.

But as he drew back and began to explain, she realized his display was not a show and glancing toward Sirex, noticed even his usual smirk had been replaced with a look of awe.

"That ring is said to hold the heart of Nisatus himself, made for his lover Syene as a token of his faith," Alopex said with the solemnness of one who believed the legend with every ounce of his being.

"Centuries ago, she sneaked from his bed in the middle of the night and fled, taking the ring with her and ever since, her line has kept it hidden, passing it down from generation to generation.

"They are the only of our kind who still live separate from the rest of us, devoting themselves to hiding the heart of the Aile. We protect them, though even we do not know where they hide.

"One thing I can tell you, is the last of their line rumored to carry that ring was Luix, and I'd be willing to bet he is the one who gave it to your mother."

It seemed like a tale told to a child around the evening fire, yet Alopex relayed it with all seriousness, not taking it lightly in the slightest.

Glad for the distraction Aster had provided, Nev took the opportunity to further study Alopex, for while his essence was imprinted in her senses, she hadn't had much chance to take him in otherwise during their confrontation.

His face showed wisdom, if not in the depth of his eyes, then most certainly in the placement of the few wrinkles she found there, a testament to the years he had squinted in study and to the emotion that had visited him.

Chiseled and framed in strong bones, there was no escaping the family resemblance they shared, departing only where his high cheeks led down to the rounded curve of a firm jaw.

Taking him in, she couldn't help but wonder if she was seeing a glimpse of herself to come.

His hair hung like a mane, clear from his face but trailing down his back, falling just below his shoulders in a straight line. It was absent of pigment, save for the black streak leading the way. And he was handsome, she noted, something in his spirit penetrating past his flesh in a way that brought it all together in one, enigmatic package that surely led people to stand behind him, if nothing else than in the hope of feeling the power he carried.

It certainly didn't reconcile – for nowhere in his presence could she find the lurking evil or the stench from the rancor of his deeds that she had imagined. Instead, she found he pulled the room inward like the center of a vortex, commanding all to look at him.

That was another place where they differed, she thought, recognizing within him the confidence of a man who knew himself, while she was yet a stranger to herself most days.

He was capable of violence, but the trained response of his muscles that showed in even the slightest gesture or shift of his body made her think any strike he made would be carefully controlled and methodically dealt, and with good reason.

No matter how hard she searched and while she had no doubt he was formidable, she could find no reflection of the callous monster that had ravaged her mother. She found before her, instead, a powerful man who acted with purpose and deliberation. Either he had changed since his abuse of Lennera or was masking the truth of himself beyond her capacity to discover it, but it didn't matter.

She would kill him, she vowed to herself, glaring as she realized he watched her study him. Yes, she thought to herself, she could get through the days or even months to come, however long it took until the truce ended and she could smell his blood once more.

The thought brought a smile to her face, set beneath the cold blue eyes she directed at his.

He smiled back, a look on his face that showed her he understood her hatred, meeting it without fear.

"How can you protect them if you don't know where they are?" Aster's voice interrupted, posing the obvious question in the way only a child could.

Alopex' smile turned into a deep laugh, his eyes breaking from Nev's to focus on the girl at her side.

Reaching out, he cupped her jaw in his large, weathered hand and looked deep into her eyes before speaking.

"We are everywhere and nowhere, waiting for them to need us. All they have to do is call and we are there," he told her intently, easing his hand from under her chin. But enamored, Aster's little face continued to stare up at him, not needing his hand to prop it.

Leaning forward until his nose was nearly touching hers, Alopex continued to speak in an even tone, like a teacher to his student.

"Tell me child, what happened in your moment of greatest need?"

Aster paused for a moment, her eyes drifting around until she found the answer.

"I cried and Nev came out of the dark and she killed them. She saved me from that man," she said, her voice a mixture of surprised pleasure at the discovery.

"Exactly. You are under our protection and we will always come. Fauho blood is never forsaken," Alopex briefly allowed his eyes to flicker up to Nev before he looked down into the child's eyes again, as if he knew the story had more meaning to her than it did Aster.

"We are born to answer that call as surely as we breathe. But you were lucky that Nev was so close. You may not be so lucky all the time and must learn to protect yourself too. Would you like it if I let Sirex show you some tricks?"

Nodding vigorously, Aster beamed, her face becoming one big smile as she looked over to Sirex, only to find him smiling as well.

"Very well, I think you'll find you have one of the best teachers the Fauho have to offer young lady," Alopex said with a gentle smile.

"One more thing," he said, his hand producing a knife from nowhere.

While Nev gasped, no one else in the room seemed to react, instead watching as the man reached up to his head and cut a strand of his own hair.

Reaching out his hand, Aster seemed to understand, placing the ring in his waiting palm.

Watching in fascination, Nev couldn't hide her amazement as he thread the strand through the ring and pinched the ends together, pulling his hand back to reveal a complete circle of hair with no end or beginning to mark the bond.

Slipping the circle over Aster's head, he tucked the ring inside her shirt and patted it gently as if telling it to stay put.

"Let's not lose that again, and don't ever let anyone take it from you ever again," he said, raising an authoritative eyebrow at her.

Nodding solemnly, Aster surprised even Alopex, wrapping her arms around his neck with no fear and no hesitation that perhaps she shouldn't.

Laughing, he recovered quickly, returning the hug, then patted Aster on the head, dismissing her to go become reunited with her prize possession.

"You had no idea, did you girl?" he said, looking at Nev, who deigned not to answer since he already knew she hadn't known about Aster or the reason for her instinctual protection of her. She had, of course not knowing the history, merely thought she was responding as she hoped anyone would to a child in need.

But the explanation had set a new frenzy of thought loose in her head. Was that instinct the reason for her change that night? The reason for her heightened senses, her increased strength, her speed … the changes to her hair and skin?

"Yes," he said, as she realized he was still looking at her.

"Though I have to say the qualities you display, having only discovered those things so recently, mark you as quite unique and far advanced." it was true admiration he expressed, making her feel embarrassed enough to avoid his eyes.

"If you had control, I might think you the best I've encountered, but that is easy enough to gain if you are willing to work at it."

She bristled defensively to see Chit nodding his head, enjoying the fact someone else was independently confirming what he had told her time and time again.

"So if Aster is Fauho, that means you are a fox," she volleyed Alopex' way, the only retort she could think of to get the attention off her shortcomings.

Her question had the opposite affect than she had hoped for, however, when Sirex and Alopex burst into laughter so voracious it seemed they might cry.

Heat rising to her cheeks, she felt anger spreading through her chest as they enjoyed what appeared to be a joke she wasn't privy to.

Rubbing his hands across his face, Alopex regained his composure and after a series of controlled breaths was able to look at Nev again. One last chuckle escaped as he opened his mouth to speak, skipping past it as if he could pretend it hadn't happened.

"That is a very simple explanation. As you can see, we are men," he said, gesturing toward Sirex, who still fought to gain control of his laughter.

"But yes, we are the people of the fox. Fauho means "fox" in the old tongue. I take it you have seen the child change?"

Nev opted not to speak, nodding curtly instead.

"But you yourself have not?"

Shaking her head, she felt a wave of near nausea move through her as she made the connection for the first time – Avec was not going to like this at all, and come to think of it, she was pretty sure she didn't either.

"I would be honored to help you learn more about our people, and yourself," Alopex said, bowing his head to her.

Nev bristled, her pride kicking in to override her curiosity.

"I've done fine on my own. I am sure I can figure it out without your help," she said briskly.

"Now what exactly is it you think the two of you are going to do to help us fight the Aile? If I remember the little history I've been told correctly, the Fauho conceded in the last battle and went back to hide in their mountain."

The insult found its mark in Sirex, who snorted in anger on the other side of the room.

But Alopex only smiled.

"Girl, I think your history lessons have failed you. In battle we found ourselves evenly matched to the Aile," he said, overlooking the way she had twisted the truth in an effort to rankle him.

"Had both sides not withdrawn we would likely still be in that valley battling one-for-one to the death."

If he had planned to say any more, he wasn't given the chance when a shriek rang through the air from outside the cottage.

"Wybert... Wybert please come help me..." she sent, relieved when the little bird darted from her hair to float in the air beside her head.

Scrambling to the door, Nev was the first to emerge into the dark, stopping dead in her tracks at the sight before her.

Standing in the middle of the grass in front of the cottage was a small cluster of men, swords drawn outward. In the center of their mass, stood an agitated and frantic Telasan, her men no more brave as they circled around her.

"I believe you have the answer to your other question, girl," Alopex's voice sounded over her shoulder from the doorway where everyone had rushed to find the source of the commotion.

Moving to stand beside her in the grass, his voice began as a low growl, then Alopex raised his fist in the air and shouted so loud the words thundered in her ears.

"We are ready..."

In response, voices answered from all around the cottage, a chorus of yips and screams that rose above the trees like a song.

And as the eerie and terrifying sound crawled through her very sinew, she knew that what she was hearing was the call of ten thousand foxes ready to die for the man that stood beside her.

●●Chapter Twenty-one●●

A full two days had passed and Telasan was adjusting better than expected to the new allies that had taken up residence around her cottage.

The explanation had been a little awkward but it was hard for her to turn down the sheer numbers that had joined her cause, though Alopex had done much apologizing for the way she had discovered their presence.

And his charms were not lost on Telasan, who already placed inordinate trust in Sirex and found comfort in the similar traits exhibited by his king. She had been angry at first, to learn Sirex had taken on with her, dishonest in the fact that his allegiance was already sworn to another.

But Alopex explained the Fauho had been looking out for her and her people since long before she rose to lead them. He said they were similarly imbedded in other regions, and had been waiting for this day, strategically forming bonds throughout Leresan.

Rylen, who, thanks to Nina's tea, had slept through the entire exchange between Nev and Alopex to include introduction of the Fauho, was just as surprised to learn it had been because of Alopex's men that he himself had escaped the fall of Kasen.

Already, word was rippling through Harren, thanks to the Fauho, and in three more days they would be in the valley waiting for Sarter and the Aile.

A message from Palynn, leader of the Logar region helped bolster trust in the Fauho, when he sent word they had revealed themselves to him as well and, along with his troops, were preparing to move in support of Telasan.

She had even accepted the truth of who Nev was, and seemed to forgive her the point, a fact for which Nev was eternally grateful.

Avec, on the other hand, hadn't come near the cottage since the Fauho arrived, communicating with Nev only from afar.

He would rather nest in a pit of vipers, he told her more than once.

But at least they were talking again, finding renewed comfort in reestablishing their connection as he flew watch over the area.

With the exception of a couple hundred of Alopex's higher ranking fighters that took up camp around the cottage, the throngs of Fauho had melted back into the woods, for the most part disappearing, something Nev was learning they had an aptitude for. But she still knew they were there and could feel their eyes upon her everywhere she went.

Even though they took their human forms around the cottage, they could smell the Aile blood in her veins and she knew it, but none would dare touch her, knowing she was under Alopex' protection – not that it made her feel any less like a piece of meat paraded in front of hungry vultures.

But it could have just been her imagining that was how they felt, for if it was, they worked hard to hide it, treating her with politeness and respect.

She learned quickly that the characteristics of Alopex and Sirex were common to the Fauho as a whole. Charming and warm, the fox people were likable and entertaining. And she discovered the flirting charisma that Sirex displayed was not owned by him, even if it did feel a little different coming from him.

Whether male or female, the Fauho interacted with seductive guile like Nev had never seen before. Entirely different than the disgusting women Delsin had enjoyed, whose efforts at flirting were about as transparent as an open window, the Fauho by contrast were skilled at making one's blood heat and skin tingle.

And they were beautiful, every single one of them.

She now saw where some of her own features came from, for in human form, the slender built Fauho all seemed to have defined facial structure that housed deep piercing eyes, whether they be blue or shades of brown and gold.

The women, called "Vixens" the irony of which was not lost on Nev, wore their hair long, with black, brown, golden and red locks flowing down the middle of their backs and many of the men did the same. The one thing she noticed, however, was that aside from her and Alopex, none had silver or gray hair.

It was a fact that even though she was curious to understand, she refused to ask, still of the mind that to accept Alopex' help equated to subjugating herself.

But Aster was reveling in her new family, now affixed to Sirex's side everywhere he went.

She was talented well beyond her years and remarkably skilled in the absence of any instruction, Alopex commented after Sirex spent a couple of hours with her to determine where to begin their lessons.

Aster's abilities with fire were unique, even among the Fauho, though the skill did crop up every few generations, Nev learned.

And Aster had a strong dose of the talent in her veins – probably traceable to Syene who was remembered by Fauho legend to have mastered the manipulation of fire so well she could walk through the sky on trails of flame she had created.

The biggest obstacle the child faced was shaking the guilt she had over her powers, the only lasting impression she seemed to carry from her human grandparents, but deep seeded just the same, Alopex had conveyed with disgust.

Interaction between Nev and Alopex had continued to be strained, but the problem was clearly hers.

Mostly because she found herself fighting to dislike him, rather than the other way around. He was warm and always smiling, taking her insults and coldness in stride, never changing his approach to her.

Even Nina seemed taken by him and Chit completely drawn in, the old soldier in him wakened by watching Alopex command with near undetectable effort.

There was no doubt his people loved and respected him, their willingness to follow him anywhere he led evidenced just by the looks they gave when he walked by, as if the fact that they were all there to begin with weren't testament enough.

The dilemma was enough to send Nev in search of Nina, hoping for a way to resolve the conflict seething within her.

"Why isn't Alopex the monster I imagined he would be," she asked, cornering the woman in the garden where she was picking vegetables for the mid-day meal.

"I don't know how to answer that girl," Nina said, looking up through Nev's shadow before resuming her search through the leaves.

"Maybe he changed or maybe he has another side that he isn't showing," she said, plucking a particularly fat squash from its vine before moving toward a patch of carrots.

It was frustrating to watch her mundane actions in the midst of such an important topic and Nev lost her temper.

"Nina, you cried with me when we talked about what he did to my mother, now you seem to be completely at ease with him and I want to know why!" she said, all but shouting at the top of the woman's head.

Her hands stopped and she sat still for a second, finally stretching to her feet to stand in front of Nev.

"Nev, he is the greatest ally we have right now and without the help of the Fauho these people don't stand a chance. That is something I can see with my own eyes and so can you," she said, her tone showing she was tired but there wasn't a hint of anger.

"Only you can resolve this. You have time to get to know him. Judge for yourself. I think the question you need to ask yourself isn't did he do this thing. Instead, ask yourself if his death will change anything for you. What is justice girl? What will give you peace? I think the answer may surprise you."

Reaching a hand out to squeeze Nev's shoulder, Nina smiled at her the way she used to when she sent her out the burrow door after tea, and, for the first time, Nev understood the expression for what it was.

It was a smile designed to tell her Nina would be there waiting when she returned to lick her wounds, regardless of what happened.

"I'm proud of you girl and I know that you will see your way through this but it's time you start thinking for yourself," she said, giving Nev a quick hug before returning to her spot on the ground.

Finding herself more confused than she had been when she sought the woman's counsel, Nev trudged back to the cottage.

All around her, she found the fervor of activity of people were getting ready for war, but the only war she seemed to care about was the one that raged inside her, and for that she felt childish and stupid.

But she didn't know what else to do.

Her bags had never been unpacked since they'd arrived at the cottage and her knife was sharp. Her travel weary clothes were mended and Telasan had even lent her a pair of her dead husband's boots – who must have been a small man, because they fit like they were made for her.

She had even checked Aster's clothes and seen to it she was ready too.

Riding Mica was a thought, but not one she dwelled on long when she looked around at all the activity she would have to weave through to get anywhere.

"Fly with me..." Avec sent, surprising her with his presence in her mind.

Nev had found that she could leave an opening in her mind just for Avec, while blocking out the rest of the Fauho around her but often found herself jolted when he connected now that she was so guarded to the intrusions of others.

Laughing, she smiled at the absurdity of his suggestion.

"Why not? They all know what you are and better to surprise them now than on the battle field the first time you spread your wings," he said.

"Who cares what they think, you don't owe them anything."

He was right, as usual.

Nev's recent affiliation with a people that made his feathers stand on end was trying, but they were making it work. The hardest part of it all was that they hadn't spent time together in more than a week and it was starting to take its toll, no matter how close their bond was.

Looking around her at the people moving to and fro, she felt a moment of hesitation and almost changed her mind, but when her skimming eyes came to rest on Alopex and Sirex talking to some men nearby, she suddenly felt emboldened.

Connecting with Avec, she smiled as he did a roll in the air that sent tingles through her and she felt her wings pushing against the flesh of her back.

Her confidence had grown through all Nina's exercises and she didn't really need his help extending her wings anymore, but she still enjoyed having him there when she did.

The familiar tingles moved through her back as she felt her wings stretching, growing to their full lengths and she found she enjoyed the looks around her as swords clamored to the ground and mouths opened in awe.

Even Sirex stared, his shock obvious. The look on Alopex' face was harder to read – It almost seemed a mixture of anger and disappointment.

Ignoring him, Nev stretched her wings as far as they would go, beating them a little more rapidly than required as she began her ascent. Once above the ground, she pushed forward, angling her body so she could turn and cut through the air, rising to meet Avec.

The people below no longer mattered the higher she rose, falling away beneath her and feeling less significant with each beat of her wings.

"This was exactly what I needed," she sent his way, feeling his agreement flood back her way.

The endless sky beckoned, Nev glad to oblige as she found a strong current of air and coasted along it, letting it bear her weight while she closed her eyes and soaked up the warmth of the sun.

It was hard to imagine how her life had been complete before she had experienced weightlessness, so hard, in fact that knew it hadn't been complete at all. If only she could stay in the sky forever, she knew everything would be perfect, for all her problems lay below her.

Crossing her arms across her chest, she folded her arms and rolled, perfectly timing the stop when she threw her wings out toward the earth. She bounced a little as they came against a wall of air but they were strong enough to bear the pressure, eliciting a giggle of pride that even made Avec laugh.

"This is my favorite way to see you," he sent, his pleasure evident.

"There's nothing I enjoy more than seeing you happy."

The hawk's words took Nev back to their early days together, before the world had changed and become so complicated – the first time he had struggled to fly, the times she had crashed to the earth in tears. Those problems seemed so trivial now and yet there was no denying the necessity that had brought her to the present.

Why was she still pushing forward? Why not just embrace the simplicity of the sky and let the world move on below without her?

What seemed simple was that had she stayed in Roden, she would have been sold to the trader, or worse yet would have fallen in the path of Sarter and the Aile, and there might have been no Nina, no Aster or Chit, no Sirex … no Alopex, and no chance.

The air rushing past her face worked to wash away all the clutter, cleansing her mind and leaving behind a clear perspective for the first time she could remember.

Even though each challenge overcome seemed to introduce a new one and despite the complexity that each addition to her life brought with it, the one thing they all offered was hope … a chance.

With all the irreconcilable contradictions Alopex presented, even he came offering a chance for something, whether it was victory in battle or the victory of revenge, or maybe both, even he held a key to something more.

Yes, that was the reason and somehow it made all the challenges that waited below seem all right.

Turning to Avec, she smiled broadly and cut sharp beneath him, doubling back in taunt.

Chuckling, he followed, his smaller wings working twice as hard to draw along side her again.

"We need to head back now before you get tired," he said, chuckling again at her disappointed groan. *"You haven't practiced in days and you're going to tire faster than you think, Nev."*

She knew he was right and looking below her, realized they had traveled quite a ways from the cottage already.

"Find a current to ride and save your energy for your landing. You pulled it off last time, but you still need more practice," he said, voicing thoughts that were already forming in her head.

Dropping down a level, she found a layer that could bear her and adjusted her wings to the perfect angle so they could cut through the air in front, while still allowing the right amount of pressure to exist below them.

"Well done, Nev," Avec watched from above, sending his approval.

But something in her face was changing and the bliss that had been there just seconds before shifted to pain.

Reaching out to connect with her, Avec found he was not alone in her mind.

"Little fox ... Little flying fox, I see you ...Where are you going little one? ...You can't outrun me ..."

Over and over the voice chanted, taunting inside her head but she had withdrawn from the intrusion, her eyes empty and her face wracked in pain.

Burrowing deeper, Avec put himself between Nev and the voice, throwing up blocks with all his strength to shield her, hoping it would work.

"Nev, you have to fight it off! I'm not strong enough to do it alone!" he called to her as the voice laughed behind him.

"Oh, Look who has a friend ... You can't keep me from her ... She's mine..."

"Nev, please, help me! I can't do this for both of us, you have to help," Avec practically cried, the pain now entering his mind as his blocks started to give way. The voice was strong, stronger than he was and he knew he couldn't keep it out much longer.

*"**Nev!**... Please...."* he tried one last time.

Just as he felt the voice push past him, a wall of force moved through him to slam against it, pushing it out, though it laughed as it left.

His own wings were failing, the strain had taken everything from him.

"Nev..." he was spiraling downward, and fighting to right himself against the current that held him captive, overpowering him.

Even in his tumble through the air, his only concern was Nev and the devastating realization that he couldn't help her. He couldn't even help himself.

The air rushed over him, consuming him as he fell and as everything went black, his last thoughts went to Nev, tumbling through the air above him.

●●Chapter Twenty-two●●

"Nev, Nev, NevNevNev..." the small, fretting voice filtered into her consciousness while she struggled to open her eyes, then gave up. Groaning, she shifted, surprised to feel softness beneath her.

"Nev!"

"Wybert..." She mumbled, half in response but more in recognition than anything – a recognition that brought forth another groan.

"We talked about this Nev! You are supposed to be caaarefull..." the little bird responded, his voice expressing reprimand and relief all in one.

"So I guess this means I'm not dead?" she muttered.

Wybert laughed.

"Silly Nev, if you were dead, you wouldn't be talking to me!"

"That's what I figured," she mumbled.

Settling back into what she had identified as pillows though she had yet to open her eyes, Nev drew a labored breath, not surprised to find it hurt.

How had she come to this, she wondered, searching her mind for her last memories.

Flying, a voice, pain and falling … it came back to her in pieces though not necessarily in order.

Falling …

"Avec!" she cried, jolting upright and opening her eyes at the same time. Looking around, she realized she was in Telasan's bed and the cottage was dimly lit, indication that Wybert was recovering at the same rate she was.

"Shhh... Nev, he's fine!" she heard Aster but took a moment to register where the voice was coming from. Turning to her left, she made out the girl's figure as she thrust her hands forward to reveal the hawk.

Bandages wrapped around both wings, he looked up at Nev with the most pitiful look she had ever seen.

"Oh no! Avec, are your wings broken?" she asked, afraid to touch him.

"No, but your little friend here seemed to think I needed bandages anyway. She made me eat mushed up carrots and gave me a bath too..." he said, the disgust clearly displayed on his face.

"Avec, the carrots were to give you energy, Nina said they're good for you, and well … You know why I gave you a bath," Aster retorted, not hesitating to join in their exchange.

"Why?" Nev asked, her curiosity piqued.

Avec looked down, not wanting to meet her eye.

"Let's just say something ... um ... squishy broke my fall," he mumbled, his embarrassment evident.

"It was really bad," Aster said, giggling much to the hawk's chagrin.

"You, on the other hand, have perfected the bounce," Nina's voice sounded somewhere behind Aster's shoulder.

Squinting to see, Nev could make out her shape but little else.

"My wings...?" Nev asked.

"They are fine, girl, in fact all of you is. You just took a hard knock to the head is all," Nina said reassuringly.

"I'm not sure how many more of those you're going to survive though. Your head is thick, but not that thick."

Groaning, Nev leaned back against the pillows, wishing she was still unconscious.

But she wasn't going to get any rest for a while yet, judging from the next voice that filtered through – this time angry.

"What the hell kind of stunt was that?"

"What are you talking about?" she said, trying to sound indignant, but she didn't have the strength to pull it off.

Aster shuffled close enough to the bed to set Avec on top of the blanket, then scurried off behind Nina, making it obvious neither of them wanted to be there for the conversation that was about to take place.

"Well you set the bait if that's what you were trying to accomplish. My people had a devil of a time fooling the Aile into thinking you were heading for the valley, but they pulled it off," Alopex grumbled from the side of the bed where he had taken the gap left by Nina's departure.

"We have enough people in place in the valley to keep them busy and buy us time to get there, but it isn't quite the advantage we were hoping for."

"What happened up there anyway? My people saw you lock up in the middle of the air and start falling. By the time they carried you and that bird into the woods, they said the air was swarming with Aile," he said.

Nev searched her mind for the memories, relieved to have some much needed assistance from Avec.

"One of them was in your mind, Nev, I tried to block him but I wasn't strong enough," he sent, the guilt of his failure clearly still with him.

Yes, she remembered. He had been inside her mind taunting her and taking over, grabbing hold until she backed into a corner trying to get away ... and it had hurt.

But Avec didn't fail, he saved her, providing enough of a barrier for her to throw up blocks and force the voice out so she could make it to the ground, even if she didn't manage to land gracefully.

Reaching out, she told him as much, glad to feel his spirit lift a little at the revelation.

Turning back to Alopex, she paused for a moment.

"It was Calvus and he knew me," she told him, waiting to watch his reaction, her vision improving with each passing moment.

"Calvus is a snake. As bad as the Aile are, he is the worst of them. What I don't understand is how he knew you, other than he might have just known you weren't one of his own," Alopex said, his eyes showing the intensity of his thoughts.

"I don't know either, but he did and it was more than me just not being one of his. He called me a, 'little flying fox'," she said.

Alopex pondered for a moment but didn't share his thoughts, instead, shaking his head.

"Well, I'm not sure it matters anymore because they've seen you, so if it was a secret, it certainly isn't now," he said.

An awkward silence grew between them.

"I know you don't want my help, but if I could just give you a little insight?" Alopex ventured cautiously.

Unable to keep from smiling, Nev nodded.

"Keep your blocks up all the time, don't ever let your guard down. You will know if someone trusted wants to connect with you, but you can't afford to be vulnerable like that again," he said, looking at her with genuine concern.

"And don't go wandering off without telling anyone."

Ashamed, Nev looked down at the blanket, nervously smoothing out a wrinkle with her hand.

"I know, I just needed to get away, I ... It was stupid, you're right," she said, the admission causing more pain that the fall had, for at least she had been unconscious for most of that.

Alopex reached out to squeeze her hand quickly then withdrew it so fast, she almost thought she'd imagined it.

"Get some rest. We leave in the morning," he said.

"From now on, if you want to be stupid, I can't stop you, just try to remember you're my only heir." And then he was gone, disappearing through the door that shut softly behind him.

Shocked, Nev looked down at Avec. She had never thought about it before, but surely Alopex had other children.

"Don't foxes have lots of children?" she asked Avec.

But another voice answered before the bird could respond.

"We can, just as humans can," Sirex said, his smirk absent as he pulled one of the chairs beside the bed and sat looking at Nev with his arms crossed.

"But foxes, and the Fauho, also mate for life – And though many would have it different, you are his only child," he said, the weight of his words sinking in as she studied his face.

"He worries about you. I've known Alopex all my life and I've never seen him quite like this before," Sirex said, his concern for his king surfacing as the reason for his visit.

"I'm not sure I understand why you hate him so much and I probably don't want to know, but I thought you should know that you are very important to him.

"He had us follow you today because he had a feeling something was going to happen, and he was right. He usually is."

Nev paused, then looked at Sirex with a new found respect, for she couldn't deny the love he obviously had for Alopex.

"Well I suppose it's a good thing he sent you, or I would probably still be laying there," she said, a hint of bitterness creeping into her voice even though she fought to keep it out.

"Not exactly," he said. "I was already trailing you before Alopex sent the order."

Looking down, her eyes stopped on a bandage wrapped around Sirex' arm, then moved back up to meet his eyes.

"Did Aster bandage you and make you eat carrots too?" she said, a smile tugging at the corners of her mouth.

Grinning in return, Sirex stood and bent down to quickly brush his lips against the top of her forehead.

"Not exactly," he said, walking toward the kitchen while she had the delayed realization Sirex' bandage had a tinge of red in its center..

The touch of his lips still burning on her forehead, Nev looked down at Avec and felt tears gathering in her eyes.

"I don't understand, why should they care about me? Aren't I the child of their enemy?" she asked him silently so no one else could hear,

"Maybe," Avec said. *"But you're one of them too."*

Sitting back against her pillows, Nev felt a warmth in her center that grew in spite of the questions that lurked in her mind.

Closing her eyes, she felt Wybert rustle a few strands of hair as he perched on top of her head and listened to the happy hum coming from the kitchen as her strange family of circumstance laughed over their evening meal, seemingly oblivious to the fact dawn was coming, and with it, a war like none Leresan had ever seen.

The thought that by tomorrow some of them may lose their lives was one she had difficulty absorbing.

What was truly ironic was that even with the unknown weighing on her heart and mind, she had less fear facing tomorrow than the fear she'd always had trudging along the path to the burrow knowing Delsin was waiting for her.

A curious thing indeed.

But this time they could, and would fight and maybe that was the difference. That in a round about way they controlled their own destiny and therefore, they had a chance.

More of a chance than she'd ever had with Delsin until the day she stood up to him.

But there was something else she'd never had in Roden and suddenly Nev understood how they gathered around the table laughing and telling jokes with the future waiting outside the cottage.

It was because in some small way, they were already experiencing victory because they had each other even if it meant they might give their lives on the battlefield.

Shifting her arm to allow Avec a spot in the hollow by her side, Nev sank down a little further, just enjoying, for the moment, the peace that had settled in her.

"Do you think we'll make it?" she asked him softly, drifting toward sleep.

"I think we already have," he said, ruffling his feathers before smoothing them back, squeezing a little closer in hope of joining in her dreams.

For once, it seemed they were thinking the same thing.